Amanda Waters

Black Rose Writing | Texas

ISBN: 978-1-68513-069-5
PUBLISHED BY BLACK ROSE WRITING
www.blackrosewriting.com

Printed in the United States of America
Suggested Retail Price (SRP) $23.95

With You is printed in Georgia

*As a planet-friendly publisher, Black Rose Writing does its best to eliminate unnecessary waste to reduce paper usage and energy costs, while never compromising the reading experience. As a result, the final word count vs. page count may not meet common expectations.

To all the places and people we call home.

With
You

Chapter 1

It wasn't so much that Kristen regretted her recent move to Riverton, Missouri. It was more that she couldn't quite remember why it had seemed like such a great idea two months ago.

At the moment, she was channeling her conflicting feelings through her running shoes, focusing on the rhythmic thud of her feet against the paved park path, and the steady in and out of her breath. It was the kind of blustery day that reminded her of Chicago, and she was happy that for the moment, the wind was at her back. A pale morning sun rested just above the horizon. Birds flew in and out and around the trees lining the path, and squirrels seemed oblivious to the early morning runners and walkers. As she approached the parking lot, Kristen glanced at her watch and decided she had enough time for a second loop around the park.

She wasn't sure why today the heaviness of her move would come crashing down on her all at once.

To be sure, once she'd decided to move, everything had happened quickly, and her final few weeks in Chicago had been a whirlwind of packing and coordinating logistics and saying goodbye, with no time for a lot of feelings. These first few weeks in Riverton had been a delight. She was staying with her dad and his new wife Rosalee while she looked for a place to live, relishing the time with them: the slow mornings, cooking with Rosalee, evening walks with the dog, playing card games on the patio, and watching baseball with her dad.

Maybe the problem, Kristen now thought, was that although she was still working and even searching for a place to rent on her own, the past few weeks had felt like a vacation. But this morning there was no getting around reality, because today was the day she and her dad were taking an in-person look at a few rental options. She'd be talking leases, and neighborhoods, and trying to imagine ordinary, everyday life in a place that wasn't her little two-flat in Chicago where she'd lived for the past 20 years. Then there was the message her friends had sent her last night—a video greeting from Liz's birthday dinner, from Nora, Liz and Kole, and their two kids, even 15-year-old Bella who was on her phone most of the time. Kristen felt her eyes prick with tears, and refocused on her breathing, on the rhythm of her feet. In-two-three, out-two-three, in-two-three, out-two-three.

By the time she'd finished her run and briefly

stretched, Kristen still hadn't resolved her cognitive dissonance, but the moving meditation and rush of endorphins had at least helped her make momentary peace with it, and had lifted her heaviness. She was going to table the uncomfortable feelings for now.

• • •

When she got back to her dad's condo, Rosalee perched on a bar stool, a triangle of toast in one hand and a paperback book in the other. She looked up as Kristen shut the front door and walked inside.

"Good morning!" Rosalee said with a big smile. "How was your run?"

"It was good. Meditative. Just what I needed."

"Glad to hear it."

She turned her attention back to her book. Kristen got a glass of water from the kitchen and thought about how Rosalee had an uncanny and admirable ability to know when to ask questions and when to give a person space.

"Has Dad left for his dentist appointment yet?"

"About ten minutes before you walked in," Rosalee slid a scrap of paper into her book and set it down. "Can I make you some breakfast? Eggs? Toast?"

"Some toast sounds good, but I can make it."

"Why don't you just put the kettle on, and I'll slice up some of that good sourdough Elizabeth gave us yesterday."

"Mmmm, well, I'm not going to say no to sourdough toast."

Rosalee stood up and began moving through the kitchen, while Kristen filled the red enamel kettle with water, set it on the stove, and turned the burner on.

Rosalee and George, Kristen's dad, had gotten married just a little over a year ago, although they had met more than forty years before, the summer before Rosalee's senior year of high school. Their summer romance had almost turned into something more until George got Kristen's mom pregnant and broke Rosalee's heart. Despite not having the romantic fairy tale ending they'd hoped for, Rosalee and George had both moved on and ended up in happy marriages and with fulfilling lives. They'd lost all contact with each other until about a year ago, when George, who'd been widowed at that point for more than two decades, moved to Riverton. He'd been pleasantly surprised to run into Rosalee Barnes—McDonnell now—at a restaurant. She was also widowed, albeit more recently than George was. It was a bit of a rocky road back to romance, but it had thrilled Kristen when they'd said they were getting married. Kristen knew her dad had been lonely–not that he'd ever have said anything–and she'd adored Rosalee from their first meeting.

Getting to know Rosalee and her family better was definitely one perk of Kristen's relocation to

Riverton. Rosalee's daughter Elizabeth and son Charles both lived nearby with their families, and every Sunday night the whole family gathered at Elizabeth's house. Kristen had met the family when George and Rosalee were dating, and while they had been mostly friendly, Kristen had definitely detected some tense undercurrents. She'd thought about skipping family dinners, not wanting to intrude or cause discomfort, but when both Rosalee and her dad had insisted, she figured she'd give it at least one shot. It had turned out to be the right decision. The McDonnell and Finch families were warm, welcoming, fun, and she'd felt at home right away.

The whistle of the kettle startled Kristen out of her reverie, and she quickly removed it from the heat and poured the water into her waiting mug, the scent of Earl Grey tea wafting into the air. She picked up the mug and carried it over to the bar where Rosalee had set a plate with two buttered pieces of thick bread and two small pots of jam.

"I wasn't sure if you wanted raspberry or apricot."

"Thank you. You're spoiling me, you know. I'm going to miss staying here with you guys, although you may be ready to kick me out and have the place to yourself again."

"We absolutely love having you here, and you truly can stay as long as you like, although my guess is that you'll be happy to have your own space again," Rosalee smiled and squeezed Kristen's shoulder. "I'm going to take Buddy on a walk. We can wait if you want to join us."

Kristen smiled as the big mutt lumbered in from the back of the condo, his ears clearly attuned to that magical word. "Thanks, but I'd like to shower before Dad and I head out."

"I totally understand. All right boy, you ready?" Rosalee bent down to clip a leash on Buddy, whose full body tail wagging seemed to indicate that yes, he was definitely ready for that walk. "See you in a bit!"

The chiming of a grandfather clock in the corner reminded Kristen that she needed to pay attention to the time. She quickly took her last bite of toast and one last swallow of tea, put the dishes in the dishwasher, and went to take a quick shower. When she walked back into the main living area 30 minutes later, Rosalee was walking back through the French doors with Buddy and her dad was walking in the front door.

"Hey, sweetie," Rosalee said, walking up to George. He leaned down for a quick kiss. "How was the dentist?"

George shrugged. "It was the dentist. Now I have clean teeth."

"Hey Dad." Kristen stepped up and gave him a hug.

"Hey, Peanut. Ready to go apartment shopping?"

"Sure, let me just grab my purse."

Five minutes later, they were in the car, but before they'd gone even a mile, her dad started fidgeting and shifting in his seat. Kristen smiled to herself. Some people thought her dad was enigmatic, but to her he was as transparent as glass.

"What is it, Dad? I can tell something's on your mind."

George smiled and shook his head. "I really have missed you, Peanut. I was just thinking... everything's happened so quickly over the past couple of months. You never mentioned how long you're staying or if everything's okay. I never thought I'd see you move out of Chicago."

"Nothing's wrong, so don't worry about that. It's just..." Kristen sighed. How could she explain it to someone else when she could barely explain it to herself? "I've been in a weird head space for a while," she admitted. "Maybe a mid-life crisis? Who knows. But I felt like I needed a big change of scenery. I don't want a career change. I didn't think a long vacation would cut it, but a wholesale move seemed like an overreaction, so I decided on a year-long experiment. Of course, I picked Riverton because you're here." She smiled at him. "Hopefully a year someplace new will have shaken loose whatever this tightness is in my soul."

"Makes sense."

"And who knows, maybe I'll love Riverton so much I'll decide to stay."

George glanced at her, one eyebrow raised. Kristen grinned and shrugged. "Could happen."

In typical fashion, her dad simply accepted what

she said and didn't see the need to analyze it—at least not verbally. He might come back to her with a few extra questions after he'd thought about it for a while. Or he might not.

As they drove, George confessed that while he had a few places they could check out, he was taking her to the best first. "It's a house in Rosalee's old neighborhood," he explained. "Most of the houses in the neighborhood are three or four-bedroom homes—much more than you need—but there are a few small two-bedroom bungalows. They get snatched up fast, but I had the inside scoop on this one. A co-worker of Rosalee's owns it. She hasn't actually listed it yet, and said you could look at it first."

He turned onto a shady street flanked by tall, leafy trees that Kristen was sure would be breathtaking in the fall. The homes were modest farmhouses or long, low ranch styles, with a few Craftsman bungalows thrown in, and most had deep front porches. Kristen saw driveways with basketball hoops, or stray bicycles, and nice sized lawns that ranged from simple and manicured to somewhat wild and almost overgrown. Since it was a weekday, there wasn't much vehicle or pedestrian traffic, although Kristen saw a couple of joggers and one woman pushing a toddler in a stroller while wearing an infant on her torso.

After a few turns, Kristen felt the car slow down and saw George crane his neck forward a bit. He pointed out her window.

"That's it. The rock house with the blue door."

Kristen peered out her window and smiled. This was it.

The tiny rock house looked almost like someone had plucked it from a fairy tale. The kind of house that fairy godmothers lived in, or princesses in hiding, or maybe a poor farmer before he finds out he's really the prince. A flagstone walkway cut through the yard in half, with the driveway on one side and a large maple tree on the other. A bench sat under the maple tree, and Kristen could picture herself sitting under the tree with a book or her laptop. There was no front porch, but a screened-in porch jutted off to one side, and Kristen thought she glimpsed a window seat in the front picture window.

She turned to George with a smile. "Do we get to look inside?"

"We do. The owners are meeting us here in about five minutes. They live a couple of streets over. They don't seem like the hovering type though, if you're worried about that."

"You forget, I spent the last 20 years living above my landlady."

George laughed. Kristen suggested waiting outside of the car, her eyes on the bench in the yard. She wanted to test it out. The two of them sat in companionable silence, watching squirrels chase each other in the yard, and listening to birdsong. Kristen took a deep breath of the distinctive late spring smells of flowers, mowed grass, and wet earth. She wondered if the landlords would mind if she put up a birdhouse somewhere in the yard, somewhere in view of this bench or maybe the screened porch.

An older model pickup truck turned the corner and rumbled slowly to the curb behind George's car. Kristen and George stood up as a man and woman climbed out of the truck. The man was tall with dark, graying hair mostly covered by a St. Louis Cardinals cap, and the woman was of average build with shoulder length silver hair, and a round face softened by a big smile. Both were dressed casually in jeans, the man in a faded plaid shirt and work boots, and the woman in striped button down with smudges of dirt on the hem and a pair of flowered clogs on her feet.

"You must be Kristen," the woman said as they walked up. "I'm Ellen Mattox and this is Randall. Do you want to look around the outside of the house first, or just head on inside?"

"I'm dying to look around inside," Kristen said. "The house is darling from out here."

Randall led the way up the flagstone walk, and Ellen explained that the current tenants were moving out next week, so the house was in a bit of disarray, but that's also why they hadn't listed it for rent yet.

"If you decide to sign a lease, we can have the cleaning crew come in the day after the Britts move out and get you settled in as soon as possible," she said.

Kristen assured her that she wasn't in any rush as long as her dad and Rosalee didn't mind putting up with her for a week. George's eyes crinkled in response and he put his arm around Kristen's shoulders.

"I guess I'll manage," he said with a wink.

The cardboard boxes, piles of stuff, and bare walls did nothing to mask the charm of the house in Kristen's opinion. It was cozy without being claustrophobic, with hardwood floors, lots of nooks and crannies, and built-in shelves and bookcases everywhere. Even the low ceilings contributed to the coziness, while the pale gray walls and white trim helped to bring lightness to a space that could have felt oppressive. Kristen particularly fell in love with the big picture window and the sunny kitchen. Randall said the screened porch was shaded most of the day, which prompted Kristen to make a mental note to find some cheap outdoor furniture first thing. She didn't plan on spending too much money for a one-year lease, but it would be a crime not to enjoy the space.

The two bedrooms were small, but Kristen just needed space for a bed in one and her writing desk in the other. George asked questions about the appliances, and whether the rental came with a lawn mower. Randall said it did not, but if Kristen didn't want to bother getting one herself, they could add

$30 to the rent and just take care of having it done. Kristen asked a few questions about the leasing terms, and the Mattoxes said since she had such good references they'd waive the deposit if she agreed not to get any pets while she lived there. Kristen agreed.

"Well, we brought the lease agreement with us, in case you're ready to sign now," Ellen said. "But it's fine if you want to take a few days to think about it or look around."

"No, I'm ready," Kristen said after a quick glance at her dad. He nodded his head. "This place seems just right."

"Oh, good!" Ellen said, her big smile reappearing. "Let's go out to the truck, then."

They filed out of the house, Randall locking the door behind them, and made their way to the truck, where Kristen quickly signed and initialed the lease.

"I'll make a copy for you to keep and give it to you when we hand off the keys," Ellen said as she took the papers and pen from Kristen. "Does that sound all right with you?"

"Of course."

"Like I said earlier, the Britts are moving out on Friday, and I've already scheduled the cleaning for the following Monday. We can meet anytime that Tuesday to hand off the keys."

"That works for me," Kristen replied.

"Do you want some help unloading your moving truck?" Randall chimed in.

Kristen shook her head. "I was planning to hire a moving company. I figure there's one of those 'college guys lift heavy stuff' companies in town."

"Nonsense," Randall replied. He looked over at George. "George, talk some sense into your girl. We don't mind helping at all, and there's no need to spend money if you don't have to."

"I tried to tell her I could get some help and it'd be easy."

Kristen rolled her eyes and waved her arm in the air. "Hello! I'm right here!"

George turned to his daughter, a twinkle in his eyes. "Sweetie. They really don't mind. You can spend the money on some porch furniture."

Randall nodded. "Yep. I can talk to Levi Blair too. I know he and Celia were hoping to meet Kristen and welcome her to town."

George nodded. "Good thinking. The Blairs were Rosalee's next-door-neighbors," he said to Kristen before she could ask. "They're good friends of ours."

Kristen shook her head. Another dilemma. It sounded nice, but it made her uncomfortable to accept help from strangers. On the other hand, they weren't strangers to her dad. George caught her eye and nodded. Well. She trusted her dad more than anyone else, so she'd let him take the lead on this one.

"If you are absolutely sure," she said to the Mattoxes, "then I will accept."

They exchanged phone numbers, waved

goodbye, and walked back toward the car, but paused with her hand on the door.

"Do you mind if we take a short walk around the neighborhood?" she asked. "I'd love to get a feel for the place."

"Of course," George pocketed his keys. "Great idea."

It felt strange to Kristen to be walking in a neighborhood that was so relatively quiet compared to her neighborhood in the city, even the neighborhood she grew up in. Large lawns and trees and other growing things muffled noise from the nearest major road. After about 15 minutes, George slowed and pointed at a dark blue house with a huge front porch and rose bushes flanking the front steps.

"That's Rosalee's old house," he said. "And that one," he gestured to a white house on the left. "is the Blairs'."

Kristen noted the swing hanging from the tree in the front yard and a scooter leaning against the front steps.

"Do they have grandkids?" she asked.

George chuckled and shook his head. "No, they've got a 10-year-old and a four-year-old," he said. "They're closer to your age than mine."

"Oh! Well, I need to reorient a little now." Would it be too much to hope that she might make a friend who lived this close?

The day was warming up and both Kristen and George were getting hungry, so they made their way back to the car and the condo. Kristen's brain kicked into overdrive, planning and dreaming, some of her residual nerves morphing into excited anticipation.

Chapter 2

The day Kristen had decided it was time to leave Chicago, the sun was shining in a cloudless sky, Lake Michigan was the perfect shade of glassy, brilliant blue, and the Cubs won their home opener.

Kirsten arrived early, which was how she preferred it. She liked to get on the Red Line near her apartment, and walk to Wrigley Field from the station. She liked to stop and chat with Segar, who had been selling t-shirts, caps, and pennants on the East side of the ball field for the past ten years. She liked to stop at the concessions and get two hot dogs and an extra large Coke before watching the pitchers warm up and making predictions on the bullpen. Most importantly, an early arrival and slow start gave Kristen time to talk with the other season ticket holders she saw at almost every home game: the Millers, the O'Shays, the Browns, the Chungs, Big Jim, and her former college roommates Liz, and Nora.

Kristen was often the first one in their sub section, but that day the O'Shays were already at their seats and halfway through their own pre-game ritual. Glen would stop at concessions and get two beers and a bottle of water. Robbie would come to the seats, wipe them down with her faded Cubs towel, then slather her fair skin with sunscreen. Usually, by the time she was done, Glen would arrive at the seats and hand Robbie her water and beer, which she would tuck underneath her seat before pulling out her black sketch pad and flowered pencil case. Glen would keep his beer in hand, tuck a pencil behind one ear, pull a folded score card out of his back pocket, then settle into his seat.

"Hi there, Kristen." Robbie tucked her towel into the pocket of her loose-fitting linen pants and reached across the back of her seat to hug Kristen. She held her cardboard concessions tray to the side and wrapped the other arm around Robbie's shoulders.

"Hey, Robbie. How're you doing? Did Glen get off early today?"

"Not hardly," Glen spoke from behind her, where he'd just walked up still in his UPS browns. "But I did luck out with a light route today, and I didn't ask for anything extra when I got back to the warehouse."

The Millers and the Chungs arrived next, Mrs. Miller and Mrs. Chung talking nearly simultaneously, yet somehow completely understanding each other and carrying on an actual conversation. They filed down the row behind Kristen, waving as they passed her. Mr. Chung, the last of the quartet, leaned down when he reached her.

"Mrs. Chung wanted me to let you know that Phil's single again. If you want her to set up a date or something."

Kristen smiled. "Tell her that's very sweet, but I'm good. I have a very strict no blind date policy." *A well-earned policy*, she thought. Mrs. Chung had been dying to set Kristen up on a date with her only son Phil, but Phil seemed to always be in a relationship and always with women that Mrs. Chung wasn't impressed with. Kristen wasn't sure if the issue was genuinely Phil's taste or his mother's unrealistic standards, but either way, Kristen was steering clear of that drama.

Liz walked up as the section filled in earnest. Kristen wrapped in a big bear hug. Liz lived in the suburbs across town, and it had been a few months since Kristen had seen her.

"Your hair!" Liz exclaimed as she walked by Kristen to her seat. "It's so long! And purple!"

Kristen made a face. "Very, very spur of the moment. I'm not sure I like it. Makes me feel like I'm trying too hard." Liz fluffed Kristen's purple-tipped curls. "Well, I love it. Hey, I haven't seen you around online much lately. Taking a break?"

"Something like that." In truth, social media had

joined the increasingly long list of things Kristen found unsatisfying and uninspiring lately.

"Enough about my hair," she said. "I want to hear about your life and your kids. And what you're watching right now because I can not find ANYTHING interesting."

They talked until the national anthem, pausing to stand as a local school choir began singing. Kristen looked around the packed stadium, soaking in the sea of red, white, and blue. The sky was clear, the breeze was cool, the atmosphere was full of hope and possibility, and a sense of contentment that had eluded her for weeks settled into her soul. She saw movement out of the corner of her eye and turned to smile at Big Jim, who had slid into his seat on the edge of her row. Big Jim was, in fact, a big man—over six feet tall and solidly built—and always came to the games straight from work, his shirt sleeves rolled up and his tie loosened. Kristen asked him once why he didn't just take the tie off and put it in his car, and he'd simply responded "I take the El," to which she'd responded "why not put it in your bag." to which he'd grinned and shrugged. "Never thought about it, I guess." Based on his unchanged look at every game, Kristen assumed he'd never thought about it again after the conversation either. That or Big Jim had a stubborn and contrary streak.

Big Jim wasn't much of a talker. He'd had his two seats for about five years, but almost always came to the games alone. On weekends, he would sometimes bring his grandson, an elfin-faced little boy with brown skin, bright green eyes, and a head full of curly hair. Zeke had been a chubby-kneed three-year-old when he'd come to his first game with Big Jim and, much to Kristen's amusement and delight, he had talked non-stop during the nine innings of the game, pausing only for bathroom breaks and drinks. Zeke was a devoted Cubs fan, and Kristen liked to imagine posters and pennants covering his room, with a growing collection of signed baseballs. Kristen often wondered if Big Jim had bought his season tickets for Zeke, but when she'd asked, Big Jim had just smiled and shrugged.

"Maybe a little," he'd said in his quiet bass voice. "Or maybe I just forgot how much I love baseball."

Nora arrived at the top of the second inning, her hands full of nachos, a large soda, and a soft pretzel. Big Jim stood up and into the aisle to let her pass, bending down with a small smile as Nora stopped to say hello and kiss both his cheeks.

"Ciao, you gorgeous people!" she said, working her way down the row. "I've missed you! I hope for your sake this game is slow and boring because I am talking the entire time."

True to her word, Nora kept the conversation flowing throughout the game, which was, if not exactly slow, slow enough for conversation between friends who hadn't seen each other in a couple of months. *This feels right*, Kristen thought. It was as if she could feel her soul exhale and settle for the first time in months. Was that all it took? Time with friends? Comforting ritual? A shout from the crowd pulled her attention to the game for the next several minutes as they all kept their eyes on a particularly tense group of pitches, and ultimately the Cubs' first score of the game.

"Okay, after that I need something to eat." Liz remained standing. "Anyone need anything while I'm up?"

They shook their heads, but Nora added, "hurry back. I have a big, juicy Italian story to tell."

"No fair!" Liz exclaimed. "you should have led with that! Not listened to my lame stories about work."

When Liz returned to their row, the Cubs had scored again and everyone was passing around high fives. As soon as they all sat down Nora's eyes got that particular gleam they had when she was about to tell a really dramatic story.

"I may have met someone."

"Ooohh," Liz said, taking a long sip of her coke. "An Italian someone? A male someone?"

"Yes and yes."

Her friends leaned forward in their seats, the game temporarily forgotten.

"Well," Kristen said. "Spill it. We all know you're dying to."

It could have been a romance novel plot: Nora had just settled into her seat on the airplane headed to Milan when a shadow fell across the page of her magazine and a deep voice said, "I have the window." Nora had looked up, up, up into the deepest, darkest brown eyes she'd ever seen, framed by eyelashes that would make a model weep on a face that she was pretty sure she'd seen on a sculpture at the Galleria de Accademia in Florence. His name was Gabriel, and they were both heading to Milan, where they ended up spending a lot of time together over the two weeks Nora was there. In true Nora fashion, the story was nearly a play-by-play of every interaction between her and Gabriel, told with big gestures and lots of details, especially of the food.

"Nora, I swear if you describe one more meal before this game's over, I'm driving to Nona's Kitchen right now." Liz glanced down at her half-eaten nachos.

Nora waved away Liz's protests but conceded with a, "fine, fine. It's not important. The important thing is that Gabriel is funny, a good listener, has a cat, loves his mother and sisters, and has season tickets to A.C. Milan. He married young, but his wife died in an auto accident about 10 years ago. No kids. He appreciates opinionated women, I got his number, and he's coming to visit this summer while he's on holiday. Now, I suppose someone should tell me what inning it is now."

"Sixth, and we're ahead."

The three friends turned to look at Mrs. Chung, who laughed at their surprised faces. "Honey, you know I eavesdropped, and that was the best story

I've heard in ages. Even better than a movie. So sad about his wife, though. I hate to hear about people becoming widowed so young. Well, anyway, you keep me posted."

"Of course, Mrs. Chung."

Kristen realized she needed to use the ladies' room. She slipped past Big Jim and headed down the stairs. She smiled to herself, thinking of Nora's story, happy that her friend had had a romantic adventure, and sincerely hoping that regardless of how the story ended, that it was a happy ending. As was her habit when meeting new people, Kristen compiled a mental list of questions to ask Gabriel. What was his family like? Did he have a good relationship with them? What was his childhood like? School? Play? Was he athletic, bookish, outdoorsy? How did he end up in a job that allowed him to travel to another country? Did he always dream of that? She always had questions.

When the game was over, the three of them looked at each other.

"Nona's?" Liz asked. "I have a craving for tiramisu."

"Agreed," Kristen chimed in. "Can I ride with one of you? I'll take the El home."

Once upon a time, the three former college roommates had crammed themselves into a tiny apartment near Humboldt Park. They'd rented the top floor of a two-flat from the elderly owner who lived in the bottom apartment. After several years together, a family emergency had drawn Nora back to her family's home base in Little Italy, and by the time life had settled down, she was content in her studio apartment down the street from her parents. Liz had eventually gotten married and moved out, but by then Kristen's freelance income was steady enough to pay the bills and Mrs. Carpenter was in no hurry to raise the rent. She had loved the "good girls" who lived above her, who helped her out when she needed a hand, who never had wild parties even in their 20s and who always paid the rent on time. So she kept the rent low because she told Kristen it felt like kicking out family, and who wanted to take a risk on new tenants, anyway?

The flat was a short walk to the El, so even though Kristen had a car she really only used it occasionally, sometimes for work if research took her outside the public transit zone, to drive out to the suburbs to visit Liz, to visit her dad now that he'd moved to Missouri, and now and then for a road trip out of town. Needless to say, she hadn't driven it to the game.

"Don't be silly," Nora said. "I can drop you off at home after. Now let's go eat."

Chapter 3

Nona's looked so much like the movie version of an Italian restaurant that the first time Kristen had eaten there she'd assumed it was a bland chain catering to out-of-towners and people looking for endless breadsticks and a Lady and the Tramp moment. Much to her surprise, Nona's was the real deal, a small, dim space filled with the smell of garlic, herbs, and wine. The tables and chairs were warm, dark wood, worn smooth and glassy from years of diners and furniture polish. Velvet drapes hung from the walls, softening and dampening the effects of the tiled floor. In between the draperies, wrought iron sconces provided a soft light, mingling with the miniature lamps that sat on each table. When they'd first started coming to Nona's many years before, the table lamps were real candles, but a fire at a nearby restaurant had inspired the owner to exchange open flames for electric light.

Nona's was an unassuming place, but you felt at

home the minute you stepped inside. The tables might contain families with small children, gray-haired couples, people gazing romantically and starry-eyed at each other, individuals dining alone, or groups of friends. Kristen always walked in feeling like she should know someone at one of the tables. The three of them had been eating there long enough, often they did. For many people, Nona's felt like an extension of their own home, and that was certainly true for Kristen, Nora, and Liz.

A somewhat tall brunette with a big smile and deep dimples greeted them at the door. Her dark hair was twisted into a low bun, and she wore a simple black dress with a pair of canary-yellow flats. Stephanie had been the hostess at Nona's for years. She was the youngest daughter of the current owner, who was the great granddaughter of the original Nona, and Stephanie was a big part of creating Nona's uniquely homey and classy atmosphere.

"Welcome, friends! It's been a while." Stephanie said with a flash of dimples. "Would you like your favorite corner booth?"

Their "yes" was unanimous and emphatic, and she led them through the restaurant to a booth in the back corner, far from both the swinging kitchen door on one end of the restaurant, and the restrooms at the other. It was the perfect booth for people watching, laughing loudly, or having deep, serious conversations, all without disturbing other customers. As the three women slid across the bench seats, it felt like coming home.

Kristen sat quietly, listening to the other two chat with Stephanie until she had to go greet some other customers. Lucas, a college-aged server, quickly replaced her spot at the end of the table. He took their drink orders, dropped off menus, and left them to make the always challenging decision of what to eat. When the three of them came to Nona's, they always ate family-style and shared everything, which meant sometimes ordering was simple, and sometimes it was more like a snake draft. Tonight was definitely a snake draft night, Kristen thought, smiling as Liz and Nora argued about how many appetizers they should get.

Normally Kristen was in the thick of the discussion, but she felt disconnected from the debate over Caprese Salad versus Prosciutto Wrapped Figs. Eventually, Nora and Liz asked Kristen what she thought, and Kristen just shrugged and said: "I'm fine with whatever." Liz raised an eyebrow at this lackluster response, so Kristen mustered some energy. "I don't know why you're even arguing. We all ate at the ballpark, so you know we won't eat full meals. Let's get both those appetizers plus the fruit and cheese plate, a tossed salad, and some desserts. We're all here for the desserts and wine, anyway."

They knew she was right. Nora waved Lucas back over and put in their order. As he walked away, the conversation turned to a popular book that was currently climbing the best-seller charts and on everyone's "What to Read This Summer" lists. Still, Kristen found herself unable to focus on the conversation. She put her elbow on the table and rested her chin in her hand, taking a drink of her wine and letting her eyes roam the restaurant. She watched a woman slice up pieces of roasted asparagus and what looked like melon for a baby that was happily gumming a hunk of crusty bread. As the woman sliced, she talked to the man at the table with her. Reading their body language, Kristen guessed it was her husband, or at the very least the baby's father. At the next table, a different kind of family sat—mom, dad, and three teenagers. Two of the teenagers — were they twins? — talked animatedly, clearly in storytelling mode. The parents listened intently, but the third and youngest teenager, maybe 14 or 15, stared out the plate-glass window of the restaurant, a look of longing on her face. Kristen watched a young man at another booth reach across the table to rest his hand on that of the woman sitting across from him; their eyes shone with discovery and new love. Kristen looked away quickly, feeling like an intruder on their private moment. She smiled at the next diner that caught her eye, a silver-haired and somewhat wrinkled gentleman in a charcoal blazer sitting alone at a table, one hand navigating his bowl of soup while the other propped open a worn paperback. Henry. That was his name, she recalled. An economics professor with a deep love of detective fiction.

Kristen watched Stephanie seat a middle-aged couple at a table by the window. The man, dressed in dark pants and a remarkably unwrinkled gray button-up shirt, pulled a chair out from the table for the woman to sit. The woman, highlighted dark hair in perfect barrel curls and wearing a flattering floral wrap dress, tilted her head toward the man and smiled. *First date*, Kristen thought. *Or maybe a very special anniversary.* She itched to go over to the table and ask. To be honest, she wanted to go to every table, find out the story behind it all.

Lucas appeared with their appetizers, and the four women thanked him and began reaching for the delicious-looking food. Kristen reached for a fig and tried to return her attention to her friends, but she couldn't concentrate. She closed her eyes and rolled her shoulders, taking a big, slow breath like she was in yoga class. When she opened her eyes, Liz was staring at her from across the table.

"You okay?" she asked.

"Yeah, I'm fine."

Liz raised her eyebrows.

Kristen's eyes slipped away from Liz's piercing gaze. Where was Nora? She spotted her across the restaurant, talking to Henry. Kristen fidgeted. She was fine, wasn't she? Why was Liz's stare making her feel like she was lying?

"Look, I'm fine, really. Just..." she hesitated, trying to find the word. "I'm feeling... restless?

Emotionally itchy? Disconnected?"

"Like... tonight?"

"Tonight," Kristen said, then thought some more. "Or maybe..." she reached around and pulled the ends of her hair up in front of her face, the bright purple tips visible even in the dim light. "Maybe not just tonight?"

"Hmmm...." Liz rested her chin in her hand and stared at Kristen as if she was staring at a modern painting and trying to work out the hidden metaphors. "Now that I think about it, you have dropped off the radar lately. Are you sure you're okay?"

Kristen thought about the past few months: her accidental hiatus from social media, her nightstand stacked with half-finished books, her email inbox with an appalling number of messages waiting for answers. She thought about how she'd logged more running miles in the past month than she had in the previous two months combined.

"Nothing is wrong," Kristen replied slowly, "but maybe not everything is fine. Does that make any sense?"

Liz took a sip of her red wine and nodded. "Yeah, I think so."

"What are you guys talking about?" Nora asked, sliding back into the booth next to Kristen.

Kristen sighed. She hated this kind of attention on her when she felt like nothing was actually going on, but weren't they establishing that maybe something was going on?

"Kristen is being weird," Liz said, her smile softening the blunt words. "Nothing is wrong, but not everything is fine."

Nora nodded. "Makes perfect sense," she said. "Not weird at all."

"Thanks, guys. I just feel a little overly dramatic talking about it."

Nora waved her hand dismissively. "It's us." The simple phrase was loaded with meaning and history, bringing to mind countless silly and serious conversations, late nights, early mornings, laughter, and tears.

"Why don't you tell us your symptoms," Liz said, "the feelings that seem out of place? Maybe we can do a little emotional diagnosing."

"Well..." Kristen took a sip of her drink, then reached for another fig. Two pairs of sympathetic eyes watched her, unhurried, undistracted. "Well... I'm having trouble focusing lately. I've been running a lot more than normal. I keep wanting to get out of my apartment, but I don't want to see people I know."

"What are you reading?" Nora asked.

Kristen shook her head. "Nothing. Or, at least, I can't finish anything. And even if I try to read short stories or magazine articles, I skim them."

"Are you watching anything?" Liz chimed in.

"Old 'comfort' shows. The occasional comedy special—although sometimes only half of it. Travel documentaries, home improvement shows, cooking shows. Nothing that I need to concentrate on, and again, half the time, I don't even finish them."

"Maybe you..." Nora started to say, but Liz interrupted. "Do you want advice?" Liz asked, "or do you just want us to listen?"

"Either way." Kristen shrugged, then laughed. "I can't even muster an opinion on friend-therapy."

Nora started again. "Maybe you need a vacation?" she suggested. "Come with me on my next trip to Italy. Italy is excellent for inspiration."

"Maybe."

"I know you're going to say it's the Gabriel factor talking, but maybe you need a little romance? A date? A few dates?"

Kristen shook her head. "No. Absolutely no, I do not need any romance in my life right now."

They continued to brainstorm, their suggestions ranging from somewhat helpful and serious (adopt a dog, volunteer, take a class somewhere) to the impractical or absurd (adopt a child, learn to sail, buy a home), and although none of their suggestions really felt like the right thing, just the act of talking about her current malaise lifted her spirits more than she expected. And like the journalist she was, she took notes on their suggestions, just in case.

They were all yawning by the time they paid their bill and said goodbye, more a testament to their busy lives than the lateness of the hour. Nora convinced Kristen to accept the ride home, and they settled into the kind of companionable silence shared by those who have known each other a long time. Kristen gazed out the passenger window, watching the city she loved tuck in for the night. Familiar landmarks and stores and restaurants flitted in and out of her view. At 10 p.m. on a weeknight, traffic was light, and it wasn't long before Nora was pulling up to the curb in front of the two-flat. She gazed up at the navy blue house, and a wistful smile crept onto her face.

"We made some wonderful memories here."

Kristen nodded in agreement but said nothing, her throat unexpectedly choked up.

"Well, tell Mrs. Carpenter, I said hello. Want to have lunch sometime this week?"

Kristen cleared her throat and made an effort to sound normal. "Yeah, sounds great!" She got out of the car, shut the door gently, and waved as Nora drove away. After the car had rounded the corner, Kristen slowly turned around and stared up at the house, taking in the freshly touched up white trim, the plethora of potted plants surrounding the front stoop, the lamp in the upstairs window that she always left on when she left, and Mrs. Carpenter's cat peeking out from under the curtained downstairs picture window. Tears pricked her eyes because on the short drive home from Nona's, it had occurred to her what she needed to do to scratch her restless itch.

Chapter 4

When Kristen pulled into the driveway of her new home on moving day, the Mattoxes were waiting on the front yard bench. They waved as she put her car in park and gathered the box full of pastries she'd picked up on the way.

"Now how did you know I was hankering after a little morning pick-me-up," Randall said with a grin.

"Nothing like a little sugar and carbs to make unloading a moving truck easier!" Kristen replied.

She followed the Mattoxes into the house and deposited the box on the counter.

"The truck should be here in the next 20 minutes. I got a call while I was on my way over."

"Excellent," Ellen said. She handed Kristen a blue folder and a ring with three keys on it. "The folder has some phone numbers for you: ours, of course, plus the plumber, HVAC company, and lawn service that we use. Obviously, you can just call us if anything comes up, but this way you can call them directly if it's more convenient or if we're not available. They all have this address on file, so they should bill us for any work that needs done. Randall does most of the general handyman stuff, so if you need anything like that just call him."

"That's really thoughtful, thank you," Kristen said, she thought she'd never have a landlord she liked as much as Mrs. Carpenter, but these two sweet souls were giving Mrs. Carpenter a run for her money. "And these are the keys?" she held up the ring. "Are all the locks on the house the same?"

Ellen nodded. "Brand new deadbolts," she said. "We have them re-keyed for each new tenant."

Kristen particularly appreciated that. She pocketed the keys and tucked the folder under her arm. "I'm going to put this in my car for now, just so it doesn't get lost amidst the moving craziness, and I have a cooler of drinks to get." she gestured to the box on the counter. "Help yourself to a pastry!" she said.

She had just set the cooler in the shade by the bench when she spotted four people coming down the sidewalk toward the little house: a man and woman holding hands, a boy about 10 or 11 on a bicycle, and a little girl in a bright green tutu on a scooter. The boy on the bike reached the house first and stopped directly in front of Kristen.

"Hi, I'm Tripp," he said. "That's my mom and dad and sister Aislinn. We live around the corner," he pointed to the far end of the street. "My mom said you're moving into the neighborhood today and that we should try to get to know you because your Dad married Mrs. McDonnell who isn't Mrs. McDonnell anymore. She used to be our neighbor and sometimes she would babysit or come over for dinner and she let me play with her dog Buddy a lot. Mrs. McDonnell, I mean Mrs. Bowen, lives in another house now but she still comes over to visit, with Mr. Bowen, and we have new neighbors now but they don't have any kids, and I was really hoping for someone to ride bikes or skateboard with, because my dad got me a skateboard for my birthday this year and I'm getting really good, but I didn't ride it here today because one of the wheels is loose and Dad needs to fix it."

"Hi!" Tripp's family had caught up, and the woman—Kristen thought she remembered her name was Celia—interjected before Tripp could continue into what Kristen was sure would be the Blairs' entire life story. "I'm Celia Butler," she said with a smile. "I see you've met Tripp, and this is Aislinn," Celia rested her hand on the little girls' head. "And this is Levi." Both Celia and Levi exuded an open and friendly attitude, a casualness that made her feel as though she already knew them.

Kristen reached out and shook Celia's hand, then Levi's. "It is so nice to meet you all," she said. She glanced down at Tripp. "And I especially appreciate your introductions," she told him. "I feel like we're friends already. And I really was hoping to make friends in the neighborhood."

"Yeah, Tripp's usually a pretty good source of information, and he's never met a stranger," Levi said dryly.

"I've got some donuts and croissants in the kitchen if you want one and it's okay with your parents," Kristen said to Tripp. "Juice and milk in the fridge."

Tripp glanced up at Celia, who nodded, "Go ahead. Take Aislinn too and help her pick something out."

The bike and scooter clattered to the sidewalk, and the two raced toward the front door, waving to the Mattoxes who were walking down the path toward the sidewalk. Ellen laughed.

"Those two seem like they have a lot of energy," she said as she joined Kristen and the Blairs.

"Oh, they definitely do," Celia replied, "But Levi threatened them pretty thoroughly to not get in the way once we start moving things. So, hopefully, they'll keep that energy in the backyard or something."

"Speaking of moving things, the truck should be here soon. And thank you both so much for coming to help. It's really above and beyond being neighborly."

Levi shrugged. "It's no problem. Rosalee and George are good friends, and I remember what it was like to move to a new town where I didn't know anyone."

"And come over for supper tonight," Celia added. "I promise I won't make you stay long, because I'm sure you'll be exhausted. I was just going to bring a casserole or something by, but I'd rather get to know you a little if you're up for it."

"Oh!" Kristen hesitated. "Are you sure? That feels like a lot for someone you don't know."

"Nonsense," Celia waved away Kristen's protest. "George and Rosalee are like our extended family, so you are too. Come over around 6:00."

"Well..." *Weren't you just saying that you wanted to make friends?* "Okay, yeah. That would be nice, thank you." Kristen felt like she should protest more, but she had taken an instant liking to this disarming couple. Was there a friendship term for love at first sight?

She saw her dad's car coming down the street with the moving truck trailing behind. George parked on the curb, and he and Rosalee exited the vehicle as the truck driver began maneuvering the back of the truck into the driveway. Once the driver positioned the pod, he went through the procedure of detaching it from the truck cab, then made his way over to the knot of people for Kristen's signature on the delivery papers. She confirmed the pickup time for the next day and then turned to her assembled crew.

"All right!" she said. "Let's do this!"

She turned and walked to unlock the truck's back, the Blairs, Mattoxes, her Dad and Rosalee trailing behind her. She heard a phone ring, and Levi say, "hello?" He walked a little ways away from the group, but was back by the time she had unlocked the padlock and raised the back of the storage pod.

"The kids asked if they could play in the backyard, and I said yes," Levi said to Celia as he walked back up. "Also, that was Jack. He just pulled into our driveway, so I told him to get down here and help."

Celia clapped her hands. "Oh, yay! It's been so long since we've seen him!"

Kristen wondered who Jack was and how Levi was so easily able to talk him into helping move a complete stranger. It still felt awkward accepting help, but at this point she figured she was committed.

George climbed into the truck and began pointing out which boxes needed to go first to unearth the furniture, saying that it would probably make the most sense to get the furniture in place before unloading the majority of the other items. Everyone agreed. Kristen grabbed a box labeled "kitchen."

"Why don't you hang out in the house," Rosalee said as Kristen passed her. "That way you can point us all in the right direction. Especially once the furniture starts coming in—no sense in moving things around more than you have to."

Kristen nodded. "Good idea. I don't want to leave all the work to you, but I'll direct traffic as much as possible."

After depositing her kitchen box, Kristen stayed in the house for a few minutes to point people in the right direction, then decided to grab another armload herself. She turned toward the front door and almost ran into someone coming inside.

"Oops! Sorry," she said, moving to the side. "Guess I'm in too big of a rush."

"No problem," the voice was deep and unfamiliar. The person shifted their armload of boxes, and Kristen looked into a smiling and very handsome face. The stranger was tall enough that she had to look up at him—which was unusual for her—and had a strong, rugged face with at least a week's worth of beard and a deep dimple in one cheek. Dark brown eyes gazed at her, one eyebrow raised. "Do you know where this goes?"

Kristen's stomach fluttered.

"Umm..." she mentally slapped herself. *Focus. Focus.* "Down the hall, first bedroom you come to."

"Thanks," the stranger winked. Kristen felt her face flush, and fought the urge to turn and watch him walk down the hall. What was even happening right now? She willed her feet to move and resumed her walk outside.

"Jack's here!" Celia said brightly as Kristen passed her in the yard. "I put him straight to work. Feel free to boss him around if you need to."

Jack. Kristen thought. *Of course.*

Kristen thanked her, told her where to set the

box she was carrying and walked up to the pod. Her dad stood inside, hands on his hips.

"Hey, Kristen," he said when she greeted him. "If you want to take these lamps here, I think we can go ahead with most of the furniture next."

Kristen quickly grabbed the lamps and headed back to the house. She lectured herself on the way inside.

You are a grown woman, she said to herself. *You have seen ridiculously good-looking men before, and there is no need to act like a teenager. No stuttering, no staring, no blushing. You have interviewed rock stars for heavens' sake, and acted calm, cool, and collected. Pull yourself together.*

By the time she'd deposited the lamps in the office bedroom, Kristen felt much more in control of herself. Jack had just startled her; that was all. She walked into the living room in time to see her dad and Randall walk in with the couch, and directed them to the spot she'd picked out. Levi and Jack followed close behind with her kitchen table, Celia and Ellen behind them with two kitchen chairs. Once Levi and Jack had deposited the little square table, Kristen stepped up to the pair.

"I'm Kristen," she said with a smile, holding out her hand. "Sorry again about almost running into you earlier. You must be Jack. Thank you so much for coming to help."

Jack shook her hand, a crooked smile lighting up his face. "Nice to meet you, Kristen. And it's really no trouble. Plus, Celia told me if I didn't help, she wouldn't feed me, so..." he broke off into a laugh as Celia punched his arm lightly.

"Whatever goofball. Now come on, no more breaks." she winked at Kristen as the men grabbed donuts, then Celia herded them out the door.

When she was alone again in the kitchen, Kristen took a deep breath and let it out in a rush. *Okay*, she thought, *See? No big deal.*

Chapter 5

Jack Blair toweled condensation from the shower off of the bathroom mirror, and scrubbed a hand over his chin, wondering if he should shave before quickly rejecting the idea. He hung the towel up on the towel bar before exiting the bathroom and heading down the hall to his room at Levi and Celia's. Technically, it was a general purpose guest room, but since he was the most frequent occupant, everyone just called it Uncle Jack's room.

The air in the hall felt cool after the steamy bathroom, and goosebumps prickled his bare torso. It felt refreshing, though. It wasn't exactly a hot day, but by the time he finished moving furniture for the neighbor and then helping Levi clean out his garage, it had felt plenty warm. In his room, Levi pulled a t-shirt out of the top drawer.

"Do you want to help me work on my Wakanda?"

Jack turned as he tugged on the t-shirt and found Tripp standing in the open doorway.

"What's that?" he asked.

"I've got a new Lego set of Wakanda. Mom said we have a little bit of time to work on it before supper. Do you want to help?"

"Sure pal, lead the way."

Jack followed Tripp to the living room, halfway listening to the boy give him a play-by-play of his favorite Marvel movies and all the Marvel Lego sets he was saving his money to buy. He loved Tripp, but the kid probably talked more in thirty minutes than Jack usually talked in a week. A large wooden tray sat on top of the coffee table in the living room, a pile of little plastic bricks in the middle next to an instruction booklet. The tray was almost as large as the coffee table, a simple rectangle with a two inch lip running all along the edge. Jack guessed Levi had made it specifically for Tripp's Lego building. Big enough to work on a project and keep the pieces contained, but small enough to move to another location if needed.

"Nice setup," Jack said as he took a seat on the floor.

"Yeah it's cool," Trip said as he knelt on the floor. "We usually keep it on the dining room table since we eat in the kitchen, but Mom said that we have to eat in the dining room tonight because of you and the new lady."

Jack raised an eyebrow, but Tripp was already focused on the Legos.

"Lady?" Jack asked.

"Uh-huh. The lady with the moving stuff today. Mom invited her to supper. She said it's neighborly because she's new and she would be unpacking all day, and who wants to cook after you've been unpacking all day."

"It's a good point."

They worked in silence for a few minutes before Levi and Aislinn walked into the room.

"Hey," he said. "I promised Aislinn an episode of *Daniel Tiger* if she cleaned her room without complaining. Do you guys mind?"

Jack and Tripp shook their heads. Jack worked on the Legos with only half his attention, the other half thinking about the "new lady" coming over for supper. Kristen. Deep blue eyes and legs for days. He smiled, thinking about how flustered she'd been when she'd almost run into him. She'd recovered well, though, no trace of embarrassment when she'd officially introduced herself.

Cheerful music came out of the television speakers, and Aislinn sang along. Jack glanced up as Levi settled on the floor next to him, reaching out to join the Lego building.

"Thanks again for helping today," Levi said.

"Happy to."

"I hope you don't mind that Celia invited Kristen over on your first night. She just wanted to make her feel extra welcome since Kristen is Rosalee's step-daughter."

"I don't mind at all."

Jack's voice must have given something away, because he glanced up to see Levi giving him a look that said, *behave yourself tonight.*

Jack just grinned and held up his hand, three fingers raised. *Scout's honor.*

Levi rolled his eyes.

• •

Kristen slung on her leather cross-body and picked up her phone, the house key, and a bottle of wine. After double checking that she'd turned off all the lights except for one lamp in the living room, she walked out the front door and locked it behind her.

She took a deep breath of the early evening air that smelled faintly of turned dirt and freshly mowed grass. The sun rested just above the horizon, and Kristen thought it might just be the perfect evening. It felt good to stretch her legs after an afternoon of bending, kneeling, and sorting. She'd gotten her kitchen, bathroom, and bedroom fully unpacked and mostly set up, and felt optimistic that she could finish the rest of her unpacking tomorrow. One perk to being single, she thought, is that there was less stuff to deal with during a move. Not that she knew that much about moving, seeing as she'd lived in the same apartment for 20 years. But she had helped Liz and Kole move from their first apartment into their current home after their second child was born, and it had boggled her mind how much stuff two tiny people added to a household.

Before she knew it, Kristen walked up the porch steps of the Blairs' house and rang the doorbell. Levi answered the door.

"Come on in," he said, stepping to the side and holding the door open.

"Thanks," Kristen replied as she walked in. "And I want to thank you again for your help today, not to mention having me over tonight. It's above and beyond."

Levi waved away her thanks. "Don't mention it," he said with a smile. "Celia's in the kitchen, or you're welcome to hang out with me and Jack and the kids in the living room."

Jack? Kristen thought. *Why was Jack here?* She immediately suspected a set-up, and bristled at the thought of being thrown at a man so soon, and by people who were practically strangers!

She forced a smile, "I'll see if I can help in the kitchen."

The Blairs' kitchen was a cheerful green room with a big window, currently full of delicious smells and upbeat music. Celia was pulling a big roasting pan out of the oven, setting it down on the kitchen table next to two round loaves of bread and a pitcher of lemonade.

"You have good timing!" she said when she caught sight of Kristen. She walked over and surprised Kristen with a warm hug. "I'm so glad you came. I hope you don't mind another stranger at supper. Jack's here to visit for a couple of weeks, but we didn't think he'd be here until tomorrow. At least he got here in time to help with the muscle work today, right?"

"Right!" Kristen said brightly, a little embarrassed about her initial assumption about Jack's presence. *Arrogant, much*? She said to herself. She handed Celia the bottle of wine.

"Here. It's not nearly enough of a thank you, but I couldn't come empty-handed."

"Oh, thank you! I was just thinking that a glass of wine would be perfect, but we're out." She walked over to a drawer and began rummaging through it for a bottle opener.

"It smells amazing in here, by the way. Anything I can do to help?"

Celia nodded to the open shelving next to the sink. "I think I've decided it's too nice a night to eat inside. How about you take a stack of plates and silverware out to the patio?"

"Of course! Good idea."

It didn't take long to set everything out on the picnic table outside, and in short order, everyone had found a spot. Although the patio space wasn't covered, a trellis that currently held some kind of barely budding vines and a plethora of fairy lights bordered it on three sides. A few battery-powered lanterns, including one bug light, hung from plant stands, and provided plenty of light as the sun dropped lower over the horizon.

"Everyone dig in!" Celia said, and she began spooning food onto the children's plates. It was a simple meal of roast chicken, potatoes, carrots, asparagus, and the crusty loaves of bread.

"Did you make this?" Jack asked Celia as he sliced off the end of a loaf of bread. Celia laughed.

"No, but I'm flattered that you think I could. I went to Flour Sack after we finished up at Kristen's today."

"It's amazing," Jack mumbled around a mouth full of the crusty bread. Kristen had to agree.

Conversation stalled as everyone filled their plates and their glasses and settled into eating. Kristen had told herself not to instigate twenty questions, which is what she tended to do in groups of new people, but after a few bites of food and silence, she couldn't help herself.

"So how do you all know each other?" she asked, glancing between the other three adults.

"Jack's my cousin," Levi said. "Practically a brother, to be honest. We grew up just a few miles from each other, and then he lived with my family most of high school."

"Here in Riverton?"

"No," Celia chimed in. "Crofton. It's a small town. Most people haven't heard of it. That's where I grew up too. My family moved there when I was in third grade, and I met Levi the first week of school in Mrs. Wilson's class." She glanced over at Levi and smiled, a small, intimate smile that spoke of a lifetime of shared memories.

"More chicken, please!" Aislinn interrupted the reminiscing, and Celia's attention turned briefly to the kids, helping Aislinn refill her plate and passing the lemonade pitcher to Tripp. Kristen turned to the still silent Jack, sitting across from her.

"So, Jack, do you still live in Crofton?"

"Hell no." The answer was simple, but Kristen sensed there was a lot more to those two words.

When he offered no further commentary, Kristen pressed in a little further. "Where do you live now?"

"Nowhere in particular." Jack quirked an eyebrow as if signaling to Kristen that he knew what she was doing, and would not make it easy on her.

"Jack," Celia said drily, "I know you've only been around roughnecks for the last nine months, but have you really forgotten how to carry on a conversation?"

"Sorry," Jack said with that same lopsided grin Kristen had noticed earlier in the day. "She's kind of right. I'm a contract welder. I take jobs all around the country, lots of construction, oil and gas, but I'm not based with any one company. I have an apartment in California that I rent out as a vacation property when I'm not using it, and I stay here pretty often too."

"Uncle Jack has his own room," Tripp interjected. "It's the smallest."

Kristen laughed. "Well, that only makes sense," she said before turning back to Jack. "Do you ever get lonely moving around so much?"

Jack shrugged. "Not really. I'm kind of..."

"A loner," Celia offered.

Jack rolled his eyes in her direction. "Sure. Loner. But in a cool way, not in a serial killer kind of way."

Celia picked up the bottle of wine that Kristen had brought and nodded toward Kristen's empty glass.

"More wine?"

"Please. But just a tiny bit." Kristen held her glass up so Celia could add a splash of the fruity red. "So, Celia, when did you and Levi actually start dating?"

Celia set the bottle down. "It's basically the plot to a coming of age novel," she replied with a smile. "The three of us were friends for a long time. Jack lived a couple of miles from Levi, and I lived just a mile past Jack's place, so it was easy. Then the summer I turned 13, I got boobs and acne, and the boys didn't quite know how to deal. Frankly," she admitted, "I didn't know how to deal either. You know."

Kristen nodded, remembering her own entry into puberty. Her dad had done his best to navigate it, but it had been a rough few years.

"So, we kind of drifted apart for a little while, friendly but not really friends. Then a couple of summers later, the three of us were lifeguards at the lake together, and by the second week were right back to being the three amigos again."

"Eh, that's a little misleading," Jack said. "We were the three amigos for a few weeks, and then Levi finally got the nerve to ask you out on a date and it was two plus one."

"Well, sure, that's true, but we never ditched you."

Jack tipped his wine glass toward her. "I'll give you that." He turned to Kristen. "They kept the romantic stuff pretty chill around me," he told her. "I was never a third wheel."

"Did you two ever fight over her?"

"Jack knew there was no chance," Levi said, his smile taking away any edge the words might have had otherwise.

Jack rolled his eyes. "More like, by the time we started hanging out again I was living with you and had more on my mind than having a girlfriend."

Kristen tilted her head and opened her mouth, but before she could explore that intriguing comment, Celia stood up and started stacking empty plates.

"Who's ready for dessert?"

"Me!" The exclamation came from the far corner of the yard, where Tripp and Aislinn—who had finished their food quickly and abandoned the grownups—were playing with flashlights in the deepening dark. They now came running back toward the pool of soft light, jumping back onto the bench seats with the enthusiasm of children who know they're about to get sugar.

"Here, let me help." Kristen stood up and gathered some empty dishes, then followed Celia into the warm kitchen. She hadn't noticed how cool it had gotten now that the sun had set, but the contrast between inside and outside was noticeable.

"I hope I'm not being too nosy," Kristen said to Celia as she deposited her armful of dishes.

"Of course not! Although I'm a little mad that I haven't gotten to ask *you* any questions," her smile made it clear that she wasn't actually mad. Levi and Jack walked in at that moment carrying the rest of the dirty dishes, and they all walked back outside with a big plate full of brownies, coffees for Celia, Jack, and Levi, and cups of milk for Kristen and the kids. Jack teased Kristen about her milk and she just shrugged. "Coffee's gross, right Tripp?" she said, clinking her glass against his with a "cheers!" Of course, Aislinn held up her plastic cup too, and Kristen happily "cheersed" with her.

During dessert it was Kristen's turn in the hot seat, but she didn't mind. At some point over dinner, she'd started feeling surprisingly at home. She wasn't sure if it was the soft lighting, the bickering children, or residual effects of the wine. It was also highly likely that Celia and Levi excelled at putting people at ease. In fact, Kristen felt so at ease, she accidentally mentioned Mike, something she never talked about.

Celia had been asking her about college, and Kristen mentioned how she technically got her

English degree in four years, even though it took her six to graduate. Celia had laughed and said, "Now that sounds like a story."

Without thinking, Kristen responded, "Yeah, a story like a gasoline fire. Short, intense, and destructive." As soon as the words were out of her mouth, she regretted the comment. It was too tantalizing. At least, it would have been for her. By the expectant looks on the faces around the table, she knew it was for her hosts too. She scrambled to think of how to provide a follow-up that was satisfying but didn't get too far into all the gory details of memories she did her best to forget.

"Well, you can't just leave it at that."

"Fair enough. Well, my freshman year of college, I met a smoking hot musician named Mike and fell fast and hard. His band was going on tour starting that summer, and of course, I wanted to go along, but I told him I wouldn't follow the band around like some groupie, so we got married." Celia gasped, and Kristen grimaced. "Yeah, it was a big mistake. Mike was... not great." *To put it mildly.* "I spent three years living out of suitcases and spending most of my time in dive bars and crappy hotel rooms before I left him. Fortunately, the divorce took about as long as it did for us to get married."

"You make it sound so glamorous," Jack said drily.

"It's true, life with a struggling, just-starting-out rock star is decidedly not glamorous, but to be fair, there were some fun times too," *Not that many* "and I have to credit my time with Mike as jump starting my current career, so... not all bad." Technically true, but it was definitely mostly bad.

"I can't believe I haven't asked yet what you do," Celia replied. "I seem to remember George saying you were a writer, but I guess I didn't think about it in detail."

"Yeah, at the moment, I write album reviews, feature articles and interviews for a few publications, and co-write or ghostwrite music-related histories and biographies. When I was on the road with Mike's band, I started writing for free for web-zines, and basement music magazines. Behind-the-scenes stuff, concert reviews, album reviews, band features, interviews. After a while, I started submitting pieces to more well-known magazines and websites, started getting paid, and eventually carved out a career for myself."

"That's so cool," Celia said with a shake of her head.

Kristen grinned. "I'm really lucky. I mean, it's hard work, and I've had to take my fair share of part-time jobs over the years to fill the financial gaps, but I love it."

At that moment, there was a shout from the swing set, and all the adult heads swiveled in that direction, unable to see much since the swing set was outside the circle of light. Levi got up and walked over to the kids, returning a few minutes later carrying a slightly teary Aislinn and trailing a yawning Tripp

"She tried to jump out of the swing, but landed on her bottom instead of her feet," Levi explained.

"Poor girl," Celia stood up and kissed Aislinn. "It's way past bedtime anyway, and we have church tomorrow. Do you guys mind if we take a few minutes to get these two settled? Don't go anywhere!" She directed the last comment at Kristen. "I mean, go inside if you want, but don't leave yet." The four of them hustled inside, leaving Kristen and Jack and a silence broken only by the sound of leaves rustling in a breeze and a dog barking somewhere in the distance. Kristen reached out and took a second brownie from the plate on the center of the table. They *were* delicious, but mostly she needed something to do. Jack took a sip of his coffee.

"Do you want to go inside?" he asked. "I think I've been sitting on this bench too long. I keep telling Levi they need some comfortable seats out here."

"Sure. Sounds good."

They stood and gathered up everything that belonged in the kitchen. Jack held the door open with his free hand and nodded his head. "After you."

"Thanks." She tried to ignore the flush she felt as she slipped past him.

A few minutes later, the two were in the living room, Jack sprawled on the navy blue couch while Kristen slowly roamed the room stopping for a while at a gallery wall hung with an attractive mix of photographs and artwork. They could hear the faint sounds of the children getting ready for bed.

"Levi and Celia really have a gift for making people feel at ease," Kristen said.

"It's true. Levi's parents were always that way too, collecting strays and befriending just about everyone who came through our podunk town. And Celia's just..." he waved his hand vaguely. "... she's just Celia."

Kristen glanced at him with a smile. "I haven't known her for more than a few hours, but I think I know what you mean. In some ways, she reminds me of my friend, Nora. Nora can pull anyone out of their shell." Kristen moved on from an adorable picture of Tripp and Aislinn at the beach, stopping at a small framed snapshot resting on a shelf. An old pickup truck filled the frame, and a teenage girl in a tank top, cutoff jean shorts, and sandals sat on the blue hood. In front of her stood two teenage boys in jeans, faded t-shirts, and well-worn baseball caps, their arms around each other's shoulders, laughter on their faces. Kristen glanced at Jack out of the corner of her eye, comparing the youthful face with the adult one just a few feet away. She decided that while she was certain he'd turned a lot of heads in high school, he was even better looking now. Rather than being tall and gangly, he was still tall and slim but now appealingly muscular too. Age had mellowed but not necessarily softened the sharp angles of his face. Annoyingly long eyelashes still framed his deep brown eyes, his smile was still crooked, and there was still that one dimple. With a start, she realized that crooked smile was now aimed right at her. Had she been staring?

"This is a great photo." She was proud of herself for sounding nonchalant.

"It is. I think that was the summer after I graduated high school. Hey, can I take you out to dinner sometime?"

Kristen turned to face him, eyebrows raised.

"I'm sorry, what?" she managed.

"Can I take you out to dinner?" Jack repeated.

She walked over to the padded rocking chair that sat across from the couch. "I don't really date much. Men my age—in my experience—are usually looking for a committed relationship, and I'm not."

"Well, I'm not looking for a committed relationship. You seem like good company, fun to talk to, and I wouldn't mind spending an evening staring at you across a table." Kristen blushed. "If you say no, I won't bug you about it, but I think it would be fun, and I think you should say yes."

He made a compelling argument.

"Okay, yes."

"I hope you're not saying yes to one of Jack's Ponzi schemes," Levi had just walked into the room, Celia trailing behind him. He settled onto the other end of the couch from Jack.

"You know I don't pitch get-rich-quick schemes

until I've known someone at least a month. She was saying yes to a date."

"That's great!" Celia exclaimed. "You should go to Thai Kitchen. We went there a few weeks ago."

Kristen fought another blush, but to her surprise, Celia and Levi were unfazed by the announcement. Was that a good thing, or did it mean Jack regularly asked women out on dates? Did it matter if he did?

The conversation meandered, from favorite foods and cuisines, to travel stories, to disastrous cooking events. Jack dodged questions about life on an oil rig. "It's both not as bad and also worse than you're thinking." Kristen told them about a couple of her more memorable interviews. They talked about movies and books, and at some point Celia disappeared to the kitchen, emerging a few minutes later with a tray containing four mugs of hot chocolate.

"Oh my gosh!" Kristen exclaimed after her first sip. "Celia, I don't believe this is hot chocolate. It's magical!"

"Thanks!" Celia responded with a smile. "I'd tell you the secret, but then I'd have to kill you."

The decadent cocoa made Kristen feel warm and a little drowsy, like a cat lounging in a sunny widow. As she listened to the others share some news about someone from their hometown, she felt her soul warming as well, but from the company and not the beverage. It was true what she'd said to Jack earlier:

the Blairs had a gift. Through her work, Kristen had met and interviewed hundreds of people, and she enjoyed conversations with strangers. People were endlessly fascinating, and Kristen often viewed meeting people like starting a new book. The difference tonight, she mused, is that she didn't just feel comfortable, she felt *at home*. She felt like she'd known the Blairs all her life.

Kristen's long day eventually caught up with her. She stifled a yawn.

"As much as I would love to stay and continue to enjoy your company, I think I hear my bed calling," Kristen said, standing and setting her now empty mug on the tray. "I truly cannot tell you how much I've enjoyed this evening." The others stood as well, and Kristen walked over to hug Celia. "Thank you all, really."

"I'm just so glad you came and stayed," Celia replied, her eyes confirming the truth of her words. "I'll call you later this week, but our door is always open. Come by anytime."

"Thank you."

"Did you walk?" Jack asked as Kristen gathered her purse and slipped her shoes back on.

"Sure did. It seemed silly to drive such a short distance."

"Can I walk you back?"

She only hesitated for a moment.

"Sure."

Jack and Kristen strolled down the sidewalk, their path lit by widely spaced street lamps and a full moon. They walked in silence, neither one willing to intrude upon the stillness of the sleepy neighborhood, but it was an easy silence. Jack wasn't entirely sure why he'd asked to walk Kristen home, but when she'd announced that she was going home, all he could think about was spending more time with her. Living such a transient lifestyle, Jack didn't meet many women, and those he did were quite different from the beautiful, self-assured woman walking next to him. Many of the women he met were waiting for something to happen to them or were constantly seeking approval. They were boring, to be honest. Kristen was interesting and smart and curious.

"What are you working on right now?" Jack asked. "Writing-wise, I mean."

"Any day now, I'll start working on revising and editing a book I'm co-writing. It's about the history of Irish music," she added before he could ask. "It's been so much fun to work on—one of my favorite projects. And I have a couple of interviews to do this week. I don't do magazine or blog-type articles as much as I used to, but there are a few editors who were really generous to me when I was just starting, so when they reach out, I say yes. Plus the interviews are usually fun. What about you?" she redirected. "How does the life of an itinerant welder work? How'd you even get into that?"

He told her about how the high school guidance counselor had encouraged him to go to trade school instead of just settling for a minimum wage job out of high school. "I was never going to college," he said in a tone that shut down any follow-up questions about that subject. Welding had been the first booth at the community college career fair. His first job had been for a short-term construction project in California, and he found that after living his whole life in the same small town, the idea of not being tied to one place was appealing. There was a little more to his rootless lifestyle than a desire to see new places, but nothing Jack thought was all that relevant to this conversation. He explained that industries like commercial construction and oil and gas often utilized short-term contract workers since their work was project based.

By this point, they'd reached Kristen's house and had been sitting on her front-yard bench for a good 10 or 15 minutes.

"Hey, weren't you tired?" Jack said with a smile. The question triggered a yawn.

"So tired," she replied with a laugh. They stood up. "Thanks for walking me back."

"Anytime." Jack pulled out his phone, opened up the contacts list, and held the phone out. "Put your number in, and I can call you about dinner."

She quickly added her number and name to his contacts and handed the phone back. There was a moment of awkwardness at the point where friends might have hugged, but Jack just pocketed his phone and began backing toward the sidewalk.

"See you later."

With a small smile, Kristen began backing toward the front door. "See you."

Once she'd reached the door and unlocked it, she turned back to him and waved, then went inside. Jack turned and began walking, whistling through the darkness.

Chapter 6

Afternoon sunlight slanted through the kitchen window, highlighting and deepening the colors in the bouquet that Kristen placed in the center of the little kitchen table. Tilting her head, she adjusted the blooms just as the doorbell chimed.

"Come in!"

The screen door squeaked, and she heard the shuffle of feet being wiped on the entry rug.

"It looks like you've lived here for months already!" Rosalee's voice called from down the hall.

Kristen hurried to meet her and George. "Thanks!" she said, hugging them both. "Toss your jackets in the living room and come back to the kitchen. Supper's almost ready."

After setting out drinks and getting the table set, George and Rosalee still hadn't made it to the kitchen. *It's not that big of a house,* Kristen thought. *They can't be lost.* She walked toward the living room and found them staring at the large framed photograph hanging on the wall.

"This is really stunning. Is it someplace you know?" Rosalee turned to ask.

"Thanks. It's actually a picture of my two-flat in Chicago. My friends there had a professional photographer come out one day while I was gone. They surprised me with it on moving day."

"I thought it looked familiar," her dad said with a nod.

"What a treasure," Rosalee added. "Your friends are pretty special."

"Yeah, they are."

•   •   •

Kristen had been unprepared for how emotional she would be the day she loaded up her moving truck in Chicago. The previous weeks had been a whirlwind, and she'd been so busy she hadn't had time to feel much of anything. Telling her friends that she'd decided to spend a year away had been hard, but once they'd processed the news, they'd rallied around her and helped her with all kinds of details, logistics, and even packing. There was no doubt that margarita and queso packing parties were a lot more fun than packing alone.

On moving day, Kristen, Nora, Liz, and her two kids were standing on the sidewalk in front of the old two-flat drinking bottles of water next to the now-full storage pod when Liz's husband Kole came walking up with a large, flat, wrapped package in his hands. Only Kristen looked surprised.

"What's this?"

Her friends grinned. "Open it and see," Nora said, clapping her hands in excitement. Kristen's hands shook slightly as she pulled the wrapping free and gasped.

"You guys! This is..." she shook her head, a tear escaping. "This is amazing. When did you do this?"

It was a photo canvas, a beautiful black and white rendering of the two-flat, the home of three twenty-year-old girls who weathered a lot of life together, who grew up together, who supported each other. Then the home of three young women, then two, then finally one. One woman whose roots were planted deep in this city on the banks of Lake Michigan, deep in the boards and beams of this unassuming house on a tree-lined street.

"I asked a favor of the photographer who shoots our commercial listings," Kole said with a smile. "She was actually pretty excited to do something besides office buildings."

"Well," Kristen clutched the canvas to her chest. "I love it. It's perfect."

"We wanted you to have something to remind you to call us and to remind you to come back," Liz said.

"All right, bring it in, gang," Kole stretched his arms out and everyone pulled in together, "You too, kids," he said to Noah and Bella, who were trying to slink away from the adults. They all stood with arms around each other, heads together, laughing at the awkwardness of huddles. "Kristen," Kole said, the mischievous glint in his eyes contradicting his solemn tone of voice. "Stop and stretch your legs often, but watch out for sketchy gas stations. For the love of God don't stop at a deserted rest stop. Never let the gas tank get below a quarter of a tank. And call us when you get there."

Kristen laughed. "I love you guys," she said. "I mean it."

Nora gave Kristen's shoulders a tight squeeze. "Same," she said, everyone nodding their agreement. And just like that, there really wasn't any more to say. Anything else felt like either too little or too much.

They broke their huddle, and Kristen hugged everyone, and they all wiped away tears. She found a spot for her new picture in the back seat, nestled safely between pillows and blankets, and slipped into the driver's seat. She waved at her friends, and slowly pulled out onto the street, tooting her horn as she drove away.

• • •

Back in her cozy rock house in Riverton, Kristen blinked her eyes rapidly and forced a smile to her face.

"Come on back to the kitchen and get something

to drink."

As they turned to leave the room, Rosalee reached out and squeezed Kristen's hand briefly.

"It's hard to be sad and happy at the same time," she said softly. "I just want you to know that I know it's hard. But you'll be alright."

Dad, you picked a winner. "Thank you."

Once they were settled at the table, the conversation turned to lighter topics. Rosalee talked about her week at the library, and her dad told them about a consulting project he'd been working on all week. They told her about a new walking path by the river and said they'd call Kristen next time they went. Kristen told them about her week spent settling in, working, and familiarizing herself with the neighborhood. Celia had been a gem. When Kristen had called her for suggestions for the best nearby grocery stores and cafes, Celia had simply offered to go along.

"My kids are both in school today," she'd said. "So unless you'd rather go alone or after 2:30—which is totally fine—I'd love to tag along. I need a few things at the store."

Kristen freely admitted that mundane errands were much more enjoyable with a friend along. Celia directed her along a route that went by the pharmacy, dry cleaners, her favorite pizza delivery, and a small outdoor shopping center with office supply and hardware stores. After that, they had stopped at District Cafe for drinks ("shopping fortification," Celia had said), and talked almost nonstop through the grocery store.

"I was really hoping the two of you would hit it off," Rosalee said. "A friend makes a move easier."

The three of them finished eating, and as they began cleaning up Kristen asked Rosalee and George if they were up for a short walk.

"Celia made a cake today and really wants some help eating it," she added. "She told me if you all were up for it, we should walk over and have dessert at their house."

"That sounds wonderful!" Rosalee exclaimed. George nodded his assent, and the three quickly finished loading the dishwasher and putting on their shoes. When they were a few houses down from the Blairs', Tripp and Aislinn, who were playing in the front yard, saw the trio and began racing down the sidewalk toward them. Tripp stopped just short of them and gave Rosalee a quick hug before launching into a story about some exciting event at school. Aislinn flung herself at George, who caught her as if he'd been expecting it, giving her a bear hug before settling her on his shoulders for the rest of the walk. Kristen smiled and shook her head. Clearly, her dad and Rosalee were favorites of the Blair children.

"Hello, you three!" Celia called from her perch on the porch swing. "I'm so glad you came over!" She stood up and walked down the steps to greet them with warm hugs and what Kristen was beginning to think of as her trademark big smile. "Let's go inside and get some cake."

"Cake! Cake! Cake!" Aislinn chanted.

Inside, Levi was elbow deep in a sink full of soapy dishwater, and Jack leaned against the kitchen counter next to him, a plate in one hand and dish towel in the other. Rosalee walked in and kissed Levi on the cheek, as George said hello and lifted Aislinn down to a chair at the kitchen table.

"You guys remember Levi's cousin Jack? He helped out on Kristen's moving day, and he's in town visiting for a couple of weeks," Celia said as she pulled plates down from the cabinet.

"Of course!" Rosalee said. "Lovely to see you again, Jack." George shook his hand.

"This cake looks amazing," Kristen said, eyeing the creamy-looking tower in the center of the table. "What kind is it?"

"Chocolate layer cake with a chocolate mousse filling and salted caramel frosting."

George gave a low whistle. "We picked the right day to come over for dessert," he said.

"Personally, I wasn't all that interested in sharing," Levi teased.

As Celia sliced and served the cake, George asked Jack about his work, and Celia alternated between keeping the kids from fighting and talking to Rosalee about a TV show she'd been watching.

"Oh! Kristen, I keep forgetting to ask: would you be interested in trying out our book club?" Celia looked up from where she was wiping chocolate off of Aislinn's face.

"It's a lot of fun," Rosalee chimed in. "You should come."

"I'd like that," Kristen said. She cut another bite of cake with her fork. It was even better than it looked. "What are you reading, and when's the next meeting?"

"We meet the fourth Saturday of the month at 10 a.m. at the District Cafe. So, a little over two weeks. We're reading *Murder on the Orient Express*, by Agatha Christie."

"We typically alternate between modern and classic novels," Rosalee chimed in. "I hope that fits your reading tastes."

"Honestly, I've been in a reading slump for months," Kristen admitted. "So, I'm up for anything at this point."

They finished up their cake but didn't linger, knowing the kids had school in the morning, and both Levi and Rosalee had work. Kristen was pleased to be included in goodbye hugs from the children, their tiny arms around her neck, warming her heart. As she said goodbye to Jack, he said quietly: "I can pick you up tomorrow at 6:30 unless you'd rather meet at the restaurant."

Kristen shook her head. "No reason not to ride together. I'll be ready."

His crooked smile caused her stomach to flutter, a fact that still surprised her. When was the last time anyone made her stomach flutter? Come to think of it, when was the last time she'd been on a date? When was the last time she'd spent time with anyone other than her best friends? Well, and the crew at the ball field. *Maybe it's time to stop this train of thought.* She followed her Dad and Rosalee out the front door.

Jack stared at the now closed front door for a moment before turning back to help Levi finish cleaning up the kitchen. He caught a look passing between Levi and Celia before Celia herded the kids down the hall to get ready for bed. It was one of those speaking-without-words looks that used to drive him crazy when they were teenagers, out of jealousy or loneliness or a bit of both. It didn't always spark those feelings in him because even as a clueless teenager he knew that the friendship he had with the two was special. He knew they had his back, no matter what; but he also knew that they had a connection that was separate from him or anyone else.

"Earth to Jack, earth to Jack."

Jack blinked his eyes, registering Levi's outstretched arm and the clean, dripping plate in his hand.

"Sorry," Jack said, taking the plate and drying it. "I was a million miles away."

"Clearly," Levi replied, "perhaps thinking about

a pair of blue eyes?"

Jack shrugged but didn't bother denying it.

They finished the dishes and hung up their towels, and as Jack turned off the kitchen light, Levi opened the refrigerator and pulled out a couple of beers. He held one out to Jack, who took it and pried the top off with a key from his pocket.

"I never could get the hang of that trick," Levi said, giving up his search for a bottle opener and passing his drink to Jack.

"It's a useful skill sometimes."

Levi opened the back door and flipped on the patio light. "It's a nice night. Want to sit outside?"

"Sure."

They settled into the Adirondack chairs Jack had bought that day. Jack relished the lack of tension in his body and mind, a tension that he never really noticed until he was at Celia and Levi's and it was gone. He felt relaxed, unguarded, and fully himself here. Tripp joked that the guest bedroom was "Uncle Jack's room", but really, this house and his aunt and uncle's were the only places that ever felt like home.

"You were right about the chairs, by the way," Levi finally said. "This is nice."

"You always forget that I'm usually right." Jack laughed when Levi tried to half-heartedly kick him from the chair. "Hey, did you make up a list for me yet?"

Levi nodded. "Yeah. I stuck it on the fridge tonight. Celia numbered it in order of importance, but you don't have to stick to that order. Anything you do while you're here will be awesome. I wasn't sure how long you're staying."

Anytime Jack visited for more than a few days, he always made Levi and Celia give him stuff to do. Projects or repairs around the house that they didn't have time for or that needed an extra set of hands. It kept him busy, which he needed; but more importantly, it gave him a way to help his friends—his family—out. He usually had a better idea of how long he had between jobs and how long he planned on visiting Riverton, but this time he felt far from sure. He'd put out a few feelers for his next job, but wasn't in any hurry. *Maybe I just needed a vacation,* he thought. *Maybe I needed some family time.* He thought about a certain pair of long legs and a smile that could light up a room. Maybe he'd get through Celia's entire to-do list this time.

• • •

Kristen glanced at the clock hanging in her bathroom. Jack would be at her house in ten minutes. She picked up her phone sitting on the counter and opened her group text with the Chicago girls.

"When was the last time I went on a date?" she asked. "Do any of you remember? And why do I feel nervous?"

She set the phone back down and pulled an

eyeliner out of her makeup bag, tracing a navy blue line across the top of her eyelids, and listening to the notification sounds chiming from her phone. After a quick application of mascara and lipstick, she picked up her phone, turned off the light, and walked toward the front room, reading the replies from her friends as she went.

Liz: "You brought a date to a ballgame three summers ago, someone you met at a writer's conference, maybe?"

Nora: "Liz is right. Also, Kole set you up with one of his coworkers, and we went on a double date. Which was a disaster. And maybe you're nervous because it's been THREE YEARS since you've been on a date?"

Kristen laughed at Nora's comment. She had a point.

The doorbell rang. Despite her pre-date pep talk, her face still flushed slightly when Jack smiled that crooked smile and flashed his dimple. He was dressed in jeans and a green button-up shirt, tucked in but with the sleeves rolled up to his elbows. His hair was just a little too long to be called clean-cut, and she noticed he'd shaved, exposing the strong planes of his tanned face. She had to admit, he cleaned up well.

"Hey," he said. "You look nice. Are you ready?"

"I am," she replied, "just let me grab my purse. You can come inside."

He followed her into the entryway, waiting by the

door as she tucked her phone inside her purse and pulled a jacket from the hall closet. His eyes wandered around the room, and she wondered what he was thinking.

"It's nice in here," he commented. "Cozy."

Kristen picked up her keys and gestured toward the door. "After you." She locked the door behind them and followed Jack to the newer model truck sitting at the curb. It had a built-in toolbox in the bed but didn't have the beat-up look of most of the work trucks she'd seen, and it gleamed as though it had been washed recently. She thanked Jack as he held the passenger door open, and as she slid into the soft leather seat, she decided he must have washed it that day because the inside was also sparkling clean. She wondered if he'd cleaned it for their date.

"This is probably the fanciest truck I've ever been in," Kristen said as Jack climbed in and started the engine. In the close confines of the truck cab, she could smell his aftershave—a citrusy, smoky scent that made her think of sitting outside with a cold drink. He pulled away from the curb, and Kristen thought the ride was as smooth as any luxury sedan she'd ridden in.

"I spend more time in this truck than I do in whatever house or apartment I'm living in," Jack replied. "It's basically home."

"Fair point," Kristen said with a laugh.

As they drove to the restaurant, they chatted about the day, the conversation casual and easy.

Thai Kitchen was near the college campus, an area of town Kristen hadn't been to yet, and while she kept up her end of the conversation, her eyes stayed focused out of her window. Riverton's college was small, but the campus was lovely, full of gray stone buildings that looked as though they'd grown right up out of the ground. The lawns were green and shaded by huge trees, and the neighborhood immediately surrounding campus was like the residential equivalent of a little black dress—classic, unassuming, and time-tested. The restaurant sat between a used bookstore and a coffee shop on a street that was an eclectic mix of storefronts, everything from dive bars and cheap takeout places to upscale restaurants, expensive boutiques, and everything in between. It reminded her of some of her favorite Chicago neighborhoods. The thought both comforted her and made her a tiny bit homesick.

If the aroma and ambiance of the Thai Kitchen were any indications, Kristen was confident the restaurant would live up to the recommendation. The waiting area was full of green and growing things, a theme that she could see carried throughout the elegant but casual space. The walls looked as though flowers and plants were growing out of them, and she couldn't wait to get close enough to figure out how they did it. She inhaled deeply as they stopped, waiting to be seated, savoring the mix of spices and tropical flowers.

"I'm already a little in love," she said, turning to Jack. His eyebrows lifted, and she rolled her eyes. "With the restaurant," she said. "It wasn't that long of a car ride."

Jack laughed, the expression in his eyes a mix of surprise and intense curiosity, but before either of them could say anything else, a hostess walked up.

"Hello!" she said brightly. "Table for two?"

"Yes, please."

She gave them an appraising look as she picked up two menus, nodded to herself, then smiled.

"Follow me."

She led them past tables full of college students, families, and gray-haired couples to a high backed booth tucked in an alcove. The hostess stood to the side as they slid into the booth then handed them their menus.

"Enjoy!" she said with a wink.

Kristen ignored her menu and examined the plant wall. It was deceptively simple: planters of various shapes and sizes built into the wall at various intervals. The genius to the design was having the right plants in the right planters. This way, none of the plants really overlapped with each other, and not much of the wall showed through unless you were right next to it.

"I wonder how long it takes to water the walls?" Jack mused.

"Maybe they have some kind of irrigation system?"

They discussed the possibilities as they perused the menu, interrupted briefly by a friendly waiter who took their drink order, and told them the daily specials. For a few moments, they focused on the menu, debating whether to get an appetizer, and discussing what looked good.

"What are your opinions on sharing food?" Kristen asked, glancing at Jack.

"Hmmm. I'm not opposed to it in theory because it usually means I get to try more. But I'm also pretty hungry."

"What if we got the dumplings, Pad Thai, and the green curry, and then share it all?"

Jack snapped his menu shut. "I like the way you think."

After the waiter returned with their drinks and took their order, there was a lull in the conversation. Kristen took a sip of her drink, internally rifling through various conversation topics. She wondered if it was safe to venture away from small talk. Before she could make up her mind, Jack broke the silence.

"Were you a rocker chick in high school too, or was that a college reinvention?"

So, we're definitely done with small talk, Kristen thought.

"No. I mean, I listened to music and had my favorite bands and all that, but I wasn't obsessed with it and definitely wasn't what you'd call a 'rocker chick.' I was always a writer, though. I took every extracurricular English class I could, wrote for the school newspaper for two years, and co-edited the literary magazine my senior year. But," she held up a finger, "what might surprise you is that I was also really into sports."

"That does surprise me, actually. What did you play?"

"Basketball and cross country. What were you into in high school?"

"Besides girls?"

Kristen rolled her eyes but laughed. "I mean, that's a given, obviously, but yes, aside from girls."

"Believe it or not, I also enjoyed all my English classes, but I wasn't really into organized school activities or clubs. We spent most of our time in the woods or at the lake." He stopped, but Kristen sensed there was more, so she waited. He looked slightly uncomfortable for the first time since she'd met him. "I played baseball when I was a kid." he continued, "but quit after my Dad died."

"I'm so sorry," she said. "How old were you? I was 8 when my mom died."

As she suspected, Jack's seemed to relax a little once she slipped in that she'd also lost a parent as a kid.

"Fourteen."

"That's a rough age to lose a parent. Was it sudden?"

Jack nodded, taking a sip of his drink. "Yeah. Car accident."

Jack's fingers folded and refolded his napkin as

he talked, and his eyes, which had previously shone with an open light, were shuttered and closed. Firmly closed and locked and no key in sight. She shifted gears a little.

"Do you still like to spend time in the woods?"

"Definitely." He shifted, and the tightness around his mouth eased a little. "Anytime I can."

They talked about some of Jack's favorite places he'd hiked and the benefits of rough backpacking versus campground camping. Kristen admitted she'd only been camping twice in her life: once as a kid in California with her grandparents and once in college.

"Liz was really into this guy who invited her to go camping and canoeing. She didn't want to go alone, so I agreed to go along. There were about seven of us, I think. It was an absolute disaster," she shook her head and laughed at the memory. "They stuck the two of us by ourselves in a canoe because we were too embarrassed to tell them we didn't know what we were doing. We kept getting stuck, got sunburned, and by the time we caught up to everyone at the campsite that night, the guys were already drunk, and other girls there weren't friendly."

"Sounds like you need a re-do."

Was there an invitation in those brown eyes?

Their dumplings arrived, saving her from having to decide, and she simply shook her head and said "Once was enough."

Over appetizers, Jack asked her more about her work, especially in the early days when she was on tour and just getting started. Kristen did not enjoy talking about those years that she spent with Mike and the first few years after their divorce, but she managed to talk about her writing without getting into personal territory she didn't want to discuss.

"Who's the most famous person you've ever met?" he asked as the waiter cleared their appetizer plates.

Kristen took a sip of her drink. "Taylor Swift," she said. "But she wasn't as famous when I interviewed her... Smashing Pumpkins... Destiny's Child."

"You interviewed Beyonce?!"

Kristen nodded with a small smile. "My famous people interview phase didn't last too long. I shifted gears quite a few years ago: classical, bluegrass, folk, world music. It was more interesting and less competitive."

"So, what do you listen to on your own time?"

"Not surprisingly, my personal listening tastes are pretty much all over the map at this point."

The waiter returned with their entrees, and they continued to talk about music as they ate—favorite artists, concerts, and memories associated with certain songs. They both agreed they preferred live music in smaller venues. Jack admitted he'd never developed a taste for classical music, even after dating a trumpet player in the Phoenix Symphony.

Kristen blinked a few times and shook her head. "I'm so intrigued," she said. "First of all, if you aren't into classical music, how did you end up dating a classical musician? Second, in my experience, professional female trumpet players are fairly rare."

"She was a cousin of one of my co-workers," Jack replied, his dimple deepening, "and while I can't really speak to her professional rarity, I will say she thought she was pretty special."

Kristen raised an eyebrow but changed the subject. Talking about exes on a first date was a slippery slope, and their conversation had already circled around her own not-to-be-mentioned ex for too long.

Their waiter appeared just as Kristen set down her utensils and asked if they needed anything else. After praising the food, but firmly agreeing that they couldn't eat another bite, the waiter slid the check on the table. Kristen opened her mouth to offer to split it, but before she could, Jack handed over his credit card.

"Thank you," Kristen said

Jack's crooked smile sent a warm flutter to Kristen's middle, but he waved away her thanks. "I was thinking of grabbing coffee next door and taking a walk through campus. Does that sound okay to you?"

"I'd love that. Especially if it's my treat. Seems only fair since you got dinner."

The waiter returned with Jack's card, and they

left to walk next door. Instinctively, Kristen took a deep breath as they walked through the door of The University Bean, filling her lungs with the scents of coffee, steamed milk, burnt sugar, and cinnamon. The big room was full of conversation, laughter, and the sounds of someone tuning a guitar. As they took their place in line, Kristen glanced around, finally locating the tiny stage across the room with a stool and microphone standing in the center. A college-aged guy with dark, curly hair sat hunched over the guitar.

"Would you rather stay?"

Kristen turned back to Jack. "No, but thanks for asking. A walk outside sounds better just now." However, as they waited to order, then waited for their drinks to be prepared, she did enjoy the music. The dark-haired musician sang unique covers of familiar songs, as well as some soulful ballads that she thought might be originals.

"One hot chocolate, extra whipped cream."

"Mmmm," Kristen took the hot cup from Jack. "I'm pretty excited about this; I'll be honest."

He laughed and put a hand to the small of her back, guiding her gently through the crowd toward the door. "I hope it meets your expectations then."

They strolled down the busy sidewalk. Turning once they reached the edge of campus, they meandered through the spacious lawns and stately buildings. The cool air smelled like honeysuckle and hummed with energy. They sipped their drinks and reminisced over their own college days, each of them with very different experiences. Kristen was intrigued by what it was like to live at home and going to classes, wondering how different it felt from high school, and surprised when Jack said it was more different than you'd think. Jack, on the other hand, thought an on-campus, full-time college experience sounded a little claustrophobic and like the perfect environment to get into trouble.

Their talk turned to the merits of big cities over small towns and the challenges of cooking for one person. Jack asked about her friends and her life in Chicago, and she talked about the challenges of working from home and how she had to make sure and get out and interact with people once in a while. He was impressed and a little jealous of her Cubs season tickets, and they talked about baseball until they were back at Jack's truck. She watched as he pulled his key fob out of his pocket and clicked the unlock button, stepping closer to Kristen so he could open the passenger door. She looked up at him, and saw a small smile touch the corners of his mouth, his eyes nearly black in the darkness. Had she noticed before how tall he was? Kristen wasn't used to being around men who were more than an inch or two taller than her own 5 foot 10 inches, other than her Dad. She cleared her throat and moved to climb in.

"Thanks."

He shut the door with a gentle thud and walked around to the driver's door, giving Kristen just enough time to breathe deeply and give herself a mental talking to.

"Home?" Jack asked as he started the truck.

Kristen nodded. "Please. I'm having a great time, but it's been a long week."

"Sounds good."

The drive home was quiet, the combination of a comfortable seat and rumbling engine made Kristen too mellow to muster up any conversation. But it was a peaceful silence, and before too long, Jack was pulling into Kristen's driveway. He put the truck in park but opened his door when Kristen did and walked her to her door, a gentlemanly gesture that she found surprising and very touching.

He waited on the front stoop as Kristen unlocked her door, but she turned to him before opening it. For the first time that evening, Kristen felt a smidge of awkwardness. Was he going to kiss her? High five? Handshake? Hug? This was the part of dating she never missed.

"Well, this was a lot of fun."

Jack's expression was mostly neutral, but something in his eyes made her suspect that he knew she felt awkward, and she silently cursed him because he did not appear to share her awkwardness, and perhaps even found it amusing. He reached out, briefly and gently cupping her elbow before sliding his hand down her arm to her hand, his touch as light as butterfly wings. Her body tingled. "It was," he said. "Want to do it again sometime?"

"Definitely."

He squeezed her hand gently and let go, taking a few steps backward. "I'll call you. Unless I see you at Levi's first." With his crooked grin and a wave, he turned and walked to his truck. Kristen returned the wave and walked inside, locking the door behind her, a huge grin on her face.

Chapter 7

With a satisfying *thud*, the final fencepost settled into the ground. Jack straightened, pulling his baseball cap off and pulling up the tail of his t-shirt to wipe the sweat off his face. He reached for the level at his feet and double-checked that this last post was in line with the rest. It was cooling off now that the sun was headed toward the treetops, but mid-day had held a hint of the summer heat to come. Settling his cap back on his head, Jack surveyed the backyard. Fence posts stood like dutiful soldiers around the yard, waiting for their planks that were currently stacked neatly on the edge of the patio. He was pleased that he'd managed to get all the posts set since he'd gotten a later start that morning than he'd intended, and it was supposed to storm later that evening. Setting fence posts in the mud wasn't his idea of fun.

Jack smiled to himself as he picked up the posthole digger and the few other tools lying in the yard and carried them toward the shed. What *had* been fun was his date with Kristen the night before. He'd had a hunch that he and Kristen would have a good time together, and it always felt good to be right. The conversation had flowed easily, and the silences hadn't been awkward. Several times she'd answered his questions but then deftly turned the focus back on him, and each time he'd find himself talking about things he never talked about with almost any woman he dated, let alone on the first date. Yet, she wasn't pushy. She just looked at you with those deep blue eyes and made you want to tell her all your secrets. He'd also never been out with a woman before who was more present than Kristen. She hadn't checked her phone or seemed to be comparing him or herself with anyone else around them. She hadn't even seemed to notice the multiple times that men had checked her out, something Jack couldn't blame them for since Kristen was gorgeous.

"Uncle Jack!"

The warning came as he was locking the shed door, and a moment before, the human cannonball collided with his leg and wrapped two arms tightly around his leg.

"Hey bug, how was school."

"Great! We got to play outside *two times*. And I got to pick from the treasure box."

"Sounds like the perfect day to me."

Jack knelt to Aislinn's eye level and smiled at her. "Did you come out here to swing?"

"Yes, yes, yes!"

He followed her over to the swing set and gave her a big push off, then chanted "in and out, in and out," as she practiced pumping her legs, giving her a gentle push when her rhythm got off, and she slowed down. The back door opened again, and Tripp bounded out followed by Levi.

"Hey, Uncle Jack!"

"Hey, dude."

"The posts look good," Levi said before Tripp could launch into one of his hour-by-hour daily recaps. "I'm impressed you got them all in today."

They talked for a few minutes about the fence, Levi's day at work, and whether there was any good baseball on that night. Eventually, the kids tired of swinging and jumped off to run to the playhouse in the far corner of the yard, and Jack and Levi made their way to the Adirondack chairs. Levi took a quick detour into the kitchen, came back with a couple of cold drinks, and handed one to Jack.

"Thanks."

"So," Levi settled back into his chair. "How'd the date go last night?"

Jack took a long drink before answering. "It was good."

There was a long pause.

"That's it? 'It was good?' Is that code for one and done?"

"No, it's code for you know I'm a man of few words."

Levi rolled his eyes, and Jack grinned.

"Okay, fine. I had a great time. The last time I went out with a woman with as many looks and brains as Kristen was that one semester of community college. Remember Kelley? The student assistant in the library?"

"The blonde?"

"No, the brunette. The one who always wore short skirts."

"Yeah, I remember her. You were pretty well gone on her."

Jack shrugged and took another sip of his drink. "Well. It was a similar feeling."

Levi raised one eyebrow. "I'll warn you, Celia will be *very* happy to hear that. So I can play it cool if you want me to."

"Maybe for now. I mean, it was just one date."

• • •

Jack sat alone in the living room, feet stretched out in front of him, staring at his phone. Searing white lightning lit up the dark living room, and a thunderclap boomed outside, rattling the windows and eliciting a child's cry from the back of the house. He did not envy his friends right now. The wind had picked up just before dinner, and by the time he and Levi were washing dishes, pebble-sized hail was drumming against the window, and the lights were flickering. By the time the kids were finished with their baths, the lights had winked out and stayed out. Levi had brought in a couple of battery-powered camping lanterns from the garage, and Jack wished his headlamp wasn't sitting in the glove compartment of his truck.

He set his phone back down on the coffee table, moved the lantern next to him on the couch so he could see his book better, and tried to concentrate on reading. He was more than halfway through the novel—a modern-day retelling of the Iliad—and until that moment, it had been extremely engrossing and hard to put down. Now, however, he sat with the book open on his lap, unable to concentrate on the words, and not because the lighting was dim.

Just call. You know you want to ask her out again.

He looked back at his phone. He should probably save the battery. There was no telling how long the power would be out.

And you don't want to seem too eager.

Jack shook his head. Forget that. He'd never played games while dating and wasn't about to start now. He looked down the hall just as a gust of wind and rain pummeled the house, and another boom of thunder sounded like it was inside the house. Another cry. Celia and Levi would be awhile. Now was a perfect time. Jack reached out and picked up the phone and dialed.

"Hello?"

"Hey. How's it going?"

"It's cozy and candle lit. And loud. How about

you?"

"About the same. Are you outside?" There was a lot of noise coming over the line.

"Sort of. I've been on the screened porch."

"Are you one of those weirdos who likes watching thunderstorms?"

"Hey! It's a perfectly normal thing to enjoy."

Jack chuckled. "Whatever you say."

"Watch it, bud. I might just hang up on you. Gotta save battery after all."

Jack could hear the smile in her voice but changed the subject anyway, asking if she had everything she needed in case the power was out all night, offering to come by with an extra portable battery charger or a lantern.

"That's really sweet of you, but I'm good. I've got a flashlight, plenty of extra batteries, some candles, and three portable chargers."

"Three!"

"Well, I do travel regularly for work. It's not something I want to be without. Comes in handy at times like this too. Do you need me to bring *you* a charger?"

They bantered back and forth for a few more minutes, talked about what books they were currently trying to read by lamplight, and then said goodnight. It occurred to Jack as he picked up his book again that he'd been enjoying the conversation so much that he'd forgotten to ask her out again. *Now I have a good excuse to call tomorrow.*

Chapter 8

The scent of cinnamon and sugar filled Kristen's little house, and her nose told her it was time to take the sticky buns out of the oven about a minute before the timer dinged. She had just finished pouring the maple glaze over the tops when she heard the knock on her front door.

"Come in!"

"Mmm... smells delicious in here," Rosalee called from the entryway. Kristen was stretching plastic wrap over the two baking pans as Rosalee walked into the kitchen.

"Hi, Rosalee."

"Hi yourself. Are those homemade cinnamon rolls? You know we don't have to bring anything to the book club, right? Did we mis-communicate?"

"No, you're fine. I was just in a baking mood today, but my recipe makes a big batch. So I'm keeping one and taking the other to Celia's."

"What a treat!"

"And don't get jealous, I'm planning to eat two myself and bring the rest with me to Elizabeth and Jonathan's tomorrow."

Kristen picked up her purse and book from the table, accepted Rosalee's offer to carry the pan of cinnamon rolls, and the two walked out the door to Rosalee's car.

"Thanks again for letting me ride with you and Celia," Kristen said as they pulled out of the driveway.

"Of course. It would have been silly for you to drive by yourself when the two of us would be coming from practically the same place. It may be a little silly for me to come over here and pick Celia up, but it's our tradition now."

Celia was waiting for them on the front porch when they pulled up. Kristen opened her car door and stepped out before Celia had made it across the lawn.

"I have a pan of cinnamon rolls for your house," she said.

"Ooohh! Yum! The boys will love them. I'll just have to threaten their lives if they don't leave me one."

Celia walked back up the porch steps and stuck her head inside. A moment later, Jack stepped out, barefoot and wearing just a pair of basketball shorts, looking like someone in desperate need of their first cup of coffee. He followed Celia to the car, and Kristen pulled the still-warm pan from the back seat.

When she turned around, Jack was so close she almost bumped into him.

"Hey," his already deep voice rumbled with the remnants of sleep and sent a shiver through Kristen.

"Hey, yourself. Have some sugar and carbs." *Because sugar and carbs are definitely the way to keep your abs looking like that.*

"Can't wait." he winked, then leaned down to say hello to Rosalee before turning back toward the house. Kristen got in the car and shut the door. She'd only just pulled her seatbelt on when there was a knock on her window. She rolled it down, and Jack stooped over again.

"You busy tonight?"

"No."

"Want to get some dinner?"

"Yes."

"6:30 sound good?"

"Sounds good."

"Great. See you then. Thanks again for the sugar." He grinned, and Kristen fought the urge to close the short distance and kiss him. *Get ahold of yourself, woman!* Fortunately, he stood up before she could give in to the impulse and waved before turning and walking back toward the house. Kristen rolled up her window, and Rosalee put the car in reverse.

"Date night!" Celia said in a sing-song voice, a smile lighting up her face.

"I hope Jack is as nice as he is good looking,"

Rosalee added. "I can say from first-hand experience that men with smiles like that are very hard to resist, even at 60." She paused. "He's in very good shape, that one."

"Rosalee!"

They laughed, and Celia changed the subject, for which Kristen was grateful, although a tiny part of her brain continued to hum in delighted anticipation at the prospect of the evening's date.

"Kristen, I don't know if I've mentioned it again, but I am so glad you came this morning! I can't wait for you to meet everyone," Celia said as they pulled out onto the street.

"Do they know you invited me?" Kristen asked. The thought had popped into her mind that morning, and she'd had trouble shaking it. It was one thing to be the new person in a group and another to be the unexpected new person.

"Mmm... most people do, I think. I know I mentioned it to Sierra and Mary. Maybe Judy too." she waved her hand in a dismissive gesture. "It's totally fine, though. It's a pretty open group. Listen, though, what I really need to talk about before we get there is your date! The last time I saw you, the guys were around, so I couldn't ask you about it. Did you have fun? I guess you're going out again tonight, so you must have."

"I had a really good time." Kristen shifted in her seat so she could see Celia a little better. "The Thai Kitchen was an excellent recommendation, and we had coffee—well, I had hot chocolate—from the University Bean after and walked through campus. It's a beautiful campus, by the way. Honestly, the evening went by really quickly. Jack's an easy person to talk to."

A strange look passed over Celia's face, puzzled, but with a hint of glee. "I'm so glad," she said. "I'm always afraid that Jack's kind of lonely, which of course he brushes off with his 'I'm a lone wolf' schtick, but I don't always buy it."

"Well, he was excellent company. We've talked on the phone a few times since then, and of course I've seen him at your house. We discussed going out again, it just hadn't happened until today."

"Our fault, I'm afraid," Rosalee said. "Dinner at our house and various family activities. Which you don't have to come to," she said to Kristen. "Just a reminder."

"Are you kidding? I love your family, and I am trying very hard to ingratiate myself." They all laughed. Kristen made light of her new family, but it was true that after it just being her and her dad for so long, a big family was a nice change.

District Cafe was almost empty when they arrived, save for a glass-walled room in the far corner. It held a mismatched assortment of about twelve chairs with a few small, low tables shoved together in the middle of the room. The room was also full of what Kristen assumed were the other members of the book club. She followed Celia and

Rosalee to the counter first, and they ordered drinks and pastries before walking back toward the rest of the group.

"Since it's not busy, they'll bring our orders back to us when they're ready," Celia told her.

Rosalee introduced her to the rest of the group, which consisted of Caroline and Judy, who appeared to be in their mid-sixties; Lois, a stooped, silver-haired lady with a huge smile that Kristen though was probably in her 80s; Sierra, a twenty-something Black woman who looked about four months pregnant; and Ashley, a Black woman who Kristen guessed was in her 30s. As she finished the rounds of introductions, Mary, Rosalee's daughter-in-law, came in. Kristen was happy to see another familiar face. Less than ten minutes later, everyone was settled in a chair with their beverages and snacks, the low tables now arranged for better sharing.

"I know Ashley's son has a baseball game to get to later, so let's get started," Celia said.

They jumped right into discussion of the book, which almost everyone had enjoyed. Judy and Mary were the only two who hadn't liked it, and both admitted that mostly they just rarely read mysteries.

"I could see objectively that it was good, but I just couldn't get into it," Mary said with a shrug. "Maybe it just wasn't the right time."

"And we all know Judy isn't going to like a book with no love story," Lois said with a smile. Judy laughed and said she couldn't argue with that.

The discussion was lively and insightful and meandered just the right amount. They talked about train travel, cruises, cozy mysteries versus detective novels, and the merits and weaknesses of all of Agatha Christie's main characters. Sierra admitted that she'd been a little hesitant to read it because she'd heard that some of Christie's books were pretty racist but had been pleasantly surprised by this one at any rate.

After a little more than an hour, just as the conversation reached a natural pause, Ashley gathered her things and stood up.

"The baseball field calls," she said with a smile. "It's been fun, ladies. Oh! What's the book for next time again?"

Celia pulled a notebook out of her bag and flipped through the pages until she found what she was looking for, naming a popular novel that Kristen had been hearing about everywhere. Caroline stood up as well, saying she'd walk out with Ashley since she and her husband had an extensive list of projects they were trying to get through that weekend. The women said goodbye, both taking a moment to stop by Kristen's chair and tell her they were really glad she'd come.

No one else seemed in a hurry to leave, and the larger conversation loosened into more intimate conversations between two or three. Kristen turned to Lois, who was sitting on her right.

"So how do you know everyone?" she asked.

"Oh, most of us live in the same neighborhood, except Caroline, Mary, and of course now Rosalee. Caroline works with Rosalee at the library."

"Then we're neighbors too! I'm renting a house at the end of Hickory Street."

"Oh yes, I know the one. The Mattoxes' house, yes?"

"That's right."

Kristen asked Lois how long she'd lived in the neighborhood and was delighted as Lois turned out to be a natural storyteller, needing little prompting to talk about growing up on a small farm outside of Riverton and how much the town had changed over the years. She talked about her husband and their four children. Lois was telling Kristen about one of her grandsons, a doctor in Kansas City, when Rosalee joined them.

"I'm trying to talk him into moving to Riverton," Lois was saying. "He's my first grandson, and we're very close. He and my husband are like peas in a pod. And he's very handsome, you know," she said, patting Kristen's knee. "And successful."

Kristen laughed. "Well, I appreciate the heads up, but I'm not really in the market for a relationship at the moment."

"Yes, you should meet Jack Blair, Lois," Rosalee chimed in with a mischievous grin. "I think Kristen's plate might already be full."

Kristen shook her head, but smiled. "That's actually not what I meant. Jack and I are going out tonight, yes, but it's nothing serious. I don't actually do serious."

"Hmm," Lois said, tilting her head. "You know, I don't often hear women say that unless they are very young or someone has hurt them." She left it at that, but her clear blue eyes seemed very knowing and wise at the moment.

"That's a very astute observation," Kristen replied. "To tell you the truth, I was hurt. It was a long time ago, but single life has been good to me, so I haven't seen a need to change that."

Lois nodded, and Rosalee's smile was easy and reassuring. "Why mess with a good thing?" she said lightly, "and who's to say you can't just enjoy someone's company with no pressure to make it permanent?"

"Exactly."

Judy joined their little circle, and Kristen deliberately shifted the conversation, asking Judy what she did for a living. Judy talked animatedly about the after-school program she ran at the community center. Sierra wandered over as Judy was finishing her story and pulled up another chair. She asked Kristen about how she'd ended up in Riverton. Sierra had come to Riverton for college and followed the tried-and-true path of meeting a boy and getting married.

"But I finished my degree," she was quick to say. "We'll see if being a CPA remains appealing after this little guy is born." she rubbed her rounded stomach with a smile.

Everyone lingered for about 20 more minutes. Kristen found the obvious camaraderie among such a diverse group of women to be refreshing, and the group's warm, unreserved welcome had made her feel instantly at ease. Before the gathering scattered for the day, she'd exchanged phone numbers with everyone and made plans to go for a morning walk on Monday with Sierra and Judy. All in all, she thought, it was a great start to the weekend.

<h1 style="text-align:center">Chapter 9</h1>

The scent of honeysuckle and roses mingled with that of hot charcoal and charred meat as Kristen sat on the bench in her front yard, eyes closed and face lifted toward the setting sun. She took a deep breath, savoring the sensations of an almost perfect late spring evening.

After book club, Kristen had spent the afternoon with her Dad and Rosalee. They'd gone for a long walk on their new favorite trail and played cards after. By the time she'd gotten home, she'd been worried she wouldn't have time to get ready for her date that evening but decided there was no need to wash her hair. The curls did better with infrequent washing, anyway. She'd had a moment of indecision as she dressed—she had no idea what they were doing that evening—but in the end went with casual and slightly edgy, which was usually her default, anyway.

The low purr of a large engine interrupted the

birdsong coming from the tree branches above her, and Kristen opened her eyes to the sight of Jack's once again spotless black truck pulling up to the curb. She stood up and walked across the lawn, arriving at the truck just as Jack was opening the passenger door for her. His handsome face was creased in a smile, which Kristen couldn't help but return.

"Hey."

"Hey, yourself."

He shut the door with a gentle thud, and Kristen buckled her seatbelt.

"So," she said once Jack slid into the driver's seat. "Do we have a plan yet?"

"I have an idea, but I'm open to other suggestions if it doesn't sound good to you."

"Let's hear it."

"There's a burger place on the edge of town that has a big outdoor patio and stage area, and they have music on the weekends. I checked tonight's lineup, and it's a couple of local alt-country bands." His eyes shifted over to her briefly before returning to the road. "It's supposed to be a nice night, and I know first hand the food is delicious. Levi said he's heard one of the bands, and they're excellent."

"That sounds perfect," Kristen said.

"Good. I wasn't sure if it was too obvious a choice."

"Obvious isn't always bad."

As they drove through town, Kristen thought

about Jack's comment about live music and dinner being an obvious choice. She thought about people she'd known who seemed to always expect each date to be creative and better than the last. It was one of several reasons she'd stopped dating. The pressure to impress was just too exhausting. Not that she didn't enjoy new experiences—she loved them, in fact—but there was something to be said for simply doing what sounded fun.

•　•　•

The parking lot at Sue's Burgers was filling up when they arrived, and Jack thought that was probably a good sign. He found a spot, and they made their way inside. The interior was dark and small and screamed "hole in the wall," but the patio easily tripled the square footage of the dining room. Tables crowded the floor, lit by strings of lights crisscrossing above, and a bar ran along the wall, cleverly designed to serve both inside and outside customers. Jack leaned closer to Kristen so she could hear him above the noise.

"Do you see a table?" He nodded toward the sign that said, "Welcome to Sue's! Grab a seat and settle in."

She nodded and grabbed his hand, leading him to the table that had caught his own eye, more than halfway to the stage and slightly off-center. Not too close to the speakers, but with a good view. Kristen sat down, and Jack slid a chair, so he was sitting next to her rather than across the table.

"Do you mind? This way, I can see, and we can talk easier before the music starts."

Her smile made him feel like he'd won a prize.

"Can I get you guys some drinks?"

The server looked to be in her early twenties, with long red hair pulled back into a ponytail and a black t-shirt with "Sue's Burgers and Music" emblazoned in white letters across the front. She set a couple of menus on the table and pulled a pen out of her serving apron.

"I heard you feature some local beers," Jack said.

The girl nodded and reached out to flip over the menu. "Yep. Full drinks menu is on the back here, but I can tell you that tonight we have Bur Oak, Exit 6, Mark Twain, and Mother's on tap. You can order a flight if you want to try them all."

Jack glanced at Kristen, who nodded. They ordered two flights and some water, then picked up their menus as the waitress walked away.

"How was book club this morning?" Jack asked.

"It was good! Everyone was welcoming, and we had a good discussion about the book. I'll definitely go back."

They read through the menu, and by the time the waitress reappeared with their drinks, they were ready to order: fried pickles to share, a green chili burger for Kristen, and a blue cheeseburger for Jack. The waitress left to place their order, and Kristen and Jack each picked up a glass from the samplers sitting on the table, two narrow wooden trays with four mini glasses nestled in cutouts.

"Cheers."

They clinked glasses and took a sip. It was good, Jack thought. Crisp and bright. He opened his mouth to ask Kristen how she liked hers when the strum of an amped acoustic guitar cut through the buzz of conversation. The opening band didn't waste time with introductions, instead jumping right into their set. As Jack sat back in his chair, he glanced over at Kristen. She was leaning forward, elbow on the table, chin resting in her hand, gaze fixed on the stage. Her deep blue eyes glowed, and Jack found himself watching her as he listened. Her body moved slightly to the music like she wanted to get up and dance but was restraining herself. Her unabashed enjoyment captivated him. Their food came, and the band played, and Jack kept watching Kristen.

When the first band finished to applause and whistles from the crowd, Kristen leaned over to Jack as the stage was being reset for the second band.

"They were so good, don't you think?"

Jack agreed and made what he hoped were intelligent observations, although he mostly listened to her and tried to keep her talking about what she thought. The second band was just as good as the first, if not better, to Jack's ears, although he still spent the entire set watching Kristen. He'd just

never realized how attractive intensity and focus could be.

It was late when the band finished. The bar had filled during the performances, and there were now more people than chairs on the patio, a lively crowd that seemed to be settling in for a couple more hours. Jack looked at Kristen. "Do you want to get some more drinks, or are you ready to go?" he said, leaning close so she could hear him without shouting. She nodded her head toward the door. "Let's go."

Jack had settled the bill a while ago, so they just stood up and began winding their way through the now crowded space. To his surprise, Kristen took his hand again as they walked, and although he assumed it was for the practical purpose of helping them stay together through the crush of people, she didn't let go once they reached the parking lot. He wished he'd parked farther away from the entrance.

"That was such an excellent idea," Kristen said once they'd gotten buckled in and Jack was pulling onto the road. Her eyes still shone. "It's been too long since I've been to a show."

"I had a good time too. Honestly, the bands were better than I expected."

"Right?!"

For the rest of the ride home, Kristen excitedly dissected the music, and Jack did his best to keep up. When Jack pulled the truck into Kristen's driveway, she was comparing the second band

they'd seen to a musician Jack had never heard of. He turned off the engine, and she trailed to a stop.

"I'm sorry, I think I got a little carried away," she looked sheepish, and her cheeks seemed flushed, although it was difficult to tell in the dark.

"No need to apologize. I've enjoyed the education."

"Well, obviously, I had a great time. Thank you for thinking of it."

"I had a great time too."

Kristen unbuckled her seatbelt but didn't make a move to get out. Instead, she shifted slightly in the seat, turning to face him and resting her head against the headrest. The night was quiet, the cab of the truck like a cacoon, and at that moment, it felt to Jack like the two of them were the only people in the world.

"Why did you move in with Levi's family when you were younger?" Kristen asked in a soft voice.

Jack stiffened slightly but tried to hide it. "My dad died."

She kept her voice low. "It was more than that."

"Yes."

Silence.

Kristen raised her eyebrows, but Jack shook his head.

"I'm not going to talk about it," he said. He spoke quietly but firmly. He didn't care how beautiful and deep and gentle her eyes were.

"Okay."

Wait. That's it? No begging? No wheedling?

Kristen smiled, and when she spoke, it was like she'd read his thoughts. "We haven't known each other *that* long. I'm not going to force you to tell me your secrets."

At that, she yawned, and Jack grinned. "I think that's a sign."

Kristen shook her head and reached for the door handle. "My all-nighters are behind me, I'm afraid."

Once again, Jack walked Kristen to the house and waited while she got out her keys and unlocked the door.

"Well," she said with a smile. "See you."

"Yep." He reached out and brushed his fingertips lightly down her cheek, tucking a stray curl behind her ear. Before he could talk himself out of it, he leaned forward and pressed his lips gently to hers.

"Good night, Kristen."

He could tell he'd surprised her. With a grin, he squeezed her hand, let go, and walked back to his truck. She was still standing on the stoop, watching him as he cranked the engine. With a wave, he backed out of the driveway and headed back home, the smile never leaving his face.

Chapter 10

The sun had just broken over the horizon when Kristen locked her door and jogged down her front steps. Judy and Sierra, her new friends from the book club, were waiting on the sidewalk. Judy and Sierra had been walking together three mornings a week for almost a year, and this was the second week that Kristen had joined them. Despite the early morning hour, it had already become one of Kristen's favorite parts of her week.

"Good morning!" Sierra said as Kristen joined them on the sidewalk. The trio began walking briskly, chatting about the upcoming day and how the rest of their weekend had gone. Sierra had been working long days, trying to get her clients settled before she began her maternity leave, and was still going back and forth on whether she would go back to work after her baby was born.

"I always assumed I would go back to work. I enjoy what I do, and it's nice to have two incomes, but one of my girlfriends just had a baby a couple of months ago and based on what she keeps telling me about newborns…” Sierra shook her head. “I don't know if I'm cut out to work and be a mom too. You've done both, haven't you, Judy?” Sierra glanced at the woman in the middle of their trio. “What do you think?”

“I think it's a personal decision, and no one else can make it for you,” Judy said firmly. “Yes, I stayed home for a little while, and then I went back to work. But that's not for everyone. My sister went back to work and then decided to stay home.”

Sierra groaned. “Why can't there be an obvious answer?”

“Unfortunately,” Judy replied, “when it comes to children, there are never obvious answers.”

They came to a hill and fell silent, their attention focused on their physical effort. Sierra and Judy's discussion about working versus stay-at-home knocked around in her head. A few relevant thoughts landed on the tip of her tongue, but she hesitated. *They didn't ask you.* She focused on steady breathing. *You don't have any experience with having kids.* A contrary voice chimed in. *You, of all people, know that you don't have to have direct experience with something to have insight. Yes, but your other friends know you and love you. These ladies don't know you that well yet.* She gave her internal critic a mental slap upside the head and reminded herself that this year was about stepping out.

"I can't speak to your dilemma directly," Kristen said as they crested the hill. "But when I have a difficult decision to make, I ask myself a couple of questions: what is the most important thing to me in this situation? What's the best thing that could happen with each choice, and what's the worst thing that could happen?"

"Those are good," Sierra said, nodding her head vigorously. "My pro-con lists aren't cutting it this time around."

"I can't take full credit for the process," Kristen was quick to add. "I got it from a book I read once, but it really does help in my experience. Especially when traditional pro-con lists don't lead to clear results."

"Do you remember the book title?" Sierra asked. "I'm not generally a non-fiction reader, but that sounds like something I might be able to get into."

Kristen said that she couldn't recall the title off the top of her head, but she'd look it up when she got home. If she found the title, she'd be sure to text Sierra. They finished their walk talking about books and reading journals. When Kristen walked in her front door, she felt a pleasant buzzing inside that had a little to do with exercise in the fresh air and a lot to do with having put herself out there and finding a welcome reception.

After eating and showering, Kristen settled onto her little screened porch with a mug of tea and her laptop. The breeze that drifted through the windows carried with it the fresh aroma from the lilac bush that grew outside the kitchen window and the green, earthy scent of the redbud tree that hugged the corner of the house and shaded the porch nearly all day. She spent an hour catching up on emails and was pleased to see that the editor for *More Than a Harp: A Brief History of Irish Music* had sent several chapters full of notes for her to look at. However, before she settled in to work on revisions, one last email caught her eye, a note from a colleague she'd collaborated with a few times. *Curious.*

"I've got an idea," the subject line read. Kristen opened the message, and in moments her heart began pounding, and a huge smile split her face. What were the odds that Lianne would have an idea so similar to the one that had been rattling around in her own imagination for the past six months? She hit reply and began typing: "I'm interested. Let's set up a time to talk soon." She included a few suggestions on when they could set up phone call or virtual meeting, then hit send. For a few minutes, she stared out over her lawn, not really seeing anything, her imagination spinning with possibilities. A succession of beeps from her phone shook her out of her reverie. It was Celia, inviting her to supper. Kristen accepted, then set her phone down and stretched her arms above her head. *Time to focus, woman.* She turned on her favorite classical playlist—perfect for helping her stay on task—and opened the document from her editor.

Several hours later, a knock at her door caused her to jump. Kristen glanced at her watch, startled to see that it was almost time for Celia and Levi's cookout. She hurried to answer the door, wincing a little as her knee protested how long she'd been sitting still. She opened the door to see Jack dressed in basketball shorts and a faded t-shirt, his slightly long hair still damp on the ends, and his strong jaw covered in a couple of days worth of stubble. His mouth lifted in his crooked smile, and her heart gave a little flutter.

"I'm not late, am I?" she asked.

"No, I just thought it seemed like a good evening for a walk."

"Well, it's good to see you. Come on in. I need to save what I was working on real quick."

Jack stepped inside, closed the door behind him, and then followed Kristen through the kitchen and onto the porch. She perched on the edge of the chair she'd been working in and began typing on her laptop, saving her work and closing everything down. Jack sat in one of the other chairs, leaning back with his legs stretched out in front of him. The space immediately felt smaller, more... full of Jack. Kristen gave herself a mental head shake and told herself to get it together.

A few minutes later, she closed the laptop and

stood up. Jack stood as well, and just like that, they were standing less than a foot apart, and Kristen was remembering Jack kissing her. She cleared her throat. "Okay, well, that's it. Let me drop this in my room and put my shoes on." She hurried through the door, Jack following behind.

"I'll wait in the living room."

Thank goodness.

The short walk to the Blairs' helped clear Kristen's head and restored her equilibrium a little, even when Jack reached over halfway through the walk and took her hand, lacing his fingers through hers. Kristen thought it seemed like Jack had something he wanted to say but maybe was figuring out how to bring it up.

"I started a job today."

"Really?" Kristen said. Her stomach sank. "When are you leaving?"

"No, I mean I started a job here. In Riverton."

"Oh!" She wanted to ask why and for how long, but it felt awkward—like maybe she was fishing for him to say he was staying for her. Was he staying for her? Did she want him to stay for her? Her chest felt tight.

"My last job was a long one, and I forgot how nice it is being around family," Jack said. "Plus, you know..." he glanced over at her and winked. "It's more fun in Riverton than I remembered."

Her face flushed.

"Well, it's..." she searched for the right words,

"I'm… happy you're staying for a while longer."

"Three months at least, and then we'll see."

They arrived at the Blairs' house, for which Kristen was relieved. The scent of grilled meat filled the air, so rather than go inside, they walked around the house—through the newly installed fence—to the backyard. Aislinn and Tripp were playing on the swing set while Celia stood at the smoking grill, a Coke in one hand and a long-handled spatula in the other. She greeted Kristen and Jack with a big smile and hugs as they walked up.

"You guys have good timing! I need to go check the tots in the oven. Do you mind keeping an eye on the grill?"

"Of course. Where's Levi?" Jack reached to take the spatula from Celia.

"He ran over to Judy's real quick to take a look at her car. She couldn't get it started and wasn't sure if it was just the battery or something worse. He should be back any minute. If you're good here, I'll finish getting stuff ready inside."

"I'll help you." Kristen smiled at Jack and rested her hand briefly on his arm as she walked by him and followed Celia inside.

Over the past couple of weeks, Celia and Kristen had started eating lunch together every few days, usually just a quick 30 minutes. It was easy and casual; sometimes Kristen brought her lunch to Celia's, and sometimes Celia and the kids showed up at Kristen's with a bag of sandwiches and fruit. It was a nice break in the day and offered some welcome social interaction on days when working at home dragged. Kristen imagined it was what it felt like working at a company with other employees and a break room—well if break rooms included children. It also meant that Kristen was beginning to feel quite comfortable at the Blairs' house. While Celia checked on the tater tots crisping in the oven, Kristen went straight to the cabinet that held plates and cups and began pulling them out. Celia shut the oven door and pulled out a large wooden tray.

"Let's eat outside," she said. "You can stack everything on there to take it out."

"Good idea."

Celia began pulling condiments and fruit out of the refrigerator, and the two talked as they got everything ready. They talked about Jack's new job and some challenges that Tripp was having with a few of his friends. Kristen told Celia about a new album she'd bought after a recent interview and promised to bring the vinyl over the next time she came. Levi walked in just as they were ready to carry things out to the picnic table, and they managed everything in one trip.

"Perfect timing." Jack slid the last burger onto the plate, turned off the gas, and closed the top of the grill.

Levi chased the kids to the table with much squealing and giggling, and in five minutes, everyone had full plates.

The food disappeared as the sun set, and the sky turned shades of purple and rose. The air filled with pops and whistles as people began setting off firecrackers in the neighborhood. Celia pulled out a handful of sparklers for the kids. Levi pulled out a lighter, and Aislinn squealed in delight when they crackled and popped with light. She and Tripp began chasing each other around the yard. In the distance, Kristen could barely see the big fireworks display at City Hall.

Once the final sparkler had fizzled out and it was well and truly dark, Celia told the kids it was time to get ready for bed, rolling her eyes at the dramatic whining and complaining. She stood up.

"I'll play sheepherder tonight," she said, gently shoving the kids toward the kitchen door while the other three adults cleaned up.

Kristen shook her head, a small smile on her face. There had been times in her life when she mourned the fact that she had never had children, especially as that window was slowly closing, but most of the time, it was easy to admit that she preferred being the really great aunt. She picked up the wooden tray, now full of dirty dishes, and her eyes met Jack's as she straightened. His mouth was quirked in an almost-smile, and his eyes glittered as though he could read her mind. Her smile widened, and she shrugged as if to say, *hey, it is what it is.*

The three of them walked into the kitchen with the remains of dinner. Jack turned on the faucet as

Levi began loading the dishwasher, and Kristen put the lone remaining burger, three slices of cheese, and condiments in the refrigerator. As he waited for the sink to fill, Jack leaned his hip against the counter and crossed his arms.

"Let's go camping."

Levi glanced up.

"When are you thinking? Not this weekend—it's always crazy this close to July 4th. Not to mention everywhere will probably be booked out."

Jack shrugged. "Next weekend? Or the weekend after? Nothing fancy. We could drive down to Table Rock."

"I'm game. Are you thinking family trip or guys trip?"

Jack shrugged, then turned to look at Kristen, who was finished putting food away. "Do you want to come?"

Kristen straightened and shook her head. "Nope. No way. I told you about my camping experience."

"Exactly, time for a re-do."

"What's a re-do?" Celia walked into the kitchen at that moment, and Kristen groaned softly, stealing herself for the enthusiasm she knew was coming. *Stick to your guns*, she told herself.

"Levi and I thought a weekend camping trip would be fun, and I'm trying to convince Kristen to come. She's only been camping once, and it was a terrible experience."

"Oh, yes!" Celia's eyes were bright. "That sounds

fun. You should definitely come, Kristen. Camping is fun with us! There's swimming in the lake, lots of hiking, card games, and I always bring way too many snacks. Sometimes we rent kayaks or jet skis. And you can sleep in the camper with the kids and me if you want a mattress and air conditioning. The guys will sleep in the hammocks."

Kristen hesitated, glancing around the kitchen. Celia's look was excited and expectant; Levi was his typical chill self, washing dishes with long sleeves of his t-shirt pushed up and waiting to see how things would shake out. Jack's dark brown eyes were glued to her, a slight challenge in their dark brown depths and a small smile on his face.

Emotions rose in her that she hadn't felt in a long time. The urge to say yes, even when she wanted to say no. The urge to please, to be accommodating at all costs, to be who they wanted her to be, even when she didn't want to. *No way. Not again.*

"It's really nice of you to ask, but I'd rather not." It took an effort to keep her voice neutral and polite. She could feel her heart pounding, and her face felt flushed. She avoided looking at Celia, afraid that if she did, she'd see hurt or confusion and that she'd cave. She avoided looking at Jack, afraid that if she saw the challenge in his eyes, or his dimple, that she'd cave. Levi continued handing Jack dishes to dry, although Jack was moving so slowly the wet dishes started stacking up on the counter.

"You don't have to come," Jack finally said. "but

it'd be a lot more fun if you would."

Kristen risked a glance and was surprised to see that his eyes had softened. She looked at Celia and saw that she was still smiling.

"Totally," Celia said. "We're not going to force you. The invitation stands, but you don't have to come."

Had they noticed her unexpected spike of anxiety? Had they heard it in her voice?

Or maybe they're just being friends?

Kristen forced her shoulders to relax and attempted a small smile.

"Thanks," she said. "I still think I'm going to pass, sorry. I really do appreciate you asking me."

Celia waved her hand at her and picked up a dishtowel to help dry the dishes. "Seriously, it's no big deal."

Levi changed the conversation to baseball, and they all finished cleaning up. Before she left, Kristen invited them to come over the next night to watch the Cubs-Cardinals game with her and her dad. "I'll even cook!" she said as she walked out the door.

She was halfway down the street, debating with Jack about which team had the most promising rookie before she realized it was the first time Jack had just started walking her home without asking first.

Chapter 11

The next night, Kristen sat curled up on her couch with a glass of wine and her laptop, talking with her Chicago friends on a video call. It had been a couple of weeks since they'd communicated, and it was even better than she'd expected to see their faces and hear their voices. They all claimed that nothing much was going on in their lives, but Kristen grilled them on all the mundane details she was missing out on: work dramas, kid activities, the Cubs games.

Kristen shook her head as Liz finished telling them about her son Noah's first date. Since he and his date were both 14, Liz had been the chauffeur, driving them to the miniature golf course where she had agreed to sit in the car and wait. It wasn't terrible, Liz admitted. She'd gotten a large vanilla Coke from Sonic and downloaded a few episodes of the show she was currently binging.

"The kids were really cute," she said. "They were so nervous, which cracked me up because they've known each other since the third grade."

"Hey, speaking of dates…" Nora said, "We want to hear about Jack. What's going on there? Your first date went well, but you haven't mentioned him since."

Liz nodded, and Kristen shifted slightly, adjusting the laptop, and suddenly a little more uncomfortable than she cared to admit.

"Well…"

"Have you seen him again? What's he like? Have you kissed him?" The rapid-fire questions came from Nora, whose impish grin was clear as day, even in a tiny digital square.

The questions helped, and she took a sip of her wine, considering. She'd been preoccupied spending time with or talking to Jack; she hadn't really thought about how to describe him. "I've told you about Celia, right? Rosalee's former next-door neighbor? Well Jack is her husband's cousin and childhood friend, and he's staying with them for a while. He's direct, observant, thoughtful, reads a lot, and has a sneaky sense of humor. He's definitely good looking. He's got this dimple… and his eyes are a really deep brown with stupid-long lashes. And he's tall. Like, I could probably wear heels around him. He doesn't like to shave very often, but it suits him. He's a welder by trade and likes to go camping and hiking and work outside, so he's got this kind of shaggy haired, tanned, flannel thing going on. And…" she hesitated.

"A hot bod?" Liz said, and they all laughed.

"Yeah," Kristen admitted as their giggles subsided, her face on fire.

Her friends were grinning, and Nora put the back of her hand to her forehead in a fake swoon. "He sounds dreamy. And it's about time is all I've got to say."

"She's right," Liz chimed in. "Fifteen years is long enough to avoid dating."

"I haven't avoided dating!"

Kristen squirmed under their pointed looks, looks that spoke paragraphs of evidence to why she was deluding herself if she really thought that. "Well," she defended herself. "Can you blame me?"

"It's true that your avoidance of relationships is understandable," Liz conceded, "Mike was an abusive jerk, and that was a dark time. But I stand by my statement. Fifteen years is long enough."

"How many times have you gone out?" Nora said, steering the conversation back into more cheerful territory.

Kristen tilted her head, thinking. "Only a couple of times," she said. "But we've hung out a lot over at the Blairs' house. They're great. You guys would love them. They're really relaxed and down-to-earth. I felt included and like part of their family almost immediately. I never thought it would be so much fun to make a new friend—I mean, I've never needed to, because I have you guys!"

"And don't think you're getting rid of us," Nora

said.

Kristen laughed. "As if. You guys are like extra appendages at this point. But listen, don't get too excited about Jack. It's just fun. He's looking for something serious about as much as I am."

Her friends nodded as though they believed her, but she could see the doubt on their faces. She didn't blame them for their optimism, though. It was natural to want to write a romantic happily-ever-after ending for a friend, but in her mind a happily-ever-after meant never losing herself in a relationship again, and she wasn't sure that was possible unless she kept a certain amount of emotional distance.

"When are you going out next?" Nora asked.

"He's coming over here tomorrow to watch the game with Dad and me. I think Celia and Levi might come. We might go out this weekend, I guess, but we haven't talked about it. I'd like to sometime this week though, since he's going camping next weekend."

"And you're not going?" Liz teased. She had been on the disastrous camping trip too.

"Well.... they did ask. But I said no, obviously."

"I think you should go!" Nora exclaimed, clapping her hands. "Time for a do-over!"

They all burst into laughter.

"No way," Kristen said. "Although I almost said yes."

Liz laughed again, but then said she agreed with

Nora and thought Kristen should give it a chance.

"It feels too much like giving in. Like... trying to conform. I don't do that anymore, not for a man."

"No one's asking you to conform to anything. Just try out something new. No harm in that. Don't you like trying new things?"

Ouch.

"Hey. Don't get that look. If I were there, I would give you a big hug so you would know I said that in love. Tough love."

"Do it. Do it. Do it." Nora began chanting, and they started giggling again. And this time, it was the kind of laughter that wouldn't quite quit—a glance at the clock told her that yes, it was much later than she'd thought and about the right time for late night punch drunk mania.

"I'll think about it," she said when the laughter finally calmed to a manageable level. "But I think maybe it's time for me to call it for tonight. As much as I hate to say goodbye and have needed this more than I knew, I know we all need to get up early tomorrow."

"And you want us to stop commenting on your love life."

"Most definitely."

They said goodbye, and after she shut down her laptop, Kristen let out a deep sigh. Part contentment, part melancholy, part contemplation. No. She couldn't think about Jack or camping or her emotional baggage tonight. Time for bed.

Kristen was the last one to arrive at Elizabeth and Jonathan's for family dinner on Sunday. Usually, she rode with her dad and Rosalee, but she had been working at District Cafe and had decided to just go straight from there. A glance at the cars parked in the driveway told her that even Jessica had arrived already. As she put her car in park, Kristen gave herself a mental head shake. She wasn't late, and everyone would be so busy talking and catching up from the previous week that she'd be able to just slip in, no fuss. She slung her leather tote over her shoulder, climbed the front porch steps, and raised her hand to knock. Her instincts seemed to be spot on because she could hear conversation and laughter behind the heavy oak door, and instead of knocking, she impulsively turned the doorknob instead and slipped inside.

She peeked into the living room first and spied the two boys sprawled on the couches with video game controllers clutched in their hands, eyes glued to the digital cars racing on the TV. Kiera lay stretched out on the rug, a book spread out in front of her. Kristen reached into her tote and pulled out three boxes of candy, which she then set down next to each kid.

"Hey, Kristen, thanks!" Chris glanced up. Keira and Austin echoed the sentiment.

"Wait until after dinner so your moms don't get mad at me," Kristen said with a wink. She walked across the hall to the large kitchen, heading first to her dad who sat on the edge of a bar stool munching on some chips and guacamole spread out on the island. She wrapped her arm around his shoulders and squeezed.

"Hey, Peanut," he said. "When did you get here?"

Kristen shrugged, "Just now. Don't tell anyone."

George just smiled, and Kristen reached for a chip and dipped it in the dip, listening to catch the drift of the conversations. *I need to get the secret to Elizabeth's guacamole. This is amazing.* Jonathan and Rosalee discussed the best place to buy plants in town, while Elizabeth, Mary, and Jessica seemed to be talking about a tough class Jessica was taking. As they talked, Elizabeth's hands were busy shredding meat, while Mary tossed something in a bowl with a pair of tongs.

"It's not that the material is that difficult," Jessica was saying, "but she has such unrealistic expectations on how long it takes to actually read and respond to everything she's giving us. Kristen," Jessica turned toward her. "You were an English major, right?"

Kristen nodded, mouth full.

"Tell me if I'm being unreasonable here. This professor assigns us two short stories each class, which we're required to read and then write a 2-3 page response to—using prompts from the professor—by the next class, and we have class twice a week! That's a lot, right?"

"Eh... it is. But, it's not an unusual amount for an English class. Is it a 300 or 400 level?"

Jessica nodded.

"Yeah... sorry, Jess, but especially at those upper levels, that's pretty typical."

Jessica groaned and lightly beat her head against the wall. "All I needed was an elective. All I wanted was to take a class with my boyfriend, and Short Stories from the Pacific sounded delightful." She sighed. "Next time, I'm picking the class."

Elizabeth rolled her eyes. "Jessica, stop being so dramatic and take the tortillas out of the oven. I think we're ready to move everything to the table."

Kristen picked up a platter full of taco toppings and followed Jessica to the dining room table.

"Speaking of that boyfriend of yours, where is he today?"

"He has a big paper due tomorrow and needed extra time in the library," Jessica replied. "But speaking of boyfriends..." her eyes sparkled. "When are you going to bring your fella to Sunday dinner? Gran says he's quite the looker. Her words, of course."

Kristen blushed. "He is a looker, but I don't know about bringing him to Sunday dinner. That seems..." she searched for the right word.

"Like a lot of pressure?" Jessica offered. "Like I'm asking you to force a conversation about your relationships that you'd rather not have?"

"Something like that."

"You should bring him, no pressure," Mary chimed in. She had followed the other two into the dining room with a stack of plates and flatware and began distributing the place settings around the table. "When Corbin was in high school, he brought a different girl to Sunday dinner almost every week. You're thinking about what it was like when George first came. There was definitely a lot of pressure on that visit, but that was different. No one will act weird or awkward if you bring Jack, I promise."

Austin and Chris barreled through the dining room, Chris's hair inexplicably soaking wet, and Mary sighed. "Well, some of us might act weird, but not any more than normal."

The three of them walked back to the kitchen to get more food.

"How about next week?" Jessica asked.

Kristen shook her head. "He and the Blairs are going camping."

"Where are they going?" Jonathan, who was setting glasses on a tray, joined the conversation.

"Umm... it was a lake, I think. Something Rock?"

"Table Rock?" Charles asked.

"Yes, that's it!"

"You aren't going?" Mary asked.

"No. They asked, but no."

Before she could explain, or anyone could ask why, Elizabeth herded everyone back into the dining room, where they all busied themselves filling plates and passing food. Eventually, once everyone had begun eating, Jessica turned to Kristen.

"So why aren't you going camping?"

Why is everyone so obsessed with whether I'm going camping?

Kristen told the story of her one and only camping trip, and by the time she was done, everyone was crying from laughter, and no one questioned her reasoning. However, later, Kristen was in the kitchen helping wash dishes, Elizabeth brought it up.

"You know," she said. "There's nothing wrong with trying something again. Believe me, I've learned that the hard way."

Kristen cocked her head, a question in her eyes.

"I don't like looking stupid," Elizabeth continued. "And over the years, I've avoided doing a lot of things because I knew I wouldn't be able to do it well, or I didn't understand it, or I felt like if I tried, I would be embarrassed. One of the things that first attracted me to Jonathan is that he's the opposite of that. He LOVES trying new things, and he hardly ever gets embarrassed about anything. He's pushed me to try things I would never have on my own, and because of that, I've had so many wonderful experiences I never would have otherwise."

"Aren't you afraid you'll... forget how to say no? That he won't respect your boundaries?" Kristen handed her a clean, wet bowl.

Elizabeth thought for a minute as she dried. "Not really. I mean, maybe when we were dating? I know this may surprise you," her voice was dry, "but I've never been afraid to speak my mind."

Kristen laughed. "It's one of the things I like most about you."

"Thank you."

They worked in silence for a few more minutes, then Elizabeth spoke again. "I know on the surface you and I don't seem much alike, but I think in some ways, we're very similar. I know what it's like to... hold yourself back. Emotionally, I mean." her voice was almost uncharacteristically hesitant, like she was afraid Kristen would get offended. "I might be wrong, but it seems like I recognize some of those walls."

If the comment had come from anyone else, Kristen's alarm bells would have been ringing, but over the past few months, she had learned that Elizabeth was never mean-spirited and that her sometimes rigid exterior concealed a very caring spirit. Plus, Kristen appreciated Elizabeth's directness. As if sensing that Kristen needed some time to process, Elizabeth changed the subject to more mundane things like a new restaurant that had opened in town and a vacation that Elizabeth's family was going on later that summer. They joined the rest of the family outside on the patio, but Kristen soon found that she was distracted and tired, so said her goodbyes.

The next morning, Kristen woke up before her alarm clock went off and took advantage of the early morning for a head-clearing run through the neighborhood. Judy and Sierra were coming by to walk, but she had time to run first.

Kristen loved running at this time of day, loved the feeling of being completely alone, yet also watching the world wake up and join her. Even though she usually ran to music, this morning she ran in silence, with only the birdsong and the occasional barking dog as accompaniment to her pounding shoes and steady breathing. She thought about what Liz and Elizabeth had said. She thought about her new friends, and about Jack, trying to think only about *him* and not her projections onto him. Three miles and her head felt clearer, her sense of self firm and whole. As she sat on her front steps with a bottle of water, waiting for her walking buddies, she pulled out her phone and sent Jack a text.

"On second thought, count me in. You're right about the do-over."

His response was swift: "cool"

She texted Celia as well, and her response was as characteristically her as Jack's had been characteristically him: "CALL ME LATER!!!!!!! CAN'T WAIT!!!!!!!"

Kristen texted back: "getting ready to walk with Sierra and Judy. Will call you after."

As she tucked her phone back into her running belt, Kristen was glad that she'd taken everyone's advice and reconsidered the invitation. Her knee jerk reaction to the perceived pressure of the moment had taken her off guard—and it really had been perceived, she realized. No one had actually been pressuring her.

To be fair to herself, she still wasn't one hundred percent sure about going camping, but it was just the weekend, and it couldn't be any worse than the last time. She hoped.

Chapter 12

Jack picked up his phone for the twentieth time, flipped over to his weather app, then almost immediately shoved the phone back in his pocket. He knew he was putting too much pressure on the weekend, but at least there were no storms in the forecast.

At that moment, Levi appeared, arms full with a cooler, which he shoved onto the open tailgate of Jack's truck.

"Don't worry; I can get it all." The smirk on his face softened the sarcasm in his voice.

Jack lightly punched him on the arm. "Okay, okay. Point me to the stuff. But it's not my fault you have to bring so much."

"I'll make sure Celia knows you're eating out of your own backpack then."

Jack just shook his head and followed Levi back into the house. Fifteen minutes later, the guys had loaded Jack's truck and Levi's camper with two coolers, backpacks, bedding, hammocks, two sleeping bags, mosquito netting, swim totes, one camp stove, a bag of charcoal, three big plastic tubs, fishing poles, a tackle box, camp chairs, and a few other odds and ends. The kids came running out of the house as Levi shut the back of the SUV, with Celia following close behind. As Celia loaded the kids in the car, Levi and Jack double-checked that they each had the campsite plugged into their GPS—although it was one they'd been to a lot and could probably get to in their sleep—then they headed out, Celia and Levi to the store to grab ice for the coolers and Jack to Kristen's to pick her up.

A few minutes later, Jack pulled into Kristen's driveway. She sat on the bench under the big oak tree in her front yard, a pillow, big duffle bag, tote bag, and a 12-pack of Coke sitting at her feet. Her long curly hair was pulled up into a ponytail, and she was wearing a blue t-shirt with some kind of logo on it and a pair of distressed jeans that looked like they probably hadn't started out that way. She sat with her eyes closed and a pair of earbuds tucked into her ears. Jake's heart thumped at the sight of her, his thoughts skittering, one part of his brain mapping their drive to the lake, while another part noted that her t-shirt was exactly the shade of her eyes, and another part wondered what she was listening to. And part of him was just... excited.

He got out of the truck, and she opened her eyes at the sound of his door closing. She pulled her earbuds out and stood up, a smile lighting up her face.

"Hey!"

"Hey, yourself."

She tucked her earbuds into her pocket and grabbed the tote bag and Cokes. Jack grabbed the duffle bag and pillow.

"Are the secrets of the universe hiding in that giant bag," Jack said, nodding at the tote slung over her shoulder.

"Haha. Very funny."

They loaded Kristen's gear into the truck, then headed down the street. Kristen asked him about his new job, and then the conversation turned toward her video chat with her friends.

"You miss them a lot," Jack commented.

Kristen nodded. "Yeah." She was quiet for a few minutes. "We've all been friends for a long time," she said eventually. Her voice held touches of wistfulness.

"Tell me about them."

She told him about how she and her three best friends met in college in a freshman English class, where they bonded over their disdain for the TA. They moved in together their sophomore year, into a dingy little apartment close to campus, where they lived until they all graduated and moved into the two-flat that she'd lived in ever since. She told him about Nora's enthusiasm for everything and Liz's straightforward lack of filter that sometimes led to misunderstandings but more often made them all crack up. She talked about how they'd all called Liz the "grownup" of their little family and that they'd thought she was virtually unflappable until she met her now husband, who turned her into a romantic pile of mush. Jack commented that it was nice to have friends like that.

"Yeah, it is." she smiled at him. "Of course, you understand."

More silence, but not uncomfortable. Jack opened his mouth to ask Kristen if she minded putting on some music when she turned toward him.

"Do you mind if we roll down the windows and put on some music?"

Jack grinned. "You read my mind."

Kristen picked a classic country music mix that provided a perfect soundtrack to the back roads and small highways that Jack drove them down. He hummed along to the familiar songs and felt himself relax as they passed by farms and small towns. The roads became curvier, the terrain more hilly, and the open farmland turned to cool green woods. As he drove, Jack glanced over at Kristen frequently. Her arm lay on the edge of the open window, chin resting on her forearm. He wondered what she was thinking.

Chapter 13

A few hours later, they pulled into the campground. Jack stopped at the welcome center, checked in, and picked up a parking pass. He waved away the offer of a map and got back into the truck with Kristen.

Their double campsite was tucked under huge oak, maple, and sweet gum trees, close to the bathhouse. A long set of railroad tie steps led down a gentle hill to the lake, where a short dock jutted out into the water, and a small strip of sand ran along the shoreline for about 100 yards.

"Wow! This is amazing. I mean, it's gotta be the perfect campsite."

Jack's heart filled with warmth at her enthusiasm. "There are several campsites with the dock and the swimming beach, but this one's our favorite with the kids since it's so close to the bathhouse. We were lucky it was available last minute." He bumped up against Kristen with his shoulder. "Maybe the universe is on board with your do-over."

"Hmmm… it's possible. But I'm not convinced yet."

After one more moment staring at the view, Jack moved to the back of his truck and pulled out two small bundles that turned out to be hammocks. Kristen helped him tie them off to the trees.

"Are you sure you guys don't mind sleeping in these?" she asked, skeptical.

"Yep. It's what we usually sleep in when it's just the two of us. They're really comfortable and less hassle than the camper. But the camper's great for the kids. Levi and Celia bought it when Tripp was little because he never slept well on the ground, and they were worried about him falling out of a hammock. And it's good for rain. It's mostly just sleeping and storage, but there is a fold-out table, and Levi retrofitted it with a little air conditioning unit."

When Levi and Celia's SUV pulled up not too much later, the hammocks were swaying gently in the breeze, the camp chairs were situated around the fire pit, and Kristen and Jack sat at the picnic table playing an intense game of Slap Jack. Tripp and Aislinn leaped out of the vehicle and proceeded to yell and run in circles as if they'd been cooped up for days rather than a few hours.

"Ha!" Kristen took advantage of Jack's momentary distraction and slapped the jack of hearts on top of a big pile of cards. "That's the last one," she gloated, "I'm pretty sure of it."

They played it out, but Jack was also pretty sure she was right.

"I told you, I have lightning reflexes," she said with a grin, waggling her fingers. Jack reached fast across the table and grabbed her hands before she could pull away, tugging her upper body partway across the table. He leaned his own torso toward her and kissed her.

"Me too."

Before she could say anything, Jack let go of her hands and stood up so he could help Levi unload. It was fun to catch Kristen off guard. Unconsciously, he reached up and ran his thumb across his lips. Her berry-flavored lip gloss made him think of the good parts of high school.

After Jack and Levi unloaded, they set to work getting a charcoal fire started in the fire pit. Next to it sat a metal grate that fit across the top and could be used for grilling. Kristen walked over and handed them koozie-wrapped sodas.

"Pretty clever setup," she commented, handing them the drinks and squatting down next to Jack. He nodded.

"If we want later tonight, we can take the grate off and put some firewood in to build up a wood fire."

Levi set the grate on top of the lit coals, and the three of them headed toward the picnic table closest to the camper. Celia had spread a plastic tablecloth across the top and set the tub full of kitchen stuff on the bench. One of the coolers sat next to it. Jack and Levi started getting out the things they needed for dinner prep, working together with the ease of two people who'd been there together a million times before. Jack gave Kristen things to do to help, knowing he always felt awkward standing around watching other people work.

The evening moved on uneventfully: burgers and hot dogs, s'mores and sticky kids, a sunset walk along the lake and watching the kids chase fireflies. Jack spent most of the evening watching Kristen when she wasn't looking.

Eventually, they finished cleaning up the last of the s'mores stuff and sealing up food, so no animals would get to it in the middle of the night. Aislinn and Tripp came running down the path from the bath house, faces freshly scrubbed and teeth brushed. Celia herded them into the camper, and Levi moved to follow and help get the kids settled for bed.

"They'll be back out soon," Jack said to Kristen.

She murmured an unintelligible response from where she sat in the camp chair, her head tilted back, eyes closed. Jack leaned forward and stirred the fire with a stick.

"If you stare at me all weekend like you did today, I'm going to get paranoid," Kristen said. Her eyes were still closed, but there was a smile on her face.

Jack chuckled. And here he thought he'd been so subtle.

"No promises," he said.

They sat enjoying the sounds of nighttime at the campground: the soft whoosh, whoosh of water lapping gently on their little strip of beach; the faint murmur of voices coming from the camper; rustling leaves and snapping twigs; the crackle of the fire; and distant sounds of music and laughter from other occupied campsites. After Levi and Celia came out, they took a lantern and deck of cards to the picnic table and played a couple of games of Hearts. Jack teased Kristen as her competitive streak re-emerged, and he was pleased when she seemed to not just take the teasing in stride but double down on her competitiveness when it became clear that nobody minded.

Normally, Jack was just as competitive but instead of getting into the game, he found himself thinking about the last few times he'd been camping. Usually, Jack went solo, especially when he was away from Missouri. It was his preference, truthfully. Woods, water, rocks, trails—in all its variations, it was his therapy, it was home. It took him a long time to see it like that though, or at least to put words to it in that way. When he was younger, he just knew that outside was where he could better deal with his emotions and frustrations. These days, it was his favorite way to explore a new place, and his favorite way to spend his time when he wasn't working. Of course, he always enjoyed camping trips with Levi, either just the two of them or the whole family. He might have liked his own company better than most, but even he craved connection now and then.

How long had it been since he'd spent this much time with someone new? Not just this weekend, but the past several weeks. When was the last time he'd gone on more than two dates with a woman, or called her on the phone just to talk? Honestly, he couldn't even remember the last time he'd made a new friend. He had coworkers and acquaintances, guys with whom he played pickup basketball, or rec league softball, but friends? He'd never felt he needed any other friends and certainly never felt like he needed any kind of real romantic entanglement. *Get yourself emotionally dependent on someone, and it only leads to heartache.*

Then came Kristen. Where did she fit in? She captivated him, and all he wanted to do was spend more time with her. She didn't ask much of him—not yet anyway—but so far, he got the impression she hadn't offered too much of herself either. They were quite a pair. He reminded himself to be careful.

Chapter 14

Kristen woke to the smell of coffee and bacon and the sounds of whispering little voices. She opened her eyes and peeked over the edge of the bunk bed. Celia was helping Aislinn get her shoes on, and Tripp was just finishing lacing his own shoes. Celia motioned with her hand for Tripp to keep his voice down, and it didn't look like the first time.

"I'm awake," Kristen croaked. She cleared her throat and tried again. "Good morning."

"Good morning!" Tripp said before bounding toward the door and practically leaping out of the camper, the door slamming behind him.

Celia sighed and shook her head. "Good morning. I hope we didn't wake you up."

"Not at all. I think it was the siren song of bacon."

"Same. I wish Levi got up early and cooked me bacon at home too, but unfortunately, it's just a camping thing."

"Well, that makes it more special, right?"

"Hmmm..." Celia tapped a finger on her chin as though in deep thought. "Maybe you have a point."

"Mama, potty!" Aislinn was hopping up and down now.

"Oh! Right. Let's go, sweetie." Celia and Aislinn exited the camper.

Kristen lay on the bed for a few more minutes before getting up, exchanging her sleep shorts for cut-offs, slipping on her sneakers, and joining everyone else outside. Levi stood by the camp stove, frying bacon on a cast iron griddle and holding a steaming stainless steel mug of what she assumed was coffee. Tripp sat at the picnic table, carefully buttering slices of bread and Jack sat across from him slicing the tops of a carton of strawberries, his own steaming mug in front of him. Jack's light brown hair told the story of a deep night's sleep, flattened on one side and standing up on the other.

Kristen stretched her arms over her head and took a deep breath. She had to admit, there was something about the smell of coffee and frying bacon mixed with the smell of fresh air, dirt, and green, growing things. Jack glanced up from his strawberries and flashed his dimple.

"'Morning."

"Good morning."

She walked over to the table, and Jack nodded his head toward an electric kettle sitting on the end of the table next to a stainless steel tumbler, a Tupperware container full of what looked like sugar, and a plastic baggie stuffed with tea bags.

"Celia packed some tea," he said. "There's milk in the red cooler."

I am going to have to think of something extra special to do for Celia. She is so thoughtful.

"You've got a keeper there, Levi," Kristen said, pushing the button to heat the kettle.

"Truest thing I know," he replied, flipping over a slice of bacon.

While the kettle heated, Kristen walked to the bathhouse, passing Celia and Aislinn on the way. When she got back to the campsite, a mound of bacon sat on a plate next to the stove, and Levi had moved on to toasting the bread that Tripp had buttered. Aislinn and Tripp were swinging and giggling in the hammocks, Celia was doctoring a cup of coffee, and Jack was lounging on the picnic bench, elbows resting on the tabletop next to the bowl of washed and trimmed strawberries, legs stretched out in front of him. Kristen made herself a cup of tea.

They took their time over breakfast, munching on perfectly crisped bacon and buttery toast with jelly, stealing strawberries straight from the bowl, not even bothering with individual plates. Celia brewed a second pot of coffee, and Kristen's one cup of tea turned into two. By the time the last bite of food had disappeared and the dirty dishes had been cleaned up, Kristen had lost all sense of time, but she was one hundred percent okay with that.

After their leisurely start to the day, they filled

the rest of it with hiking and swimming, peanut butter sandwiches, sausage and potato foil packs cooked in the coals, and more s'mores. When the sun had nearly disappeared, Celia and Levi started getting the kids ready for bed. Kristen carried a chair and one last s'more down to the dock, where she settled in with a little sigh of contentment to watch the last of the day's fire sink behind the trees, the lights of other camps winking around the lake.

When the gentle and subtle motion of the dock became more pronounced, Kristen turned to see Celia walking toward her. She felt a pang of disappointment, then was immediately embarrassed to admit that she'd been hoping it was Jack. *What's wrong with you?* Kristen scolded herself. When Celia reached her she held out a hand, offering Kristen one of the two long-necked bottles she held.

"May I join you?" she asked.

Kristen smiled and accepted the drink. "Of course, and thank you."

Celia sat down next to her in the chair she'd carried down in her other hand, and for a while they simply enjoyed the lake-cooled evening breeze and the sounds of crickets.

"I guess the kids settled pretty quickly?" Kristen finally asked.

"Eh, sort of," Celia said. "Levi has it under control, and they prefer him at bedtime." She let out a long sigh, leaning her head back in the chair. "I apologize if this hits a nerve or anything, but can I just admit to you that kids are exhausting, and as much as I love mine, sometimes I secretly envy my carefree friends."

"To be fair," Kristen replied, "I'm not exactly 'carefree,' my cares are just... different. But I get what you mean. Parenting is a really hard gig."

Celia laughed. "True enough," she said. "Let's just say adulting is hard, no matter what that looks like."

Kristen grinned and stretched out the hand holding her bottle. "I'll drink to that." Celia clinked her bottle against Kristen's, then they sat in companionable silence as the dusk deepened.

It had been such a fun day, Kristen thought. The weather had been perfect, wildflowers had been blooming along the trail they'd hiked, and the lake had been cool and refreshing. There had been no agenda and no expectations, and she marveled at how at ease she felt, and how the Blairs treated her like family. Kristen felt Celia shifting in the chair next to her. She turned, although it was now too dim to see Celia's expression clearly. Celia cleared her throat.

"I don't know..." she began, then hesitated. "I'm not sure how much you and Jack talk about your... relationship?" she framed it as a question. "I mean, I don't even know if you call it a relationship, because historically Jack doesn't 'do' relationships—

his words," she was quick to add. "And, I know it's early days and you've only gone out on a few dates. I promise I'm not trying to put any pressure on you or anything. But Jack seems really... happy, and in the past that usually precedes a... quick exit."

Kristen drummed her fingers against the arm of her chair. This was unexpected. Despite Celia's assurances that she wasn't trying to put pressure on whatever was going on with Jack, her words kind of did. Mostly, Kristen was just confused. *Was Celia warning her away from Jack?* She opened her mouth to ask, but Celia continued.

"I'm not saying this well. I don't want to steer you away from Jack—we like spending time with you and getting to spend time together all four of us, well, it's been really nice for Levi and me." she cleared her throat again. "I guess, I'm saying, if Jack distances himself, don't be surprised, but maybe don't write him off right away? And I hope...well, Levi and I both hope you'll still hang out with us, even if Jack doesn't."

The last bit of what Celia said came out in a rush, and Kristen relaxed.

"Hey, you've fed me and invited me into your home, and now you've somehow talked me into going on a camping trip," Kristen grinned, even though she knew Celia probably couldn't see her. "You won't get rid of me that easily."

Celia let out a relieved sigh. "Okay, good. I love

Jack and all, but he can be a real pain sometimes, and I didn't want him to ruin a new friendship for me."

The two laughed, then spent another hour chatting about favorite TV shows until their yawns drove them to bed.

Chapter 15

"Maybe we can just send the kids home with the guys and stay here until next weekend."

Celia waved to the four small figures that were just visible at the end of a dock. She and Kristen were floating in kayaks in the middle of the lake while Tripp and Aislinn fished one last time with Levi and Jack.

"Hmm, well, that's entirely your call, but it sounds good to me. Except for the whole needing Wi-Fi to work."

They sat with their oars resting across their laps, faces tilted toward the sun, eyes closed.

"Have you finished the book for book club next weekend yet?" Celia asked after several sun-soaked minutes. She reached up and tucked a stray blonde curl into her messy bun.

Kristen shook her head. "Almost. I actually brought it with me, but I've been too tired by the time we lay down at night to read anything. I'm enjoying it a lot, though. I can't wait to hear what everyone thinks about it."

"Me too!" Celia said. "I finished it a few days ago, and I'm dying to talk about it now. I won't spoil the ending for you, but I found it very satisfying." She lifted her oar off her lap. "Let's paddle some more. I'm thinking we have less than an hour left before we need to think about packing up, and I want to soak up every second of lake time."

Kristen agreed, and they began drifting through the water, no destination in mind, just enjoying the movement and the breeze, the sun and the water. Kristen would never have thought of herself as an outdoors person, but she was certainly enjoying herself now. As they paddled, she thought about all the times as a kid her dad had taken her to Lake Michigan for a picnic or a bike ride. She thought of her countless hours running along the waterfront and the time she and Nora had rented paddleboards almost every weekend for a month. She still didn't know if that qualified her as being an "outdoors person"—not like Jack was, for example—but maybe she wasn't as far off as she'd thought.

Thinking about Jack made her think about last night's conversation on the dock with Celia and she frowned. All day, she'd been on edge, wondering if Celia's warning was going to prove true or not. She'd tried to keep her uncertainties to herself, but there had been a few times that morning when Jack had caught her staring at him and given her a strange look. Once he'd even asked if there was something wrong, but she'd redirected the conversation. Frankly, when Celia had suggested the two of them kayak, she'd jumped at the chance, eager to be alone with her thoughts and shake off her paranoia. What she really needed was something else to focus her attention on.

"Is it ever hard having known Levi for so long?" she asked Celia as they paddled. "And dating for so long? Do you ever feel like you can't be your own person? Like you only exist as half of 'Celia and Levi'?"

Celia glanced at her. "That's a good question." she adjusted her rowing pace to match Kristen's. "Sometimes it's hard, if I'm honest. Or at least, it used to be. That's partly why we moved to Riverton."

"Really?"

Celia nodded. "Definitely. It's hard enough being an adult in the same small town you grew up in. It's hard to grow up or change. And then add on to that doing it with a high school sweetheart..." she shook her head. "After we had Tripp, Levi and I went through a really rough patch. We were both growing, changing. We had a lot of unspoken expectations after having a baby that just didn't line up with reality. Both of us did. But when I'd try to talk about any of that with a friend, or my mom, or anyone really, it just felt like no one was listening. Anyway, eventually, Levi got the idea to move. Try a fresh start."

"Fresh starts are very underrated."

Celia looked at her with a smile—a smile of understanding—but said nothing. A few minutes later, they rowed up to the dock where the guys and the kids were packing up fishing gear. Kristen and Celia dragged the kayaks out of the water, tucking the oars securely inside. They padlocked it to the post in the ground near the dock, ready to be rented by the next round of campers.

Before they'd set out on the lake, Kristen had gathered her things and put her bags in Jack's truck, so while everyone else continued to pack up, she grabbed a trash bag and recruited Tripp and Aislinn to help her do one last pass through the campsite to ensure they left the area spotless. In less than 30 minutes, the gear was loaded, the kids were buckled in, and Levi was backing the SUV up to the camper to re-hitch it. Kristen was standing next to Celia, watching, and reached out to give her new friend a hug.

"I know I'll most likely see you or talk to you in a few days, but I want to say thanks for inviting me along this weekend. It was fun."

Celia hugged her back. "I'm glad you said yes." She pulled back and grinned at Kristen. "A good do-over, yes?"

"Definitely."

Kristen waved to Levi then walked to join Jack at his truck. He smiled at her as she walked up and slipped his arm around her waist.

"Ready?"

"I am."

He leaned down and kissed her, making Kristen's toes tingle. *He didn't* act *like someone who was getting ready to run away.* Jack pulled away to open her door, and Kristen gave herself a mini pep talk as she climbed inside: *don't assume the worst, just be prepared.* She watched Jack walk around the driver's side. He cranked the engine and reached for his seat belt.

"Levi and Celia are heading straight home, but I have a personal tradition of marking the end of an outdoors trip with the best burger I can find. You game?"

"Absolutely. You know, if you'd led with that, I might have said yes to the whole camping thing a lot sooner."

Chapter 16

Jack stretched out on a chair in the backyard, combing his fingers through his wet hair and wondering if it was time for a haircut. He pulled out his phone and pressed a few buttons.

"Hello?"

His heart thumped.

"Hey. How's it going?"

"Hey, you." Kristen's voice went from sounding distracted to happy. He pictured her in her little house, sitting at the writing desk that faced the window, with her hair pulled off her face, her fingers tapping across her laptop, and a half-empty glass of Coke sweating next to her. "What's up? How was work today?"

"It was fine. Hot."

"But I bet you're sitting outside right now, aren't you?"

He smiled. She knew him well. "It's different when you're lounging in the shade. And there's a breeze."

"Mmhm, well… I'm glad I get to work inside."

"I'm heading to Tripp's baseball game in a few minutes and wondered if you wanted to come with?"

"Normally I would, but I'm really in the zone right now with these chapters I'm editing, and I think I should channel that energy while I have it. What are you doing tomorrow evening?"

"Nothing, I think."

"Do you want to come with me to Dad and Rosalee's for dinner?"

Jack hesitated. Was this a loaded question?

"It's not a big deal," Kristen said into the silence. Had her voice cooled off, or was it his imagination? "But we can hang out later this weekend if you'd rather."

"No, no, dinner tomorrow sounds fun."

"It's really not a big deal if you don't want to." There was definitely some frost in her voice. Jack felt like he'd made a misstep and then somehow made it worse. Frustration welled up inside him, and he fought the urge to say "forget it" and hang up.

"I do want to, I'm positive."

"Okay, I'll let them know. If I pick you up at 6:00, will that give you enough time after work?"

"6:00 is perfect."

"Okay, well, I should probably get back to work. Thanks for calling."

Jack suppressed a sigh. How could a conversation that ended in a dinner invitation still feel like it had gone sideways?

"See you tomorrow."

"Bye."

• • • •

Jack felt a small measure of uncertainty as he got dressed for dinner the next night, although the uncertainty was unrelated to George and Rosalee. He was looking forward to spending time with the couple, but after the way his conversation with Kristen had ended the night before, he wasn't sure what to expect from her. Would she be aloof? Act like nothing had happened? Had he read too much into the conversation in the first place? Logically, he knew he had met George and Rosalee previously, had even spent an evening watching baseball with George at Kristen's house. He couldn't explain his hesitation except that for a brief second going to dinner at George and Rosalee's had felt different— like "meeting the parents." And for a second, that had felt strange. He sighed as he tied his shoes. This was why he never went out on more than a few dates with a woman.

Several minutes later, he heard her pull into the driveway and went outside to meet her.

"Hey," he said, tucking himself into her little Honda.

Her answering smile was bright and warm, and

Jack felt some of his uncertainty fade away. That smile was a good start to the evening. "Hey yourself," she replied, shifting into reverse and backing out of the driveway. "How was your day?"

Before long, they were pulling up to a small cluster of two-story buildings surrounded by tall trees. While the buildings looked like fairly generic multi-family construction, Jack could tell that the management of the complex had made a point to provide beauty and character through the landscaping and outdoor environment. He reached for the door handle, but before he could open his door Kristen put a hand on his arm.

"I'm sorry if I was weird last night on the phone," she said. "I'm not sure why I got so..." she trailed off. "Anyway. I'm glad you're here." She squeezed his arm as if to emphasize her words. Jack leaned over and kissed her.

"Me too," he said.

Rosalee was putting the finishing touches on supper when they went inside, so after the initial greetings George got drinks and they settled around a platter of hummus, pita, and vegetables set out on the bar. Kristen began talking to the other couple about their week while Jack sat back and mostly listened. There was a familiarity in the way the three interacted that spoke of lots of time spent together and a genuine affection for each other that wasn't always guaranteed, even with blood relatives. *Sometimes especially with blood relatives.*

He watched Rosalee put the lid back on the pot on the stove and set a timer, then she turned toward him.

"Help me set the table?" she asked.

"I'd love to."

He slid off the barstool and walked around Kristen, resting his hand briefly on her back as he passed by. Rosalee handed him a stack of plates with napkins resting on top and he turned to walk the handful of steps to the table, and she followed him with silverware and glasses. As Jack walked around the table placing plates and napkins, he admired the smooth, dark wood of the farmhouse table.

"This table is amazing," he said, running his hand along the edge. "Is it walnut?"

Rosalee nodded. "Yes, it is. It's a little big for the condo, but my son Charles made it, so it was a non-negotiable in the move."

"I don't blame you, it's beautiful work. Is he a carpenter by trade?"

"No, just a hobby, but one he's enjoyed for a long time."

Jack followed Rosalee back to the kitchen where she was spooning heavily spiced roasted and sliced chicken onto a serving platter next to little bowls of what looked like picked vegetables. She nodded to the pitchers of water and tea on the counter and he picked them up and walked them to the table. At a word from Rosalee, George and Kristen followed Jack, carrying the hummus plate and the pot of rice from the stovetop. Rosalee was close behind, setting the platter on the table then gesturing to ladder-backed chairs.

"Let's eat," she said.

As they passed dishes and ate the delicious food, Rosalee asked Jack what he was reading. "Kristen tells me you're an avid reader." She nodded at George and smiled "that one over there pretty much only reads newspapers and sports magazines, despite my best efforts." she winked at George, and he shrugged.

"It's still reading," he defended himself.

"I do like to read books," Jack admitted, "I also like to read sports magazines and newspapers, so I get the best of both worlds I suppose. Recently, I've gotten really into Japanese mysteries. Kind of a random niche, but there are some really fantastic authors whose work has been translated recently."

He enjoyed talking books with Rosalee as they ate, Kristen chiming in occasionally. Talk eventually turned to George and Rosalee's upcoming vacation to Wyoming with Rosalee's kids and grandkids.

"We're staying at a lodge near the Grand Tetons, and plan on hiking until our feet fall off," Rosalee said. "The older grandkids may spend a couple of days backpacking on one of the trails, but I like the idea of a hot shower and a mattress at the end of the day."

"It sounds amazing," Jack said. "I've been to the Grand Tetons once, and it was incredible. I'd love to go back one day."

George glanced down the table at Kristen and then back at Jack. "We tried to talk Kristen into going with us, but she said no."

"I really need to work. I've got multiple deadlines looming, otherwise I'd love to. Maybe Jack can go in my place," she added with a cheeky smile.

Jack returned her smile, but shook his head. "Sadly, I need to work as well, otherwise I'd be happy to be an honorary Bowen-Finch-McDonnell."

"Well, you would be more than welcome anytime," Rosalee said as she stood up and started clearing empty dishes. The others stood up to help her, and soon they were back at the table with warm cherry pie and ice cream in front of them.

"What projects are you working on right now?" George asked Kristen. "You mentioned more than one deadline."

"I've got final edits due on the Irish music history book, two features for British & International Music Yearbook, and a book proposal."

"What's the book proposal about?" Rosalee asked.

"It was actually an idea that a colleague sent me a few weeks ago," Kristen replied. Jack watched her eyes light up as she explained the idea. "She's a food writer and photographer based in Chicago, and got the idea to write a book that combines the food and music scenes of Chicago. She's going to a big agents and editors conference in September, so we need to get a solid proposal finished before then."

"That sounds fascinating!" Rosalee exclaimed. "But it sounds like a really broad topic. How are you approaching it?"

Kristen shook her head. "We're not one hundred percent sure, yet. So we brainstormed a few different proposals and will see what rises to the top. It's a lot to figure out though. History or modern? Neighborhood or genre? Do we go broad strokes, or pick out a handful of venues and restaurants, and if so, what's the thread that connects them?"

Jack listened to Kristen talk about the ideas she was working on, thinking that it sounded a complicated process, and not one he would want to tackle. He liked to read books, but if putting one together was like that... he'd leave it to someone else. However, he enjoyed watching Kristen talk about the project. Her eyes seemed to glow, her whole body full of energy, hands gesturing as she explained her ideas. He honestly couldn't seem to take his eyes off of her.

After finishing their dessert and cleaning off the table, they debated playing a game of Hand and Foot, but Jack said he'd have to bow out because he had to work early in the morning. He apologized to Kristen for not thinking about that when they'd decided to ride together, but she waved her hand in an "it's nothing" gesture. Rosalee wrapped the rest of the pie and handed it to Jack to take with him, which he accepted with a wide smile and without protest. He kissed her cheek as he took the pie plate.

"Thank you for the wonderful evening, and for the pie. I promise I'll bring back your dish."

"I trust you."

Kristen hugged George and Rosalee and Jack shook George's hand. Rosalee asked Kristen if she wanted to ride together to book club the next day, and after a brief discussion about what time and who was driving, she and Jack were out the door.

"Thank you for coming with me tonight," Kristen said as they drove through the late summer twilight.

"It was nice. Thank you for inviting me." Jack glanced over at Kristen with a smile, but she was focused on the road, tapping her fingers against the steering wheel, her body curling slightly forward. Jack furrowed his brow slightly. Her words said one thing, but her body language said another, and considering that the road conditions were ideal, he was pretty sure she wasn't stressed about driving.

"Everything okay?" he asked.

"Hmm?" she straightened and glanced at him, eyebrows raised. "I'm sorry, I missed what you said."

"I was just asking if everything was okay. You seem..." *Tense? Sad?* "Lost in thought."

"Oh! Yes, everything's fine."

Once again, Jack got the impression that her words said one thing, but that there was more going on below the surface. He was tempted to push her and dig a little deeper, but chose silence instead, knowing that's what he would have wanted for himself if he was working something through.

"Do you ever think you know yourself, and then some... feeling comes over you, and you wonder if you really know yourself at all?"

Jack hesitated, then said, "To be perfectly honest, I try to avoid introspection that deep. But I can understand what you're saying. It sounds frustrating."

"That's a good way to put it," she shrugged. "I'll get over it. I don't know if you're a genius for avoiding introspection or if I should be telling you to give it a try sometime."

Jack chuckled. "Probably both."

Kristen pulled into the Blairs' driveway and put the car in park. Jack leaned across the center console and cupped his hand around the back of Kristen's head, pulling her toward him for a kiss. Her hands came up to the side of his face, her fingers a gentle pressure against his jaw as she returned the kiss.

"If you want to process something out loud, you have my number," he said a moment later, their faces still close, breathing the same air. "No pressure. Just... if you need me."

"Thanks."

At that, he slipped out of the car with one last wave, and walked up to the front door, pausing in the deep shadows of the porch to watch her drive away.

Chapter 17

Celia's green and white kitchen was full of sunlight and smelled like freshly squeezed lemons. She and Kristen sat at the table eating lunch, a pitcher of homemade lemonade between them. The faint sounds of squeals and laughter from the backyard were the soundtrack to their conversation, and Kristen soaked in the feeling of peacefulness.

"How long have the kids been playing in your sprinkler?" she asked as she took a bite of her toasted tomato sandwich.

"Mmm.. about 30 minutes, I think. They'll probably last another 30 or 45 minutes, then Tripp will take the sprinkler off the water hose, and they'll play with just that for another 30 minutes. If I'm lucky, they'll also set up the slip and slide."

Kristen glanced out the kitchen window. "It's nice your backyard will get watered like that."

Celia laughed. "Yes. And they get some sunshine and physical activity, so I don't feel as bad letting them watch a movie this afternoon. I'm definitely reaching the end of my summer energy. I think afternoon movies are going to be a regular thing until school starts."

"Sounds like a pretty good plan to me."

Celia took a bite of her own sandwich and closed her eyes. "There is nothing like homegrown tomatoes. Seriously, you are a true friend for sharing."

Kristen's landlords had dropped by the day before with a basket full of vegetables from their garden: tomatoes, cucumbers, and zucchini. She'd known there was no way she'd be able to eat the generous gift before some of it went bad, so she'd made a lunch date with Celia to pass along some of the bounty.

As they ate, they talked about their respective plans for the next few weeks. The Blairs were planning a week-long visit to Crofton before school started at the end of August, and Kristen was looking forward to the last of her looming deadlines. She'd already turned in her book edits and was currently dividing her attention between the articles, due the next week, and the book proposals that she needed to turn in to her colleague by Labor Day. Besides simply looking forward to work slowing down to a more manageable speed, she was also excited about a recently planned visit from Nora and Liz Labor Day weekend. They were planning to come on a Thursday and leave the day after Labor Day.

"I'd like to have everyone over while they're here," Kristen said. "You guys, Jack, Dad and Rosalee, the Finches, and the McDonnells. I'd like to invite the ladies from book club, but that feels a little overwhelming on top of everyone else." she hesitated. "Do you think it would be okay if I invited Sierra and Judy? I feel like I've started getting to know them through our walks every week. But I don't want to... break any unspoken social rules among book club members."

Celia waved away her concerns. "Invite whoever you want. None of the women at book club get offended by that kind of stuff."

Kristen nodded. "That was my instinct, but I wanted to make sure. Anyway, it will be great to see the girls, and I can't wait for them to meet everyone and for everyone to meet them."

Five minutes later, the women were finishing up their sandwiches and began clearing the table. Kristen turned to Celia to ask if she wanted to keep the rest of the tomato slices and was surprised to see her dabbing tears from her eyes.

"What's wrong?" she asked gently, trying not to sound too alarmed, even though she felt a tiny pang of worry.

Celia sniffled and gave a small laugh. "Nothing, it's fine. Hormones, maybe?"

"Nope, don't do that," Kristen replied, stepping closer to put a hand on Celia's shoulder. "Don't play off emotions as something not worth taking seriously. What's wrong? Did I say something?"

"No," Celia's reply was firm. "Well, yes, but no. I just..." she searched for the words. "This summer has been particularly exhausting. Work has been tough for Levi the past few months—more responsibility and more hours—and that trickles down to home life. The kids are great but needy in different ways, and I get overwhelmed with mom life. Last summer, I had Rosalee next door and, I just really miss her." Celia blinked away fresh tears. "I mean, I know she's not gone, and we see each other and talk a lot, but it feels different, which is understandable and, I don't begrudge her newlywed status. All that to say, I was just thinking about how I'm really, really glad you're here this summer."

Kristen didn't know what to say. *You're welcome* seemed weird, and *same here* seemed trite, even if both sentiments were heartfelt; but she was touched by the trust Celia had just shown her. In the end, she opted for a hug and a simple "I'm glad I'm here too."

Although she wouldn't have minded sitting on the back porch with Celia and another glass of lemonade, Kristen knew she needed to get back to work. She invited Celia and the kids over to her house for lunch in a few days and promised to make her famous-in-certain-circles chocolate oat cookies.

With one last hug for Celia and a wave to the kids out the backdoor, she left.

• • •

When Kristen's phone rang, it startled her to see how late it was. She picked her phone up off the table, where it sat next to a cup of cinnamon tea, an empty can of Coke, and an open box of shortbread cookies. She stood up and stretched one arm above her head while her other hand held the phone to her ear.

"Hello?"

"When was the last time you ate?" the familiar deep voice skipped the pleasantries.

"Why hello, Jack. I'm fine thanks, how are you?" Kristen teased. She heard a soft chuckle.

"Hello, Kristen. I'm doing well. Still wondering when you ate last. And cookies don't count."

Busted. How had he picked up on her habits so quickly? They hadn't even seen each other in almost two weeks, although they'd talked on the phone almost every night.

"If cookies don't count, then I think 11:30 this morning," Kristen admitted. "Maybe noon." Her stomach growled so loudly that she almost wondered if he could hear it over the phone.

"Celia made fajitas tonight. Can I bring you some? I promise not to stay long."

Kristen hesitated. She was so tired and disheveled. If she counted right, the only people she'd seen in the past four days were Sierra and Judy that morning for their walk. And when was the last time she'd showered? She'd gotten inspired and jumped right into work after walking. But she was also hungry, and hadn't been to the grocery store in... a while. Her stomach growled again.

"That would be really nice, thank you."

"No problem. I'll see you in a few."

They hung up and Kristen began closing programs and shutting down her computer, then sorting through the mess that had accumulated around her spot at the kitchen table. She threw away trash, set dirty dishes in the sink, stacked research and notes, laughed at the fact that she had six pens sitting out, and moved her work—and the pens— back to the desk in her office. Although she frequently ended up working in various locations around the house, she always enjoyed starting the day off at her desk, a mental trick she'd adopted when she'd started writing freelance full time to help her focus and get a solid start to her workday.

By the time Jack arrived with food, Kristen felt ravenous and vowed to herself to set a lunch alarm the next day so she didn't end up in the same predicament. She also made a mental note to go to the grocery store.

"I am so glad to see you," she said as she opened her front door. Jack was dressed in basketball shorts and a faded t-shirt, sporting his usual four-day scruff, and holding a sealed container in one hand. Kristen squinted at him. Had he gotten a haircut?

Jack grinned, his dimple giving him a rakish air. "I'd say I'm flattered, but I know you're probably just glad to see the food."

She opened her mouth to protest, but before she could speak, her stomach growled loudly and she winced. "I'd like to deny that, but it's probably true." It was also true that it really did feel good to see him in person. She stepped to the side. "Would you like to come in?"

"Not this time," Jack handed her the sealed container. "I have to get up extra early to get my truck serviced before work."

"Oh! Well, now I feel kind of bad you walked over just to give me food."

"Don't feel bad. I was happy to do it. Plus, it gave me an excuse to see your face, and I'd *almost* forgotten how beautiful it is."

Kristen blushed and felt a little lightheaded. *You're lightheaded because you haven't eaten anything, genius.* Before she could come up with a reply, Jack spoke again.

"I know you're busy right now, but do you want to go out tomorrow or Sunday evening? Just dinner or tea or something?"

"Dinner tomorrow sounds great."

Jack's eyes lit up. "Great! I'll come by around 6?"

"Perfect."

He turned and jogged down the steps, then waved as he backed across the yard. She waved back and watched as he turned at the sidewalk and began jogging up the street. Her stomach growled again. *All right, all right, I'll eat now.*

The next night, they ended up at Thai Kitchen. As they sat sharing a bowl of mango sticky rice at the end of the meal, Kristen realized that the evening hadn't felt like a "date." It felt less like an event and more like a continuation—another bead on a string full of evenings together, dinners with friends, walks, ball games, and conversations. And so as he dropped her off at home, she found herself saying,

"Are you busy tomorrow evening?" She was pretty sure he wasn't, especially since Celia, Levi, and the kids left that day for Crofton.

He shook his head.

"Would you like to come with me to the Finches' for Sunday Dinner?"

He raised an eyebrow, and she clarified. "Rosalee's daughter Elizabeth and her husband, Jonathan. I think I told you they have family Sunday Dinner every week."

"That sounds familiar now that you mention it. Sure, I'm game. Are you sure it's okay since I'm not family?"

His voice and body language were casual, but

were they *too* casual? Kristen thought. Were the same alarms going off in his head that went off in hers when Jessica had suggested she invited him weeks ago? She mentally slapped herself. After the whole misunderstanding of inviting him to eat at her dad's, did he suspect an ambush? Did he think she was trying to push the seriousness of their relationship? She told herself to stop being too sensitive, or she was going to make things weird by trying too hard to not make things weird. He was an adult. If he had something to say, he could say it. If he was worried, he could bring it up.

"It's very low key," she responded, keeping her tone light. "The kids bring friends all the time, and I think Caroline and her husband have gone a few times. It's a broad definition of family."

"Sounds fun then," Jack said with his dimpled half-smile. "Do you want me to pick you up?"

Kristen had hesitated. "No, I'll just text you the address and meet you there. I have some errands to run beforehand."

Chapter 18

Kristen ran a few errands, partly because they needed doing and partly so she wasn't a liar. She'd also called Elizabeth on the way, and at her request, had stopped to pick up a couple of baguettes, some aged parmesan, and a jar of olive oil from a nearby Italian bakery. As she'd planned, she arrived before anyone else, hoping she'd be able to casually set the stage before Jack arrived and make sure no one acted weird about it.

When she reached the front door, Kristen knocked lightly, then turned the knob and walked in.

"Hello!" she called.

The answering greeting came in stereo, Kiera from the couch where she lay sprawled with her ever-present book, and Elizabeth from the kitchen where the scent of homemade Bolognese sauce drew Kristen like a magnet.

"It smells amazing in here," Kristen said as she entered the spacious kitchen and set the grocery bag on the island counter. Elizabeth glanced up from where she was stirring the sauce on the stove.

"Thanks! It's Corbin's favorite, and this is his last Sunday before going back to Columbia."

Kristen nodded in understanding, then let out a low whistle as she noticed little wooden racks set up on the counter near the stove.

"Are those *homemade* noodles?!"

Elizabeth smiled and nodded. "Yes, it's my first time making them! It was pretty fun, actually."

"I am officially impressed. Now, tell me what simple and very unimpressive thing I can help you with."

Elizabeth gave Kristen the task of making bruschetta, pulling out a big cutting board, bread knife, sheet pan, and a bowl full of perfectly ripe tomatoes. Kristen began slicing up the baguettes.

"I invited Jack to come for dinner today. I hope that's okay," Kristen said, watching carefully to gauge Elizabeth's reaction. She was comforted by the fact that Elizabeth didn't even glance up from the salad she was making.

"Of course it's okay. The more, the merrier." A minute later, she added, "Actually, it's a good week for it because Jess is bringing her boyfriend for the first time." Elizabeth gave Kristen a sly smile. "Less pressure on you."

It shouldn't have made a difference, Kristen thought, but it really did make her look forward to the evening more. After a beat, Elizabeth's full comment sunk in.

"Wait, Braden is coming? Tell me all about it! How do you feel?"

For the next half hour, Kristen and Elizabeth worked together in the kitchen and talked about Jessica and Braden. Elizabeth admitted that George and Rosalee had met Braden weeks ago, even though Elizabeth hadn't.

"Does that… upset you?" Kristen asked gently.

Elizabeth shrugged but also nodded. "A little."

Kristen had the feeling that wasn't entirely true, but she let the moment breathe and kept dicing tomatoes.

"Actually, it does. Or, at least, it did." Elizabeth sighed. "I'm working on it."

She finished mixing salad dressing and began filling a giant stockpot with water to boil the pasta.

"It wasn't on purpose," Elizabeth continued. "Actually, it was right when they first started dating. They'd fought, and Jessica had gone to stay overnight at Mom's—which she does regularly. He came over to apologize and—from what I gather, declare his feelings for her. I also know I have a history of being critical. Especially toward Jessica. I haven't met anyone she's dated since high school."

"Maybe she hasn't dated much the past couple of years," Kristen offered.

"That's a nice thought, but I don't think it's entirely accurate. Either way, I'm just looking at today as a chance to set a different tone."

Elizabeth stood up straighter, and Kristen changed the subject.

The scent of toasted bread drew Keira and Corbin into the kitchen, and shortly after, the rest of the non-residents began arriving. Kristen kept one ear tuned for the sound of a knock on the door, knowing that Jack would be unlikely to just come in like everyone else.

Despite her best efforts, Mary was the one who first welcomed Jack into the house. Kristen was talking with Jonathan about a waterfall hike they did when Mary led Jack into the conversation-filled kitchen.

"I found a stray," she said, with a wink at Kristen. "Do you want to keep this one?"

Before Kristen could make a move, Rosalee, who was standing nearer to the hallway, reached out to hug Jack.

"What a pleasant surprise!" she said. "It's so good to see you, Jack. Here, let me take that and introduce you to everyone." She took a potted basil plant out of Jack's hands and led him further into the kitchen.

Kristen reached out and grabbed Jack's hand for a quick squeeze as they passed by. He winked at her, and her heart fluttered.

"Nice choice on the basil," she whispered.

"I figured it was a good guess for a person who regularly cooks for people for fun," he replied before following Rosalee.

Kristen watched them for a minute before turning back to Mary, who was looking at her with a slightly amused expression. She raised an eyebrow, and Kristen shook her head.

"Don't say anything," she said.

"If you say so."

Kristen burst out laughing, but before she could respond, Elizabeth began directing traffic toward the dining room, and Jessica and her boyfriend arrived. Braden was of average height and build, with brown skin and a head full of dark brown curls. He had an open but also slightly shy smile, and his hazel eyes were mostly glued to Jessica, whom he clearly adored. He looked vaguely familiar, but Kristen couldn't quite place him.

Dinner was lively, and Kristen was happy to sit next to Braden. She found out he was a musician and realized that she'd seen him play at University Bean. They talked music for much of the meal, and as people began clearing their plates, she apologized for monopolizing him.

"It's okay," he smiled. "Honestly, I was pretty nervous coming tonight, and now I feel a lot more relaxed. So you really did me a favor."

"Happy to help."

Kristen stood up with her own plate and realized Jack was no longer sitting next to her. She walked to the kitchen and saw him talking to Rosalee by the sink, so she continued to help clean off the table until Elizabeth handed her a tray full of cookies to take into the living room. In the living room, she got into a discussion with Keira about what she was reading, which led to talk about the upcoming school year as nearly everyone trickled into the room. Jack eventually joined the group, grabbing a couple of cookies and settling on the floor next to Kristen. He chewed and listened, an unreadable expression on his face.

Conversation swirled the way it often does in a large group of people, with little pockets and pools that changed and shifted constantly. Elizabeth pulled out the photo album she'd had printed from their trip, and Kristen had to laugh at how quickly Elizabeth had completed that task, thinking about the hundreds of pictures stored on her computer that she always intended to put into albums. She got up from her spot on the floor and went to lean over the back of the couch where Elizabeth sat. The pictures were stunning. Several of them prompted stories, each one making Kristen regret—just a smidge—that she'd stayed home. Maybe she'd just plan a visit on her own. She turned to say something to Jack, but he wasn't sitting where he had been, and a quick scan of the room showed her he wasn't there at all.

Weird. Maybe he went to get a drink?

Kristen tried to rejoin the conversation, but when several minutes went by, and Jack didn't return, she excused herself and began searching the house. He wasn't in the kitchen, or bathroom, or even the currently quiet upstairs game room. She checked the back porch, kicking herself for not thinking of that first, but all she found was Corbin's Golden Retriever and a yard full of fireflies. *Where is he?* A small inner voice whispered a possible answer, and suddenly, the delicious Italian feast felt heavy in her stomach. Slowly, she walked around the yard to the front of the house and stared at the collection of cars, none of which were Jack's truck.

He left?

Waves of emotion washed over Kristen: embarrassment, confusion, worry, and a white-hot anger. Her heart pounded and her skin felt prickly with a sudden heat that had nothing to do with the late August weather. With effort, she unclenched her fists and forced herself to breathe slowly—in for four, out for four. In. Out. After a few minutes, she felt in control enough to go back inside. Fortunately, no one seemed to have missed her—a side effect of a large family gathering. She also breathed a prayer of thanks that Jessica had brought Braden to dinner.

After grabbing her purse, she made her way around the room, quietly saying goodbye to her dad, Elizabeth, and Mary. She hurried, not wanting her controlled facade to crack, and for that very reason, she avoided Rosalee, knowing that Rosalee would be the one to ask where Jack had gone. Instead, she waved from across the room, hoping her smile looked genuine from that distance. She saw her dad looking at her with a slight frown as she left but put it out of her mind. If he wanted to ask her about it, he could call her later, and by then, she would have her emotions firmly under control.

Chapter 19

Jack knew that leaving the Finches' without telling Kristen was a bad idea, but when had knowing something was a bad idea ever stopped him? His anger and frustration lasted approximately a mile.

There was still time to turn around, slide back into the chaos.

She probably hasn't even noticed I'm gone.

The thought reignited his anger, and he kept driving. He knew he was acting petty and passive-aggressive, but at that moment, he didn't care. Instead, he just drove. He drove past the city limits, along the river until the back road hit the Interstate. He filled his gas tank at a service station by the highway, bought a large cup of burnt-smelling coffee from a gum-chewing teenager watching YouTube videos, then sat in his truck at the station exit, his gaze toggling right and left. He could turn left toward Riverton, back to a small room in a house that felt awfully crowded at that moment. Back to a fight, ordinariness, routine. Or he could turn right, see what was over the horizon... spend a few days on the road... check on his condo in California. Alone.

Jack drummed his fingers on his steering wheel and thought about his friends—his family—who always put up with him. He thought about his work contract and whether he wanted to keep his professional integrity. He thought about long legs and blue eyes. With a deep sigh, he turned left and drove with the windows down, music loud.

The neighborhood was dark and quiet when he pulled onto his street. *His street?* For the first time in a long time, the days left on his contract felt as tight and itchy as an ill-fitting sweater.

A familiar car sat parked in the street in front of Celia and Levi's house, and as he pulled into the driveway, he could see the chains on the porch swing moving back and forth in the dim light of the street lamp. Shadows hid the swing and its occupant, but he knew who it was. He turned his key and sat listening to the ticking of his engine cooling down. Eventually, he got out of the truck and climbed the porch steps. He wanted to sit next to Kristen on the creaking swing, but he stood, leaning against the railing.

"You could have told me you wanted to leave."

"I know."

Creak

Creak

"Well, why didn't you?" there was heat in

Kristen's voice now.

"It was crowded."

"It was crowded?" the heat intensified. "Look, I'm not upset if you weren't enjoying yourself and wanted to leave, but you could have said something."

"You didn't seem to be all that concerned that I was there, so I didn't think you'd be all that concerned if I left." His voice was cold steel.

"Are you kidding me? You left without telling me because you thought I was ignoring you?! How old are you, 12?"

He felt his hackles rise. "No. I'm not 12. I'm a grown man, and I don't have to get your permission to leave someone's house when I'm ready to go. I enjoyed meeting everyone and had a lovely time visiting with Rosalee, but I'm not really into spending a long time with large groups of people. I thought you'd figured that out about me."

"It's just rude!"

"So is ignoring someone you asked to come!"

She recoiled at his words. "I wasn't..."

"And for the record," he interrupted her protests, knowing what she was going to say, and lacking the patience to hear her try to defend herself. "I thanked Jonathan for having me and told him goodbye. I'm not a complete neanderthal."

She stood up and balled her fists. "You're not acting like a neanderthal; you're acting like a child. I'm sorry if you felt ignored or unimportant, but I won't sit here and soothe your ego."

She walked past him, not running, but fast enough that it was clear she wanted to be anywhere else but there. A part of him wanted to stop her, to apologize, and admit he'd been petty. But his hurt feelings and pride won out over his logic, and he turned away, and went inside.

• • •

The next morning, Jack cursed his beeping alarm clock. He'd been too worked up to sleep the night before and had stayed up way too late reading in an effort to turn off his brain. He got dressed without turning on the light, and headed to the kitchen to start coffee. While he waited for it to brew, the fight with Kristen replayed in his mind, and he felt like a jerk. He *had* felt hurt, and he wouldn't apologize for feeling that way. He could admit that it was possible he hadn't handled things very well, and that maybe when Kristen called him a child it had set him off more. He could also admit that she wasn't entirely wrong about it either.

Jack sighed. Maybe he should have kept driving last night instead of turning back. He pulled out his phone and scrolled through his contacts until he got to Kristen's name. His thumb hovered over the delete button. It would be easier... less complicated.

He shoved the phone back in his pocket without changing a thing and tried desperately to think of something else just to give his mind some peace and quiet. How slow was this coffee maker, anyway? Maybe he should get Levi a new one.

His gaze drifted around the still-quiet kitchen as the apparently geriatric coffee maker continued its gurgling, and his eyes landed on the bulletin board that hung by the doorway. It was crammed full of snapshots, school notes, and event flyers, but what caught his eye was a picture he hadn't seen before. He stepped closer to get a better look, and the corners of his mouth lifted. It was from their last camping trip. Jack sat in a kayak, Aislinn nestled in front of him, her little hands resting on his as they held the paddle, a grin splitting her face. Next to it was a photo of him, Levi, and Tripp, all three flexing their muscles and making goofy faces. Finally, there was a picture of Kristen and Celia on the kayaks, stretched out like movie stars sunning themselves, hats pulled low, and fingertips grazing the water. His heart constricted.

The coffee pot beeped, and he filled his to-go mug, telling himself to just put Kristen out of his mind and focus on work. *Easier said than done*, he thought. Despite his internal protests, deep down, what he really wanted to do was to call her, to work things out, and get back on friendly terms. He just... didn't know how to do that. He had to admit that the only person he'd ever fought and made up with was Levi.

Jack thought back to times he'd fought with Levi. How had they worked things out? When they were in elementary school, they'd fought with their fists, punching, wrestling like wolf cubs trying to establish dominance. It worked, though. By the time the dust settled, their anger had abated, and nine times out of ten, they didn't remember what they were fighting about. As they had grown older, their arguments still turned physical occasionally, but they were much less frequent. These days, if one of them was being an idiot, the other simply called them out, and the idiot apologized. But Jack knew that was a conflict resolution method that only worked because of the decades of trust they'd built between each other.

Unfortunately, he didn't have decades of trust built with Kristen, but maybe taking a direct approach was still a good idea. He could admit that his actions Sunday evening had been extremely passive aggressive, and had only made things worse. Maybe if he started with an apology, it would ease some of the tension. With a plan in mind, Jack was better able to focus on his work for the rest of the day.

•　　•　　•

"Girl, you're gonna have to slow down. My lung capacity isn't what it usually is."

Heavy puffs of air punctuated Sierra's words, and Kristen realized she was a good two steps ahead of her walking partners. With a grimace, she slowed down, reaching up to adjust her hat.

"I'm sorry. I'm kind of distracted this morning. I didn't realize how fast I was going."

Sierra shook her head, her face flushed and glistening with exertion. "You're mad about something this morning, I can tell."

Judy, whose cheeks were also rosy, nodded in agreement. "You're pounding the pavement, for sure," she said. "Want to talk about it?"

Did she want to talk about it? On the one hand—definitely not. She wasn't even sure what she thought about the fight with Jack. It all felt so... confusing. On the surface, it seemed so stupid, like such a little thing to fight about. But she'd still tossed and turned all night. She had a few unformed thoughts about why she was so mad at Jack, but she wasn't typically a verbal processor. Sharing unformed and unedited thoughts made her feel uncomfortable... vulnerable. She glanced at the women flanking her and thought about all the conversations about Sierra's work vs. stay-at-home dilemma, and Judy's troubles with her kid in college, and drama with her sister. She thought about her elevated heart rate and the spinning thoughts that had kept her up all night.

"Jack and I had a fight last night, and I'm really not sure what I think about it."

"Mmm hmm." Sierra nodded. "Man troubles. I should have guessed. Jack is Celia's cousin, right?

You guys are dating?"

Kristen nodded. "Sort of."

"So what happened?" Judy asked.

Kristen gave the briefest rundown of the evening before, camping out the longest on details of the fight itself. As she retold the story, a small part of her realized that even just summarizing the events had the effect of crystallizing her muddled feelings.

"I know I was partially in the wrong," Kristen admitted, "and his behavior reminded me a lot of... a painful experience. Which, of course, he doesn't know about. But still. Even without my baggage, the fact that he didn't seem to understand *at all* made me even angrier."

"I know it goes against common advice," Judy said, "but honestly, it sounds like maybe you did the best thing by going home. Hotheads need a chance to cool off."

"You think so?" Kristen asked, her voice full of doubt.

"Definitely. It already sounds like you have a clearer head. And from what you said, it sounds like last night you were just talking in circles."

Kristen nodded, her ponytail swinging. "Yes, exactly."

"And, forgive me if I'm misreading the situation, but it sounds like maybe neither of you has much experience fighting with a significant other?"

Kristen's laugh was tinged with bitterness. "You read that correctly," she said. "From things Celia's told me, Jack's never been in a relationship long enough to fight, and the last time I was in a romantic relationship, I was in my early twenties, and it was an emotionally abusive one." Instinctively, Kristen clenched her teeth to stop any more words from coming out. She hadn't meant to say that much.

To their credit, neither Judy nor Sierra reacted to what she'd said.

"Well then, I definitely think you both needed a little time to cool down. Get your perspective back," Judy said. Sierra nodded.

They turned a corner, and Kristen's house came into view at the end of the street. She slowed down a little more. She had one more question, one she didn't want to ask but knew she needed to.

"So... what do I do now?"

"Give it until tomorrow," Sierra advised. "If he hasn't called you, call him after work. You've already said you were a little in the wrong, so apologize for your part—just your part—and see what happens. If you feel comfortable, maybe clue him in on some of your past. If he doesn't also apologize, well... cross that bridge when you come to it. But I'd be wary of a man who can't apologize."

They'd reached Kristen's driveway.

"Thank you, guys," she said. "I'm not... used to monopolizing a conversation with personal problems."

Sierra raised her eyebrows. "Yet you listen to us do it all the time," she said, then grinned. "I'm glad you felt comfortable letting us weigh in."

"Good luck, and keep us posted," Judy added, reaching out to give Kristen's arm a gentle squeeze. "We'll see you Wednesday."

When Jack climbed into his truck, he checked his phone, half hoping maybe Kristen had taken the first step and called him, but she hadn't. *Doesn't matter*.

As he drove, he wondered if he should call her from his truck or as soon as he got home, or maybe go home and shower, then go talk to her in person. He drummed his fingers against the steering will as he thought, his whole body vibrating with energy. No. Now that he had a plan, he wanted to execute it.

Twenty minutes later, he pulled into Kristen's driveway, behind her car. With quick, purposeful movements, he got out, strode up to her front door, and knocked. A moment later, Kristen opened the door, a range of emotions playing across her face, too quickly for Jack to get a feel for what she was thinking.

"I'm sorry for leaving without telling you, and I'm sorry for getting angry about it later. You're right. I was being petty and passive-aggressive."

"I'm sorry I hurt your feelings, and I'm sorry I called you a child. You're right—I'd invited you somewhere with a lot of people you'd never met, and then kind of abandoned you."

Jack felt knots of tension release in his shoulders. He took a deep breath and exhaled slowly, then smiled. Kristen leaned against her door jamb, arms crossed.

"This feels like a momentous occasion," she said with a smile. "The only people I argue with are my dad and the two friends that are more like sisters at this point."

"So you know they won't leave?"

"Something like that."

Jack nodded. "It's kind of like that with me and Levi. He's the only person I fight with. Look at us. Just a couple of grown ups."

Neither of them spoke for a minute. Jack felt more at ease, but also a little awkward and emotionally wrung out. And really hungry.

"Do you want to grab some food?" he asked, stuffing his hands in his pockets. "Someplace with a TV turned to sports so there's no pressure to talk if we don't want to?" He hadn't meant to say that last part out loud, but he thought maybe she was feeling vulnerable too.

Kristen hesitated, then shrugged. "Sure. I don't feel like cooking tonight anyway."

He waited while Kristen grabbed her purse and locked the door, then the two of them walked to his truck. He asked her if she had a place in mind, and she shook her head, so he drove them to a Chicago-style pizzeria near downtown Riverton. It was a tiny restaurant that also served as a sort of neighborhood pub. They made amazing pizza, plus Jack knew his grunginess wouldn't raise any eyebrows.

The pizzeria was in an old building with high ceilings and decorative molding from an earlier era, in pleasant contrast to the black and white linoleum floor; dark, high-backed wooden booths; and simple, sturdy wooden tables. When they walked in, there were only a few people sitting at tables and at the bar. Two television sets were turned to a baseball game, and the entire room was full of the warmth from the pizza ovens and the smell of tomatoes, garlic, and charred bread. Jack led Kristen to one of the booths, sitting on the side with his back to the tv. Kristen glanced up at the game as soon as she sat down, then looked at Jack, raising an eyebrow.

"This is a close game," she said. "And while I typically make fun of people who sit next to each other at a restaurant table, I suggest tonight that either you sit over here with me and we can watch the game together, or I sit over there with you so neither of us is distracted."

"Are you sure?" Jack asked. "Do you want to talk or anything?"

Kristen shook her head emphatically, but also shifted her eyes and tensed her shoulders in a way that made it seem like maybe she had something on her mind.

"Maybe later, but not right now."

She scooted over, and he went around the table to sit next to her.

They spent the next thirty minutes simply watching the game, and the mundane activity and space without pressure to say anything seemed to diffuse the lingering awkwardness from their earlier vulnerability. The drinks were cold, the pizza extra cheesy and delicious, and it really was a good game. Jack settled into a feeling of contentment.

After a few slices of pizza quieted his growling stomach, he leaned against the back of the booth and stretched his legs out under the table. But when he reached up to rest his arm behind Kristen on the back of the booth, she shifted away from his touch, turning her body to face him. Her brows furrowed.

"Can I tell you a story?" she asked.

A wariness settled over Jack, but he nodded slowly. "Okay," he said.

<h1 align="center">Chapter 20</h1>

Kristen drained her glass, using the moment to give herself a quick pep talk. She had not planned on telling Jack about Mike. Frankly, she hadn't expected Jack to show up that night. She'd expected him to ghost her, and be conveniently absent from any future gatherings at Celia and Levi's. He'd surprised her, and her gut told her that as uncomfortable as it made her—sweaty and clammy and shaky—unless she was planning to ghost *him*, it was time to get a little vulnerable.

"Do you remember when I told you I'd been married briefly in college?" she asked. Jack nodded, his expression neutral. "Well, I want to tell you a little more about that. I met Mike at a very questionable dive bar near the college my freshman year. His band was the last one of the night—the worst slot—but as soon as he started playing and singing... he was electric. I've never seen a crowd so captivated. I couldn't keep my eyes off him. And he had this way of making eye contact from the stage that was so... personal. The band was fine, but I could tell that it was Mike's energy that was going to take them places. And that intensity was so attractive. It was like getting swept up in a raging river current. Being near him I felt so alive." Kristen shook her head, and gave Jack a small, wry smile. "Of course, you know that while raging rivers can be exciting and exhilarating, they aren't always safe." She turned her gaze away again and gathered her thoughts before continuing.

"Everything was about him, what he wanted, and I was happy to comply, as long as I got to be near him. For a little while, I felt like I was living the dream: girlfriend of a rock star. All his intensity and energy and passion were for me. And, like I mentioned before, we got married. It was so dumb. We were in Atlantic City, we were impulsive. Our brains weren't fully developed. And we were 'in love.'" She rolled her eyes. Distance gave the story humor, but she always felt a brief pang of pity for young Kristen. "Not long after that his narcissism started showing. He was jealous anytime I talked to another man—even guys in the band—but craved the attention of all the female fans. He was always criticizing me, comparing me to other women, belittling me. If he thought I was flirting with someone, he'd scream at me, really hateful, ugly things. And the longer we were on the road, the more he started drinking, and the more he drank, the meaner he got. The meaner he got, the more I tried to change myself to keep him happy. To just keep him, frankly. I pretended he didn't start cheating on me, and in the meantime I didn't recognize myself anymore, and I'd cut myself off from every other person in my life." Kristen paused, taking a sip of water and shoving down the lump in her throat, being careful not to look at Jack as she continued.

"Then one night we were in Milwaukee. He'd had a bad show and disappeared after. I went looking for him and found him in a storage closet at this bar hooking up with some random girl. The really embarrassing part," Kristen tried to keep her voice neutral, and hid her trembling hands. "Is that my initial reaction was to be upset not that he was making out with another girl, but that now that I'd seen it I couldn't live in denial anymore. So I told Mike he was a jerk, and he backhanded me in the face."

"What?!"

It was Jake's first audible reaction to her story, and the pure outrage in his voice calmed and grounded her back in the present. "Yeah, I know. But it worked out, because that was what I finally needed to leave. He literally knocked some sense into me."

"Please tell me you hit him back. Or that someone did."

"I wish I could, but no. We just stared at each other. And then I turned and left. I grabbed Chad— the drummer. He was usually the most sober—and asked him to drive me to our hotel. I got my stuff, what cash I could find, and bought a bus ticket home."

She glanced at Jack, then turned her eyes away, not wanting to add "soul-searching gaze" to an already excruciatingly vulnerable moment.

"And was that.... was that it?"

Kristen shrugged. "Sort of. When I say I went home, I mean really home. To Dad's house. He kept Mike away, and he helped me get a divorce without having to even talk to Mike. And he made me go to therapy as a condition of going back to school. Which I desperately wanted to do. I wanted everything to be normal again."

"And was it? Normal again?" Jack's voice was low, the question heavy with something besides just a curiosity about her story. Had something she said touched a nerve?

"Not really," she admitted, "but I got better. It ended up better than before."

Jack nodded, but his brow was still creased with frown lines, and he didn't say anything, seemingly lost in his own thoughts. Kristen shoved away her curiosity. *Not the time.* "I wanted you to know why I am the way I am. Or, partially anyway. Why I'm not... experienced at relationships. Why I value my independence. Maybe that's why I read a little too much into things."

Jack covered her hand with his and squeezed.

"Hey," he said. "I only have two friends and I'm related to one of them. I'm an ace at first dates, but until recently, the last time I went on a third date was in high school, and all we did was get Sonic and make out in a corn field. I'm a jerk sometimes, it's just a fact."

Kristen laughed. "Maybe we were destined to be friends," she said. "Two socially stunted weirdos."

Jack's dimple flashed. "I can think of much worse things," he said.

Kristen sighed and shifted so that she and Jack were facing the same direction again, and before she could overthink it, she rested her head on his shoulder, closing her eyes. She was suddenly exhausted.

"Thank you for listening," she said.

Jack kissed the top of her head. "Thank you for sharing," he replied.

Kristen nodded, too tired to speak, ready for a good night's sleep and a new day.

Chapter 21

Kristen peaked out her front window for what was probably the hundredth time, then once again told herself that watching wouldn't make the time pass more quickly. She sat back down on the couch and picked up her laptop, but after staring at the screen without moving for a solid five minutes, sighed, snapped it shut, and set it aside. Unfortunately, even if she wasn't watching out the window for her friends to arrive, that didn't mean she could concentrate.

When in doubt, get busy, she thought. Normally, she'd put on her running shoes in this kind of distracted mood, but she didn't want to be away from the house when her guests arrived. After thinking for a moment, she pulled her hair back in a ponytail and picked up her phone, scrolling until she found her 90s alternative playlist. She then connected it to a set of Bluetooth speakers in the kitchen, turned it up loud, and opened the door to her tiny pantry. It seemed like the perfect time for a little bit of reorganization.

An hour later, Kristen closed the pantry door, tossed her cleaning rag into the washing machine, and gave a contented sigh. Yes, that had been a good idea. And NOW she could look out the window again.

They were here!

Kristen flung open her front door and ran down the steps toward the silver hatchback that had just pulled in her driveway. Nora and Liz practically jumped out of the car and met her in the yard in a laughing group hug.

"Oh, I have missed you!"

They disengaged and went back to the car, pulling out their weekend bags before following Kristen to the house, everyone talking at once the whole time. Kristen showed them to the guest room where they deposited their things, and ended up sitting on the bed and desk chair, still talking. Between phone calls and text messages, it hadn't really been that long since they'd talked, and yet being in the same place for the first time in months was different, especially just the three of them. Kristen thought it felt like their just-out-of-college days, when that light and carefree feeling was bigger than whatever worries or challenges they faced.

Eventually, Nora declared she was famished, and Kristen herded them to the kitchen where she started pulling lunch out of the refrigerator. The conversation paused as they made plates of chicken salad, crusty rolls, and fruit, then gathered around the kitchen table.

"So," Liz said. "What's the plan this weekend?"

"Well, I thought it could be just the three of us the rest of today. We can hang out at the house, maybe go down to the riverfront later and have dinner out. Tomorrow we're having a cookout here so you can meet everyone, and the rest of the weekend we can play by ear! Oh, and Dad wants to have us all over for brunch on Sunday. He and Rosalee go to early service at their church, so they're usually home by 10."

"Sounds perfect," Liz said.

They spent the rest of the afternoon wandering around town and going for a stroll along the river. When it was time for dinner, Kristen took them to Thai Kitchen, where they oohed and ahh'd over the foliage just as much as she had on her first visit, and where the three of them ordered enough food for a table full of teenagers. The waitress raised their eyebrows at their huge order, and Nora just smiled sweetly and said, "You can probably just bring us some to-go containers with our food."

Late that night, when Kristen lay in her bed she couldn't stop smiling. It had been a fantastic day. Both her little house and her heart felt full.

•　　　•　　　•

Kristen had picked up sourdough bread from her favorite bakery in town, and the next morning she served eggs, toast, and farmer's market blackberries out on her screened porch. She dug her French Press out of the cabinet for Nora and Liz, and brewed a pot of Earl Grey for herself. The porch was perfect in the mornings. It was perfect at all times of day, really, but Kristen had discovered that mornings were special. In the morning, the dew-wet flowers planted just outside smelled like heaven. The sweet gum tree filtered the light of the rising sun, and the birds were busy and talkative around the bird feeder that stood tall on that corner of the house. Nora commented that she felt like she was having breakfast in a treehouse.

Nora, who was sitting on the love seat next to Kristen, took a sip of her coffee, then turned to face her. "So you've been here... approximately four months, right? How's the experiment going so far? Are you glad you came?"

Kristen admired Nora's tendency to say exactly what she was thinking, but sometimes when those unfiltered questions were turned in her direction, it was decidedly uncomfortable. And it felt important to answer this question honestly. She took a sip of her tea.

"Yes," she said finally. "I'm definitely enjoying myself. I'm making friends and getting to spend a lot of time with Dad. I think I'm learning some things about myself that are long overdue. I don't feel as restless as I did. So, I guess you could say that so far it's a success." One corner of her mouth turned up in a wry grin. "I mean, ask me again in six months. A lot can happen in that amount of time."

For a wonder, Nora didn't have a response to that. Liz looked like she wanted to say something, but she simply drank her coffee and ate her breakfast. Kristen wondered if she wanted to talk about Jack. *Maybe I should bring it up first,* she thought. *But what would I say? I know we're technically "just friends" but I really like him and we had our first fight because I subconsciously thought he was acting like Mike, but then he apologized, and I never realized how attractive it is when a man apologizes? Maybe I should say: hey, I thought I had fully dumped all of my Mike baggage, but it turns out that maybe that's not entirely true? But you probably knew that already?*

No. They had a busy day ahead, and she was sure they'd want to talk about Jack after they actually met him. The morning of a party day was not the time for friend therapy or analyzing relationships. There'd be plenty of time for that tonight.

After breakfast, Nora and Kristen went shopping while Liz cleaned up from breakfast and started setting up the backyard. The shoppers filled their cart with burgers, bratwurst, buns, and chips. They stopped at the farmer's market to pick up a watermelon, corn that had been picked fresh that morning, and a basket full of sweet baked goods from an Amish baker's booth: three pies, strawberry rhubarb cake, lemon bars, zucchini bread, and chocolate muffins.

When Kristen and Nora got back to the house, Liz had set up two long folding tables and chairs that Kristen had borrowed from Judy, and spread red checked plastic tablecloths across those as well as the wooden picnic table that lived in the backyard. A large galvanized metal tray sat at the end of one table, loaded with paper plates, napkins, and plastic cutlery. Two coolers—borrowed from her dad—sat at the other end of the table, ready to be filled with ice and stocked with bottled water and pop. They had hung paper lanterns from the trees and strategically placed Citronella candles and potted Citronella plants around the tables. They'd even pulled out Kristen's ancient croquet set from college and set it up behind the tables.

"It looks great, guys!"

"It's just missing one thing," Liz said, standing with her hands on her hips, surveying the scene.

"What? I think it looks pretty perfect."

Liz turned to her, eyebrows raised. "Umm... maybe a grill?"

Kristen laughed. "Okay, you've got me there. Levi's bringing his down later."

"Ah, ok. Well, then, yes, it looks perfect and perfectly ready."

When Jack's truck pulled up a couple of hours later, grill loaded in the back, Kristen felt butterflies flutter in her stomach. Would her friends like him?

Why did it matter so much? Would he like them? Would they act weird? Again, why did it matter so much? The questions swirled around her brain in a never-ending loop. With great mental effort, she took some deep breaths, shoved her questions aside and walked up to the truck. The doors opened and Levi and Jack stepped out.

"You guys are the best," she said, "Thanks again for helping me out. It's probably a little misguided to host a cookout with no way to actually cook out."

Levi grinned. "It's ambitious, let's say. And it's not a problem at all."

Kristen walked over to where Jack was lowering his tailgate and leaned in to give him a quick kiss. He smelled like citrus and wood smoke, and his hair was slightly damp. He put a hand on her waist and pulled her closer to return her kiss, letting it linger. When he pulled back, his mouth held its usual crooked smile and lopsided dimple, visible despite his stubble. Kristen's face felt flushed, and she returned his smile.

"When you're finished getting the grill down, I want you to meet my friends," Kristen said.

"Definitely."

She left the men to their work and walked down the driveway to the sidewalk, glancing down the street to where Celia and the kids were making their way. Tripp was zooming on his scooter, Aislinn doing her best to keep up on her own scooter, her rainbow tutu fluttering behind her. Kristen waved to her friend. *New friends, old friends, she thought. I can't decide if this is going to be the best party ever, or a complete disaster.*

Chapter 22

Three hours later, Kristen stood by her back door, gazing out across the yard, pleased that the party seemed to be a solid success. The light was fading, and she had to agree with Aislinn, who'd exclaimed, "the air is purple!" The paper lanterns glowed softly, and the smell of citronella mingled with the lingering scent of charcoal and grilled meat. Kristen had pulled out her weather-resistant Bluetooth speakers and had asked Liz to put together a playlist. Her mix tape skills were as sharp as ever, and the Backyard Party Playlist was the perfect soundtrack. Keira Finch and the McDonnell boys played croquet with Aislinn and Tripp, who thought they were in heaven getting to hang out with teenagers. Kristen had asked everyone to bring lawn chairs, and little knots of people dotted the yard. She was pleased—and a little surprised—to see that the conversation groups were entirely mixed. New friends, old friends.

She let herself linger in the good feelings, taking

it all in like a home movie in her mind, then scanned the yard for a certain tall, lean figure. She spotted Jack sitting with Rosalee, Sierra and her husband Jeremiah, and Celia. Sierra's hands were gesturing broadly, and everyone leaned forward slightly in their chairs, eyes on her. A moment later, they all burst into laughter. Kristen walked over to the little group.

"Okay, I really need to know what's so funny," she said, resting her hand on Jack's shoulder as he wiped tears of laughter from his eyes. He reached around and tugged her across his lap. Kristen stiffened in surprise, but no one else batted an eye or even seemed to notice.

Sierra grinned at her. "I was telling them the story about the singing toddler in the post office that I told you yesterday morning."

"No wonder! That had me crying."

Kristen sat with those four until the moon peaked above the trees. She loved seeing the deep affection and camaraderie between Celia and Rosalee, and Sierra's husband—an English professor at Riverton College—quickly developed an easy rapport with Jack that mostly involved talking smack about each other's sports teams while also discussing the lack of diversity classic literature curriculums.

The small circle broke up when Sierra had to use the ladies' room, complaining of her giant baby squeezing her bladder, and Celia got up to grab another drink. Kristen started to stand, but Jack kept his arm around her.

"Hey," he said. "I'm feeling a bit tapped out. Mind if I take off? I can come back tomorrow or Monday to get the grill."

"Of course," Kristen replied. "You don't need to ask my permission, but thank you for letting me know." She smiled and made a point to look him in the eyes to make sure her sincerity came through loud and clear. His dark eyes, nearly black in the dim lantern light, were warm and steady as they returned her gaze. She gently touched her forehead to his, then stood up.

"See you later," she said.

"See you."

Kristen began walking over to where Nora and Mary sat, watching the kids play with sparklers Celia had saved from the Fourth of July. She watched as Jack stopped to say something to Levi and George, who looked like they were finishing off the desserts, then as he continued down the driveway. She smiled as she realized he'd moved his truck to the street, anticipating being the first to depart. For a moment, she considered whether she should be upset that he hadn't said goodbye to anyone else but decided that it wasn't his party, so that would have been a very unrealistic expectation. She'd seen him visit with her out-of-town friends, and really that's all she'd wanted.

"I think you've managed a successful party, friend," Celia said as she walked up behind Kristen.

She righted a lawn chair that had fallen on its side and sat down.

"Thank you. I'm happy with the way everything turned out. I was a little worried there wouldn't be enough mingling, but everyone seems to be getting along and having fun."

"No cliques at this party," Nora agreed. "But I'm not surprised. You have good taste in friends." She winked.

"Levi and I will probably head out in a few," Celia said. "We've gotten lazy this summer with bedtime routines and Aislinn really needs to get back on schedule now that school's started."

"Of course."

The three of them chatted until the kids walked over, out of sparklers, and asking for more, which Celia took as her cue to round up the family. George and Rosalee followed them out, confirming their brunch date for the next day before waving goodbye. Sierra, Jeremiah, Judy, and her husband weren't far behind. Kristen smiled at the distant sounds of laughter from the two couples as they began the short walk home. Mary put her boys to work helping with clean up, although Kristen told them to leave the lanterns and croquet. They carried trays inside, emptied the coolers and set them next to the back door, folded up the tables, and bagged all of the trash.

"I'm impressed," Kristen said to Mary and Charles as she watched the boys work.

"Thanks," Charles said. "We have a work hard, play hard attitude around our house, and it seems to suit the boys. It took a while to get to this point, but the effort has paid off. For us anyway," he added with a grin.

"And when he says 'a while' he means lots of years of bribery, just to be clear," Mary said with a grin.

A few minutes later, the boys were done and Kristen was waving goodbye to the McDonnells as they pulled out of the driveway. She wrapped her arms around herself and took a deep breath, glancing up at the half-moon and the sky full of stars. The heat of the day had faded into a memory of warmth. It wasn't cool yet, but summer's intensity had gone, leaving behind the promise of fall to come.

Thinking about fall made Kristen think about some of her favorite fall traditions—visiting the apple orchard in Frankton, their neighborhood fall festival, going to see a musical at the Lyric theater. She thought about watching the leaves change color just a little more on each run along Lake Michigan. Her throat felt tight, and she felt a wave of homesickness wash over her.

The front door opened and a long rectangle of light appeared in the yard to Kristen's left. She looked back to see Liz framed in the doorway.

"What are you doing?"

And really, she didn't need Chicago when Chicago came to her.

"I was saying goodbye to Mary and then got caught up in my thoughts."

"Dangerous," Liz said. "Come inside. We have time for two movies, and we need to vote."

Kristen closed her eyes and took another deep breath, letting the air out in a rush, then turning to walk toward the house and a double feature movie night. Maybe if they all got up early enough, they could fit in a little croquet game before brunch. Stranger things had happened... although not many.

Chapter 23

The next morning, Liz, Nora, and Kristen slipped sandals on with their pajamas and took their mugs of coffee and tea outside for a game of croquet as the sun rose above the sweet gum and redbud trees.

"Remember when you and Kole bought your house, and we used to do this almost every weekend because we were so enamored with your yard?" Nora asked as she tapped her mallet against her red striped ball. It clunked against Kristen's green ball, but didn't make it through the hoop.

Liz laughed. "Yes! I also remember Kole asking me how long you all were going to keep sleeping over every Friday night. Fortunately, the novelty wore off before I had to start uninviting you."

"If I remember correctly, we stopped because it got cold, and the fun was PJ croquet tournaments, not spending the night," Kristen chimed in. "And I remember it was fall because Kole always made us the most amazing apple cider mimosas. Honestly, you could have probably kept me from coming sooner if he'd stopped making those." Her one-handed swing went wide and barely grazed her ball.

Liz shook her head. "He talked a big talk, but he loved having you guys. I think he was just jealous his friends didn't come over for sleepovers."

The three of them giggled, then told each other it was time to focus if they actually wanted their game to get anywhere.

Nora eventually secured a victory, and as they packed up the game, Kristen searched for the words to ask the question that had been on her mind since last night.

"You know, we got so wrapped up in our movies last night, I didn't get a chance to ask you if you had fun. If you liked everyone." There was the barest hesitation before 'everyone.' Had they noticed?

"Everyone?" Liz teased.

Of course they noticed. Kristen let the question breathe and chose not to rise to the bait.

"I loved meeting your new friends," Nora said. "You have surrounded yourself here with people who are lovely and kind, which of course, is to be expected. I thought the evening was relaxed and light and happy."

"I had a blast," Liz agreed, "and it was... pleasantly surprising, to be honest."

Kristen paused from where she was lining up the balls in the box. "Surprising that you had fun?" she asked.

"No, not that. Just... okay, don't take this the wrong way, but it was surprising to see that you seem to be actual friends with the people who were there, not just acquaintances."

Kristen reminded herself not to get offended. Her friend must have a good point; she just needed help to get there. "I have friends," she said. "And not just the two of you."

Liz just looked at her, but Nora put a gentle hand on Kristen's arm. "Think about our season ticket holder friends," she said. "You've known them for years, you know all about them and their families and jobs. You talk to them every spring and summer, but how much do they know about you? I think it's more accurate to say you have a lot of acquaintances, but very few friends."

Kristen held her back very straight. "Is that a bad thing? I'm a good friend, aren't I? And who says a person has to have a boatload of friends to be happy?"

"You are the best friend!" Nora assured her. "And there's nothing wrong with having a small, tight circle. I think what I'm trying to say is that I'm *glad* you've made actual, real friends. I don't have to worry about you being down here lonely. For whatever reason, you feel safe here and willing to let your guard down with the people we met last night. And I'm just glad, that's all."

"We both are," Liz said, squeezing her arm. "Now, unless we want to go to brunch in our pajamas, we should get changed. And don't worry... we'll talk about Jack in the car." her eyes twinkled.

Less than 30 minutes later, the three of them were buckled into Kristen's car heading to George and Rosalee's. Before they'd even fully exited the driveway, Nora clapped her hands together.

"Okay!" she said. "Let's discuss that tall, scruffy woodsman of yours."

Kristen rolled her eyes. "He's not a woodsman, nor is he mine."

"On that point, I beg to differ," Liz said. "You two may think you're keeping it fun and casual, but that man is smitten with you. For one thing, unless my radar is broken, he's an introvert, yet he spent hours at a party at which he engaged both of us in conversation, and for more than just a 90 second hello-how-are-you."

"For another," Nora interjected, "Even though you didn't spend the whole night side by side, I'd bet money that he knew where you were the whole time."

"And of course, he had that unmistakable look in his eyes when he looked at you," Liz said.

Kristen shifted, her skin feeling too tight all of a sudden. "I'm still not sure," she said, "but regardless, I also want to know what you actually think about him."

Nora and Liz agreed that they liked Jack a lot, that he seemed kind, funny, and unpretentious.

"I like how he paid attention," Nora added. "He

really listened when he talked to you. And he seemed to notice things—like what you were drinking, or when something on the table needed refilling. And he didn't wait for someone else to take care of something that needed to be done."

Nora and Liz agreed. They also agreed that he was extremely attractive, and that Kristen needed to—as Liz put it— "lock that man down."

Fortunately, Kristen pulled up to her Dad's condo at that point of the conversation, and the talk shifted to the present. She'd asked their opinions and shouldn't be upset when they gave them, even if some of their observations made her uncomfortable. Even if she was increasingly uncomfortable with how much she cared what they thought about Jack— what anyone thought about Jack. If they were just casually dating, then it shouldn't really matter, should it?

Chapter 24

"You're awfully quiet this morning, Kristen."

Judy nudged Kristen with her elbow. The two of them and Sierra were halfway through their walk, and Kristen realized she had no idea what the other two had been talking about. She shook her head.

"I'm sorry. I don't know where my head's at today."

"Happens to the best of us," Sierra said. "I don't know what I'm going to do when I can't blame pregnancy brain."

"Oh, don't worry, you get to keep blaming your kids," Judy assured her. "You just call it baby brain, lack of sleep brain, toddler brain...you get the picture."

They laughed.

"So, what were you talking about?" Kristen said. "Did I miss anything important? Everything going okay with you guys this week?"

Hm. Was that the kind of deflecting Liz was

talking about?

"Oh, we were just talking about the odds of Sierra going into labor before her due date, and whether I'll find enough volunteers for the community center's Halloween Party."

"I could help." Kristen said it without thinking, but it felt right.

"Oh, really?! I wasn't fishing for help, I promise."

"Yes, really! I'd love to."

"I'll text you the details of the first planning meeting later today if that's all right."

"Sounds great." Kristen was about to ask Sierra—who was due in just three weeks—whether she had had signs of early labor, when Sierra spoke first.

"How are you doing after your visit from your girlfriends? Has it made you homesick?"

Kristen formed the briefest of replies, to be followed by her question for Sierra, but stopped with her mouth gaping open slightly, as the thought struck her: *It's just like they said. I was just about to ask her about herself to avoid talking about myself.*

"Sort of," she admitted. "But, mostly I've been very preoccupied thinking about a conversation we had while they were here." She paused, and her two companions waited patiently for her to continue. Kristen tucked a stray curl back under her headband and relayed the conversation from yesterday.

They turned a corner and began hiking up the longest hill on their route, so for a few minutes the only sound was that of their breathing and the soft thud of their walking shoes on the pavement. As they crested the top, Sierra put her hand on her chest and shook her head.

"It's crazy how much harder my heart is pounding up that hill right now."

"No, I think it's normal, mama, not crazy," Kristen said.

"Going back to what you were saying a minute ago," Judy said. "Does it bother you, what Liz and Nora said?"

Kristen was sweating, and not just from the brisk walk and steep hill, but she pressed on. "I don't know. I know they didn't mean it to be offensive, but it has me questioning whether I'm a good friend, or destined to be lonely one day. I guess it just has me questioning myself in general."

"You seem like a thinker," Judy said, "like you tend to look back and analyze previous conversations and events?"

"Guilty."

"No, it's not necessarily a bad thing. I bet it's something that helps you out in your writing, not to mention in your relationships. The only problem is if you get so consumed with analyzing the past that you can't be present, or look ahead."

Kristen nodded. Judy had a point.

"Anyway, I'm taking a roundabout route to my point, but here it is: maybe instead of worrying about what they said and how you feel about it, you could take the opportunity to realize that the conversation has brought to light that what you want is to be in genuine relationships with people and to be a good friend. And if that's the case, then just start asking yourself how you can do that."

Kristen nearly came to a complete stop. It was such simple advice, and yet so profound at the same time.

"Judy, did I miss the part where you said that you're a therapist?"

Judy laughed. "Actually... I AM a licensed marriage and family therapist. I just choose to use that degree at the community center after-school program instead of in an office."

"And on walks in the neighborhood," Sierra chimed in. "I try not to take advantage of the free therapy, but some weeks that is easier said than done."

They chatted about lighter topics for the remaining 10 minutes of the walk, but later when she was showering Kristen couldn't stop thinking about what Judy had said. It was true that she tended to look back rather than forward, but maybe it was time to work on staying grounded in the present. It's why she'd moved, wasn't it? Partly anyway. Well, she'd work on it, starting with a surprise coffee drop off to Celia that afternoon to celebrate back to school week. She had work to do that morning, but she set an alarm so she wouldn't forget.

. . .

Kristen could hear laughter and squeals coming from behind the Blairs' house when she knocked on the front door. Should she walk around to the backyard instead? Before she could decide, the door opened and Celia appeared in front of her.

"Kristen, hi! What's up? Oh, sorry," she stepped to the side. "Come in, come in."

Kristen straightened her arms in front of her, a whipped-cream topped clear, plastic cup clutched in each hand. "I come bearing an afternoon pick-me-up."

"Girl, you are the best." Celia accepted the cup Kristen offered and took a long drink. "Ahh...now that hits the spot. What'd you get? I know it's not coffee."

"Iced chai with whipped cream."

"Mmm... good one. Well, the kids are outside and you caught me lounging on the couch with a magazine and the windows open."

"Rough day?"

Celia shrugged. "Not really, I just love a good nap now and then, especially with the windows open. How about you? How's your day been? Are you feeling sad that your friends went back home?"

"It's been fine," Kristen said. *But was it really*? A voice in her head whispered. *A good friend doesn't just bring coffee. A good friend is honest and genuine, the way Celia is with you. Is this what they were talking about?*

"Actually, it was kind of weird day, and I have been a little...off since the girls left. We had a somewhat difficult conversation on their last day, and it's had my head spinning."

"Want to talk about it?"

Kristen hesitated, then went for honesty, despite the butterflies careening around her insides. "Not really," she admitted. "But only because I'm still processing, and I don't really like processing out loud to someone else."

"Fair enough. I can't say I relate, but as Anne Shirley so rightly points out, I can imagine how that feels." Celia grinned and Kristen laughed.

They talked about their upcoming book club selection, a restaurant that Kristen wanted to try, and whether they should go camping again in a few weeks. Celia told Kristen that she had to try fall camping to really have the full experience, and Kristen had to admit that it sounded kind of nice. When Celia glanced at the clock and said that she needed to start supper, Kristen stood up to go and invited Celia and the family over for Friday night pizza night.

"If I'm on top of things, we'll make our own, but I make no promises," she said with a smile.

"Hey, we could eat frozen pizza, and I'd be happy. I guess if I don't see you before then, I'll see you Friday around 5:30?"

"Sounds good."

They hugged, and Kristen left with a big smile on her face. As she pulled out of the Blairs' driveway a minute later, she gave in to an impulsive feeling and turned her car toward the main road rather than her own house. It felt like the perfect evening to drop in on Dad and Rosalee.

Chapter 25

Kristen zipped up the knee-high black boots and double checked her outfit in the mirror. She'd found a good deal on vegan leather leggings, and thought it gave her Black Widow costume a more authentic look. She heard the familiar low hum of Jack's truck pulling into the driveway, grabbed her bag, and turned the light out as she left her bedroom.

Jack was standing on the front stoop when she opened the front door, hand raised in a pre-knock pose. Like her, he was wearing layers of black, plus heavy black boots, and fingerless leather gloves. He took a step back as she walked outside and closed the door behind her and gave a low whistle.

"Superhero superspy looks good on you," his voice rumbled and his mouth lifted in a crooked smile. Kristen blushed and tried to cover it up with an eye roll.

"Thanks," she said. "You make a pretty good Hawkeye."

They turned to walk across the yard. "Looks even better with the bow. I'm glad I was storing it in Levi's attic."

The two were headed to the Riverton Community Center's Youth Program Halloween Party. Judy had assigned Kristen to the ring toss booth, and Kristen had recruited Jack to help her out. He'd resisted when she'd told him he'd need to dress in a costume, but she'd convinced him that a Hawkeye would basically look like regular clothes, and he probably already had a bow (which had been true). She'd also brought the subject up during supper at Celia and Levi's, so the peer pressure from the rest of the family had definitely worked in her favor.

Levi took the back way, driving through neighborhood streets that were packing away their summer wardrobe in favor of fall colors and coziness, accessorized by mums, pumpkins, and the occasional grinning scarecrow. It was a beautiful October day, the sky a clear, bright blue. The crisp breeze marked the season, while the beaming sun promised a warm afternoon. Yards were full of people taking advantage of the remarkable day to do yard work, play, or take dogs for extra long walks. As they drove, Kristen fidgeted in the silence. The atmosphere in the truck held a tinge of awkwardness, very faint, but still there. *Why is that?*

"Did you change your soap or shampoo?" Kristen blurted out.

Jack glanced at her, eyebrows raised. Kristen

blushed again. "Your truck smells different," she said, mentally giving herself a head slap. It was true. Instead of cedar and citrus, his truck smelled like...mint and grapefruit, maybe? But still. *Your truck smells different?*

"Last week," he said. "I ran out of the old stuff and bought some new stuff. I didn't really think about the smell."

"Oh. Well, it's nice." *It's nice?* She felt as articulate as a 15-year-old on their first date. Then it hit her. When was the last time she and Jack had been alone together? On a date? She went back through the past two months and realized that she'd dragged him to a local music showcase at the end of September, but other than that they'd been spending all their time with other people. Even when he'd come again to Sunday Dinner at the Finchs' they'd driven separately. *Huh.* She glanced at Jack who seemed fully relaxed, and told herself she was just being silly.

"Did you find anything good last weekend?" Jack asked, turning out of the neighborhood.

"Hmm?" Kristen was so caught up in her thoughts, she wasn't sure what Jack was talking about.

"On your flea market hunt," he clarified.

"Oh! Yes, actually. I found a big blue and white soup tureen that I will definitely not use for soup, some candlesticks, and a gorgeous vase that I think I'll save for Rosalee's Christmas gift." Kristen, the

Blairs, and Jack had all gone camping again the previous weekend. It had been gray and cold, and Kristen had started out the weekend with doubts—would camping be as much fun without swimming and sunshine?—but the hiking and campfires and plentiful hot beverages had made for a delightful if different camping experience. Kristen had driven her own car so she could take her time and stop at some flea markets on the way home, and secretly enjoyed that part of the weekend almost as much as the camping itself.

They arrived at the community center and spent the next half hour setting up their booth then helping get the rest of the party ready for their small guests. The party was set up in the parking lot of the community center, and Kristen was thankful that the weather had cooperated. Although knowing Judy, she was confident that her friend had had a fully formed backup plan at the ready. Kristen smiled as she watched Jack pull his tool belt from the back of his truck and follow Judy around securing and fixing things. She thought she finally understood the trope of the attractive handyman.

Around 10 o'clock, the first round of kids arrived, little pumpkins, princesses, super heroes, and monsters giggling and laughing and running their way from booth to booth, bags growing increasingly heavy with candy and prizes. Kristen and Jack's Black Widow and Hawkeye costumes were a hit, and a lot of tiny Avengers asked to take pictures with the two. Kristen was impressed with Jack's commitment to the character, although having watched him interact with Tripp and Aislinn she wasn't too surprised.

Around 11:30, the smell of charcoal filled the air, and Batman and a zombie began grilling hotdogs. During a lull in their visitors, Jack went to grab hot dogs and cokes.

"Thanks," Kristen said when he returned. "Are you surviving?"

His dimple appeared and her stomach fluttered. "It's fun," he admitted. "So yes, more than surviving."

They sat eating, and this time the silence felt as comfortable as a well-loved sweatshirt. Kristen wondered if Jack had also felt the awkwardness earlier. Had it been her imagination? *No*, she told herself, even *if I was the only one who felt awkward doesn't mean I imagined it*. She shook her head, forcefully enough that Jack turned from where he'd been watching some teenagers play a game of Knock-out at the basketball goals. He tilted his head in concern.

"Everything ok?"

"Yeah, I'm fine. Just..." *wondering if you felt as awkward as I did this morning being alone together and realizing we haven't been on a real date in weeks* "in my head a little too much today."

"Well, I know of one sure fire way to get out of your head."

Kristen raised an eyebrow. "Oh?"

"Move your body."

Jack stood up and grabbed her hand, pulling her to her feet and dragging her, laughing, over to the basketball goals. He let go and picked a ball out of the big bin sitting nearby and tossed it to her without warning. Her reflexes kicked in and she caught it just before it hit her face.

"Fifteen minutes," Jack said as he pushed a few buttons on his watch and walked over to the half-court line of the nearest empty goal. She followed, dribbling the ball as she did. "Winner buys dinner tonight, and I'll even let you have the ball first."

"Deal. And I think you're going to regret your misplaced chivalry."

She barely waited for him to look up and get set before sprinting around him and executing a nearly flawless layup. She grinned at him as he caught the rebound, but mentally shifted her strategy because running in heeled boots and leather pants was not as easy as the movies made it look. However, she was pretty confident in her three-point shot, as long as she could get enough space out from under Jack's long arms.

Halfway through their 15 minute game, Kristen's cheeks were flushed and she could feel sweat prickling on her scalp. Jack had shed his jacket, and was breathing hard. A small crowd had gathered to watch, and the young bystanders seemed to have divided themselves into girls vs. boys. Jack had pulled ahead, but just barely, and Kristen once again cursed her heeled boots. She debated taking them off and playing barefoot, but she didn't want to give up any height to Jack, and—more importantly—didn't want to risk one of his lug-soled feet tromping on her toes.

Just focus, she told herself. *You can't beat him physically, so just play smart. You can give your feet an ice bath tonight, so suck it up for 8 more minutes.*

They were at the half court line, and Jack currently had the ball. Kristen dug into her mind, attempting to activate her muscle memory from the years of early morning practices and evenings playing with her dad in their driveway. Her weight rested on the balls of her feet, her knees were slightly bent, and her eyes were locked onto Jack's not the ball. She saw his eyes flick slightly over her left shoulder toward the hoop. He leaned to his left, but Kristen shifted her weight in the opposite direction, and when he redirected from his attempt to fake her out, she caught the ball out of his hands and spun around him, three steps getting her clear enough to make another three pointer, putting her ahead by one point now.

Jack got the rebound and sprinted back to the half-court line. Kristen could tell by the set of his face and the focus in his eyes that he was planning a fast break, and instead of trying to block him or turn the ball over again, she focused on keeping him inside the three point zone and pressuring him into a layup. She positioned herself to recover the ball quickly and raced to half-court, trying to keep her movements precise to give her more time. She managed another three point shot that almost bounced off the rim, dropping in at the last second. However, despite her best efforts, Jack scored one more basket before the timer on his watch began beeping, ending their competition with just one point difference.

The kids gathered to watch came over to offer excited congratulations or good-natured ribbing, and Kristen gratefully accepted a cold bottle of water from Judy, who had a smile on her face.

"Next year we may have to add a little basketball tournament to the festivities," she said, handing Jack his own bottle of water as he walked up. Kristen was gratified to see that his face was also flushed, his hairline damp with perspiration. At least if he'd won she'd made him work for it.

Jack thanked Judy for the water and took a swig from the bottle.

"You owe me a rematch when I'm not wearing heeled boots," Kristen said.

He grinned. "We'll see." He drained the bottle. "We should probably get back to ring toss."

The Halloween party lasted another hour, and it was a busy one. Kristen and Jack stayed to help clean up—the tool belt reappearing for tear down— and by the time Kristen gave Judy a hug goodbye and followed Jack to his truck, she was exhausted and her feet ached. She also felt happy and content, like her spirit was full of effervescence.

"I'd like to go shower before dinner, if that's okay with you," Jack said as he pulled out of the parking lot. "I can drop you off at your house and then pick you up in an hour or so. How does that sound?"

"Sounds great. And I know that I'm buying dinner tonight, so it should technically be your pick, but I could really go for a giant pizza and pint right about now."

"It's like you can read my mind."

Chapter 26

Orange and red flames licked at the shredded newspaper and dryer lint resting at the base of the log pyramid Jack had just constructed in the backyard fire pit. As his stay with Levi and Celia had extended, he'd finished his to-do list pretty quickly. For a while he'd enjoyed simply filling his after work time with reading, spending time with Levi and the family, Kristen, and long walks along the river trails when he started feeling restless. Lately, though, his restlessness had grown, and he'd asked Celia if she had any big, dream projects that she'd been wanting to do. Her eyes immediately lit up, and she said, "A fire pit! I would love a fire pit."

He and Levi had sat down the next night and sketched out a plan, and the two had worked together on it over the next few weekends. Tomorrow was Thanksgiving, and the fire pit was making its official debut. As he cracked twigs and medium-sized sticks and fed them into the fire, Jack admired their work. It really was an excellent fire pit. They'd found a good deal on river stones, and used them to extend the existing patio. Jack had also built a simple bench with a storage compartment to hold roasting sticks and firewood.

He heard the back door open and close, and glanced toward the house. Levi walked toward him.

"Testing it out?" he asked.

Jack nodded. "Yep. Didn't want anything to go wrong tomorrow."

"Hey, who needs an excuse to build a fire?"

Celia's parents were coming up for Thanksgiving tomorrow, as well as a couple of cousins and their kids. Jack had felt a brief pang of nervousness the week before as the holiday approached, wondering what expectations Kristen would have for Thanksgiving and the two of them. For a moment, he had panicked, wondering what his *own* expectations were. He'd never been even casually involved with a woman over a major holiday—by design—and it had snuck up on him. Fortunately, Kristen was going with her dad to visit her mom's family in California, something they apparently did most Thanksgivings. When she'd mentioned it to him, he'd noticed a wary look in her eye, but when he'd simply said that he hoped she had classic California weather for her trip, she'd relaxed, as though she too was hoping to avoid any awkward conversations about the holidays. At least, that's how he'd interpreted it. Of course, the next thing would be Christmas, but he was putting that conversation out of his mind for at least another couple of weeks.

Jack and Levi sat gradually building and tending the fire until the sun went down. They talked some, about nothing much, but they mostly sat in the silence of old friends. The fire was warm and bright and steady when Celia opened the back door to tell them it was time for supper.

"Ah, this is a nice fire!" she said. "You guys want to eat out here tonight?"

"Yeah, probably shouldn't leave the fire unattended for that long," Levi agreed. He stood up. "But we can help you carry things out."

"Great! It's all on the table. I'll go get the kids."

Aislinn and Tripp squealed and hollered when they ran out the back door, running straight toward the fire pit. Jack, who stood closest to the fire, reached out and snagged them, wrapping his arms around their waists.

"Hold on there, little fire walkers," he said with a laugh.

Levi was right behind them. "Remember the fire pit rules?"

"No running near the fire. No fire without a grown up. No putting anything in the fire without asking a grown up," they recited in unison.

"Good job. Now, let's eat, and maybe we can toast marshmallows for dessert."

After the chili pot had been cleaned out, sticky

marshmallow fingers washed, and two excited kids put to bed, the three adults settled around the fire. Celia tucked a battered quilt around her legs and let out a big sigh, leaning her head back against her chair.

"I think next year if I decide to make all the pies, I'm definitely buying pre-made crust."

They stayed outside until the fire burned down to coals, then Levi stood up and reached for Celia's hand. "I think we need to turn in," he said, grinning as Celia's protest was cut short by a jaw-cracking yawn. "Want me to get some dirt for the coals?"

"I'll stay out a bit longer and make sure I smother it before I head in," Jack replied, nodding toward the pile of dirt relocated from the fire pit project to a corner by the back fence.

Levi nodded and pulled the still yawning Celia behind him toward the house.

Several moments later the ring of his cell phone cut the stillness. Surprised, Jack reached in his pocket for his phone, a warmth unrelated to the dying fire spreading through his chest when he saw the name his caller id.

"Hey, you. How's the sunset right now?"

"I don't even want to tell you, you'd be so jealous."

Jack laughed.

"So what are you up to? Has the company arrived?"

"No, they're coming tomorrow just for the day.

I'm sitting around our first fire in the fire pit. Levi and I finished it last night."

"Ooohh! I can't wait to see the finished product! Can I book a campfire date for when I get back?"

"Absolutely."

Jack asked her about what she'd been doing aside from bragging about the sunsets, and she told him a little about her family and some of their fall traditions. By the time they said goodbye, the embers had lost their glow and the neighborhood dogs had gone quiet for the night, but Jack found that he didn't much feel the chilly night air.

The next day was full of delightful smells, full bellies, laughter, slamming screen doors, and muted Christmas movies on tv. Levi built a fire before lunch, and the adults took turns monitoring kids who had fun keeping the flames fed. By the time everyone was on their second cup of after-dinner coffee, almost everyone had found a spot on the patio, the fire seemingly as central to the family celebration as it had been to people whose lives had depended on it.

Jack debated taking a walk around the neighborhood—more for the alone time than anything else—as he sipped his second cup of coffee. He watched idly across the fire pit as Celia pulled her phone out of her pocket, glanced at the caller id and then put it away as she finished listening to what her cousin was telling her. A moment later, she frowned, pulling the phone out again, this time giving Jill an apologetic look and answering. Her frown lifted, but only briefly, then she stood and stepped away from the circle of people. Jack's eyes continued to follow her, his senses telling him something was wrong. Celia had turned her body away from the group, so he could only see her profile; but he saw her hand fly to her mouth, and her shoulders hunch in a self-protective gesture. When she turned her head and looked straight at him, he could see her eyes glistening with tears. She began walking toward the house, and Jack stood up to follow.

"It's your mom."

"On the phone?"

Celia shook her head. "No, it was Levi's dad on the phone. Your mom is sick. Well... she's dying, actually." "Dying" came out as if it had been choked and strangled before emerging limp and quivering on some conversational shore. Jack's mind fixated on the word. Dying. Dying. It lost all meaning, the syllables merging with the ticking sunflower clock hanging in the sunny kitchen. Celia laid a hand on his arm.

"Jack?"

"What's wrong with her?" His voice was cold and flat.

"Lung cancer. Apparently, she's been sick for a long time, but never went to the doctor, and now it's too late for any kind of treatment."

"Figures."

"Jack." Celia's voice was gentle, but still held a touch of reproof. Jack didn't take it personally.

"I just mean, if Jules had continued smoking as much as she did the last time I saw her, I'd be more surprised if she hadn't gotten cancer. And we never went to the doctor. Ever. So I'm not surprised, that's all."

Celia stared at Jack for several heartbeats, her expression solemn. "Jack," she said quietly, putting a hand on his arm. "Are you okay?"

Was he okay? Was he sad that his mom, whom he hadn't spoken to in 25 years, was dying of cancer? Was he shaken? Distraught?

"I'm fine," Jack said, gently. "I'm sorry for her, of course, but I'm fine."

Celia opened her mouth, then closed it again. Jack waited.

"Henry and Susan will have more details if you want them. Dad said you can call whenever."

"Did he also say I shouldn't call if I don't want to?"

Celia nodded, a small smile touching her lips if not her eyes. "Yes," she admitted. "You know him well. He knows you well."

Jack nodded. "Okay then. Hey, will it bother you if I go take a walk?"

"Of course not," she said. "Take your time."

He started to correct her—he didn't want to walk

because of the news about his mom—but decided it wasn't worth it. Instead, he said, "I know people will be curious about what happened, but could you maybe not get into it? Except with Levi, of course. Do your best anyway."

"Of course," Celia said. "It's your private business, don't worry." She gave him a hug then slipped out the back door. Jack walked out the front.

# Chapter 27

The sun was just a faint glow above the horizon when Jack pulled into the driveway after work Monday evening. He felt grimy from a long day that had started well before dawn. It was the final push on a project that had a December 1 deadline. The project managers were hoping to finish early, and Jack expected that this was going to be his shortest day of the week.

With a deep sigh, Jack turned his truck off and gathered his lunch cooler and backpack. His work boots felt like they carried 10 extra pounds. He'd been tired all day, despite the long weekend and plenty of rest. Maybe that was the problem. Maybe his body had forgotten what a day of work was like.

"Uncle Jack!"

Aislinn sprinted down the hallway toward Jack where he stood just inside the front door. He held out a hand to stop her.

"Aislinn!" he snapped. "The door's not even shut

yet, and I'm filthy besides."

If she'd been a cartoon, there would have been an audible *screech* as Aislinn skidded to a stop. Her lips trembled. "I'm sorry, Uncle Jack." Her voice was shaky.

Jack stifled another sigh and squatted in front of her. "Hey, sweetie, I'm sorry," he said, his voice gentle. "I'm just really tired, and wasn't expecting you to come running at me when I walked in. But I shouldn't have yelled at you. Forgive me?"

Aislinn nodded.

"Thanks, Pickle. I'd give you a giant hug, but I really am very dirty. I'll play after my shower, ok?"

"Okay."

Jack hurried down the hall, on a mission to avoid the rest of the family until after he'd sorted his mood out a bit. A blistering hot shower and clean clothes did wonders, and when he walked into the kitchen looking for Aislinn 30 minutes later, he felt a little more like himself.

"Smells good," he said to Celia. She stood over a pot of what smelled like chicken soup. Tripp sat at the table shredding cheese, and Aislinn was setting the table.

"Hey! Thanks! Nothing fancy, but it felt right for a cold night."

"You want some help there, Pickle?" Jack asked Aislinn. "Then maybe we can play a quick game of Skip-bo before dinner?"

"Yes!"

Jack picked up the stack of bowls. "I think you counted wrong," he told Aislinn. "There are six bowls here."

"Nuh uh. Kristen's coming over for dinner, mama said."

Right, Jack thought. He couldn't believe he'd forgotten, and he'd even talked to her yesterday. He was happy to remember it, but his anticipation was not as high as he thought it would be. *I need a vacation*, he thought, ignoring the fact that he'd been off work for the past five days.

No, a tiny voice in his head replied. *That's not it.*

He told the tiny voice to shut up and focused on setting the table and playing with Aislinn.

Celia was just putting dinner on the table when Kristen arrived, breezing through the door bringing crisp air and a good mood with her. She greeted Jack with a warm hug and a kiss on the cheek. "I missed you," she said softly. Before he could respond, she was moving around the room, hugging the rest of the family. They all sat down the table, and Jack tried to engage in the conversation, but found that he just couldn't focus on what everyone was saying. Fortunately, Celia and Kristen had enough catching up to do that he didn't think his quietness was too noticeable, although he caught Kristen giving him a few inquisitive looks. He also noticed that Levi and Celia pointedly did not give him strange looks, and while their acceptance of his behavior was a comfort, it was also irritating. Everything was irritating.

Kristen helped clean up after dinner, but headed home right after that since she was still tired from travel. For the first time in almost an hour, she asked Jack a direct question:

"I walked, would you like to walk me home?"

"Of course."

They put on coats and hats and waved goodnight. At the bottom of the porch steps Jack held out his arm and Kristen linked her elbow with his. They'd walked half a block before either of them spoke.

"So, what's going on with you tonight?" Kristen asked, her voice neutral.

"Nothing, just a long day."

"Hmm."

She didn't believe him, he could tell.

"Do you think you guys will finish up the project by the time Steve wants it done?" she asked.

"I think so. But it's going to be a hell of a week."

He felt her nod her head. "Anything else interesting happen while I was gone?" She was fishing, he could tell, unsatisfied with his responses and her assessment of his mood.

"My mom's dying."

"What?!"

He hadn't meant to say it, and he regretted it as soon as he had. He didn't want to talk about it, or think about it, or even have the thought take up one millimeter of brain space. But there it was.

"Aunt Susan called Thanksgiving day. I guess Jules just found out she has cancer, but it's too advanced to do anything about."

"Oh, Jack. Oh, I'm so sorry." She linked their arms a little tighter, pulling as close as she could without actually stopping to embrace him. He thought she might, but he maintained their momentum.

"Thanks, but it's fine."

This time even Jack's intention to keep moving couldn't keep Kristen from stopping abruptly. Locked arm in arm, the two of them stumbled.

"Seriously?"

Too late, Jack remembered that Kristen's mom had died of cancer, and that she didn't know the history between Jack and his mom. He suppressed a sigh.

"My mom and I have been estranged for 25 years at least, and we haven't spoken since I was 18. She came to my high school graduation, and I told her I never wanted to see her again."

Kristen stood like a rabbit trying to appear invisible. Jack could see that she was trying not to react visibly, and he loved that about her. Still, he could see it all play across her face and in her eyes—confusion, shock, sadness, sympathy—and he took pity on her.

"I know it's far from your own family experience," he said, his voice gentle. They were still standing close together on the sidewalk, and he reached up to adjust her hat over her dark curls. "You're right. It's probably not fine, but it hasn't been for decades. It is what it is,"

"Do you want to talk about it?"

He shook his head, and she searched his face for a long moment. He could see she still wasn't satisfied, but eventually she nodded. "Okay. Well, if you change your mind..."

I won't. "Thank you."

They walked the rest of the way hand in hand, and also in silence. It wasn't exactly an awkward silence, but they were each clearly preoccupied and lost in their own thoughts.

Chapter 28

Kristen sat at her desk, a pile of notes in front of her, laptop angled at her elbow. Rather than working—which is what she should have been doing—she sat with her chin propped in one hand, staring out the window in front of her. A redbud tree sat outside her guest room window, but a blustery rain the night before had stripped the last of the leaves from the branches. The bare branches were framed by a sky that couldn't decide whether it wanted to be gray and dreary or bright and sunny.

The view didn't matter though, because Kristen wasn't really looking at the view. Her gaze was entirely introspective, her mind trying to figure out just what was going on with Jack. She was almost certain that the news about his mom had put him out of sorts more than he wanted to admit, but maybe it really was just work stress. Maybe she was projecting. She picked up her phone from where it sat on the corner of the desk and held it up. Almost immediately, she set it face down on the desktop, and pulled her notebook toward her. Ten minutes later she was staring out the window again. Twenty minutes later, she was knocking on Celia's door, a container of cookies in her hand.

"Come on in, it's open!" the call was faint but clear through the closed front door, and Kristen walked inside.

"I'm in the kitchen!"

Kristen walked through the now familiar hallway into the sunny yellow kitchen where Celia was pulling a steaming teakettle off of the stove top. Two mugs sat on the table next to a stoneware bowl of sugar and a carton of half-and-half.

"Does Earl Grey sound okay?" Celia asked. "I think I have some peppermint tea if you'd rather have that."

"Earl Grey is perfect," Kristen said.

"I decided to embrace this as tea time myself too," Celia said as she poured the steaming water into the mugs. The tea bags that had been resting in the bottom bobbed gently in the water. "Seemed appropriate with cookies, anyway."

Kristen popped the lid off of her container, releasing a spicy, sugary aroma. Celia took a deep breath.

"Mmm. Gingersnaps?"

Kristen nodded. "Yep. Doesn't feel like fall unless I have a jar full of homemade gingersnaps on the counter. I made these last night—my second batch since October, actually. My mom made them when I was a girl, and it was one tradition my dad and I kept going after she died." Kristen reached for the half-and-half and poured some in her tea.

"Speaking of moms," she said, hesitant. "Is Jack...?" She trailed off.

"Fine? In denial? Acting like a grumpy bear?" Celia sighed. "I don't think so, probably, and yes." She took a bite of cookie and took her time chewing, swallowing, and sipping her tea, wincing only slightly at the still scalding hot liquid.

"Has he told you about his relationship with his mom? About when his dad died?" Celia asked.

Kristen shook her head. "Not really. He told me they were estranged, but nothing more than that."

"I can't really say much more than that either," Celia said, her face creased in a frown, and her eyes brimmed with sadness. "It's not my story to tell." She hesitated. "I think... I think you could ask him. To be honest, I think it might be good for him. He says he's fine, but he's not. He won't like it, and it might lead to a fight."

"I can handle that."

Celia sighed and took another bite of cookie. "Levi and I have tried, but it's too easy for him to ignore our concern. We're too much a part of the story."

Kristen reached forward and picked up a gingersnap. "Well, I feel better knowing it's not all in my head, thanks. Now, let's talk about something else."

Kristen perched on the edge of her wing-backed chair, watching out the window. She hadn't been this nervous on their first date, but she felt like she was preparing an ambush, and there was no way of knowing how Jack would react. *Scratch that. I'm pretty sure I know* exactly *how he's going to react.*

Right on time, Jack's truck pulled into her driveway, headlights sweeping across the yard. Kristen stood up, grabbed her purse, and walked out the door, locking it behind her. Jack stood by the passenger door, holding it open. His hair was still damp from a shower, and his eyes looked tired, but his smile was genuine as she approached. Her stomach churned, but she tried to ignore it. Jack pulled her close before she could step up into the truck, and gave her a long, lingering kiss. She clung to him, inhaling the spicy, clean scent of his soap and savoring the embrace.

"Hey," Jack's voice rumbled when they finally pulled apart—but not too far apart.

"Hey," Kristen was slightly breathless.

"I'm glad you called."

"Me too."

He kissed her again, briefly this time, and helped her into the truck, shutting the door behind her. Kristen closed her eyes and took a slow, deep breath as Jack walked around the truck. She opened them when Jack climbed in next to her.

"U-Bean?" he asked, buckling his seat belt.

"Sounds good."

The coffee shop was blissfully warm and only moderately full when Kristen and Jack walked inside. Kristen took a deep breath of the richly scented air, thinking for probably the hundredth time that it was too bad she didn't like coffee. Jack leaned toward her and asked if she wanted her usual. She nodded and said she'd go find an empty table.

Kristen wound through the room, noticed the young man tuning a guitar on the small stage, and waved as she recognized Braden, Jessica's boyfriend. Good, she thought, pleased that the music for the evening would be enjoyable. Braden had just begun his second song—an acoustic cover of a Billie Eilish song that worked surprisingly well—when Jack set two steaming mugs on the table and sat down across from her. Kristen rubbed her hands together in delight.

Jack handed her a spoon and took a sip of his cappuccino. Kristen thanked him and scooped up a bite of the double whipped cream on her hot chocolate. After two more spoonfuls of sweetness to bolster her courage, Kristen broke the silence.

"Why won't you contact your mom? I know you keep saying it doesn't matter to you that she's sick, but I can see that it does. That, or there's something else majorly wrong right now. And don't," she held up a hand as he opened his mouth, "tell me it's work. It's not work." She kept her voice gentle, but her gaze held steady on his. She watched him clench his jaw, his lips compressing in a thin line. She saw his gaze flick briefly toward the door and knew he was contemplating walking out. Would he? Would he leave her there? Or were they good enough friends that she could push him on this?

"Why won't you let this go?" His voice was so low that Kristen had to lean forward to hear him.

"Because I care about you," she replied, her voice lowering to match his. "Because I recognize the signs of someone who is ignoring something important." She reached out and laid a hand gently on his clenched fist, letting her words linger in the silence.

"If I agree to go, will you back off?"

Kristen recoiled at the acid in his voice, jerking her hand away and almost knocking her hot chocolate into her lap. She fought back an angry retort. Jack let out a deep sigh and rested his head in his hands.

"I'm not trying to be hurtful," he said to the table.

"You could have fooled me." Kristen's voice was brittle.

He looked up at her, and his eyes were full of such confusion and anguish that her anger softened.

"I know you're right and Levi and Susan and Henry and every person who keeps telling me to go see her is right. She doesn't have anyone. Uncle Henry and Aunt Susan do what they can, but she's done her best to push them away and there's only so much she'll let them help, and frankly only so much they'll put up with." He seemed to grow more weary with every word, as if even this took everything he had. "I don't want to see her, and I don't want to talk about her. Frankly, if I could pretend she doesn't exist, I would." The words were harsh, but Kristen could see the pain behind them. "I'll go. Because I don't want to deal with it anymore. I'll go, and we'll call it closure."

Encouraging words welled up inside of Kristen. She wanted to tell Jack that maybe reconciliation was possible, and this illness would bring healing to his and his mom's relationship. Instead, she kept quiet and took a drink of her hot chocolate. The truth was, she didn't know if reconciliation was possible, because she didn't know what had happened between them. On some level, she understood. Goodness knows she could relate to having a story she never wanted to revisit again, and until she'd told Jack about Mike, she hadn't talked about that part of her past for *years*. That was the rub: she had told him about her past. She had been vulnerable with him, but he shut her out. It stung.

"I'm sorry," he said again. "It's not about you."

She shrugged, working hard to hide her hurt. "Okay."

"I'm going to finish this job, and head to Crofton next week."

Kristen forced herself to believe that it really wasn't about her. She reached out again to squeeze his hand. "I'm glad, and I hope you will be too."

A week later Kristen sat under the big maple tree in her front yard, waiting for Jack.

Between Jack's heavy work schedule and the fraught nature of their conversation at U-Bean, their interactions over the past week had been minimal and tinged with coolness. To his credit, Jack seemed to realize he'd hurt her feelings, and had done his best to smooth things over. Kristen had worked hard to be compassionate instead of angry, and despite her lingering hurt she was glad he'd wanted to stop by and say goodbye in person.

She stood as she saw the familiar dark pickup pull into view and walked down to the sidewalk as Jack pulled up to the curb. He left the truck running and rolled his window down. Kristen leaned her arms on the window frame.

"I'll be sending you good thoughts," she said. "How long do you think you'll stay?"

"Not sure. I guess it depends on... well, on a lot of things. I'll call you," Jack replied. They leaned toward each other and kissed lightly. Kristen stepped back, and Jack put the truck into gear and pulled away, his arm waving out the window as he turned the corner. Kristen lifted her own arm in reply, then lowered it with a sigh.

Chapter 29

Kristen adjusted her yellow knit hat and pulled her gloves out of her coat pockets. As she got out of her dad's car, a gust of wind nearly pulled the door free from her hands, and she shivered.

"Great day for cutting down a Christmas tree, Dad," she said wryly as she shut the door.

"At least it's sunny," Rosalee said as she pulled on her own gloves. Her voice was muffled by the dark gray scarf that wound around the lower half of her face. Kristen wished she'd brought a scarf of her own, but settled for zipping her coat all the way up to her chin.

"Don't whine," her dad teased, a smile softening his words. "We've hunted for trees in colder weather than this."

"Yes, but I don't have the excitement of youth to keep me warm."

He laughed, and Rosalee linked her elbow through Kristen's. "Don't mind him. Let's stay close to keep warm."

They crunched through the gravel parking lot to the barn that served as the hub of the Wilson Christmas Tree farm. A tall chalkboard sign displayed prices for trees, fresh wreaths, and also directed customers inside to the work table where a smiling, rosy-cheeked woman in a red apron stood next to a cash register, busy with gardening shears, wide ribbon, twine, and a mountain of green. Kristen took a deep breath of the pine and cinnamon scented air, and beelined toward another table where cambros of complimentary coffee, hot chocolate, and spiced cider sat next to paper cups, sugar, and creamer. After a brief internal debate she opted for the cider, then prepared two cups of coffee for her dad and Rosalee: two sugars for her dad, black for Rosalee. Rosalee walked up next to her just as Kristen was putting the lids on the cups. She accepted the coffee from Kristen with one hand and pulled her scarf below her chin with the other.

"Thank you, dear," she said. "This will hit the spot today. Plus, Mr. Wilson always makes the best coffee." She gestured to the shelves behind the drink station. "And Mrs. Wilson keeps the beans stocked."

Kristen leaned forward to inspect the bags. "I recognize this!" she said. "I've seen it at your house."

Rosalee nodded. "We always buy several bags when we get our tree at Christmas and ration them out the rest of the year."

"Do they not sell them on the off season?"

"No. I've never asked why, I just snatch them up when I can!"

Kristen also saw attractively packaged bags of mulling spices and gourmet hot chocolate mixes sitting on the shelves next to the coffee beans, and made a mental note to stop back by the barn when they were finished and grab some Christmas gifts. Her dad walked up and Kristen handed him the coffee.

"Thanks, pumpkin." he took a sip. "You ladies ready to head out to the fields? Mrs. Wilson said Landon should be back with the tractor any minute."

Kristen saluted with her cup. "Feeling fortified and warming up from the inside. Let's go hunt ourselves a tree!"

Despite the icy wind, it really was a beautiful December day. The clear, pale blue sky was a beautiful backdrop to the deep greens and browns of the farm, and the crisp air smelled clean and fresh. The trio had taken advantage of Kristen's flexible schedule and the Barnes' retired status to come out on Friday morning, so they had the farm to themselves.

Just as Mrs. Wilson had predicted, a bright green and yellow tractor crested a nearby low hill, trailing a small flatbed trailer. As it pulled up in front of them, Kristen saw it had benches built along the sides, and pine needles in varying shades of green, yellow, and brown covered the wooden floor. Kristen and Rosalee climbed up into the trailer as George told Landon, the Wilson's college-aged son, which size tree they were looking for. Kristen saw Landon nod and George walked back to join the women.

The ride was quieter than Kristen expected, the rumbling of the tractor dissipating in the wide open space of the farm, nothing around to hold it in or reflect it back to them. It amused Kristen to think that it was her first time to visit a Christmas tree farm. She and her dad had always gotten a live tree for Christmas, but they'd always just walked down to the nearest parking lot tree seller. It was its own kind of fun tradition, but Kristen was happy to get to experience something new.

"How is Jack doing?" Rosalee asked as they bumped along the path.

"Better," Kristen said. "He and his mom seem to have... gotten used to each other." She gave a wry smile. "At least, that's how he put it."

The first time Jack had called her, he'd sounded like a caged animal, full of fight and tension. He'd called her from his aunt and uncle's house, ranting about how his mom wasn't willing to talk about anything, and that as he had suspected she wasn't taking care of herself, and she met any attempt to help her with derision or refusal. Jack declared he was going to stay one more night then come back to Riverton, but once he'd finished his rant and seemed calmer Kristen spoke quietly,

"She's really sick, isn't she?"

"Yeah." Jack's voice was so quiet she could barely

hear it.

Kristen hadn't known what to say. It was difficult enough to speak into someone's grief, and she felt even more at a loss not knowing the situation fully. She'd thought back to the time Nora's dad had a massive heart attack, and how Nora had told her that sometimes the best support she'd gotten was from people who weren't constantly trying to "fix" her sadness. It seemed appropriate in this situation as well, and Kristen remained silent. Eventually Jack spoke again.

"I'm going to stay a little longer," he said.

"You know what you need to do," Kristen replied, "and you know I am always willing to be a container for your frustration and rage."

Jack chuckled. "Thanks."

Sensing that he was done with that topic of conversation, she asked if he'd started the new book he'd been talking about, and they talked about lighter topics for a bit before hanging up.

The next time Kristen had talked to Jack, he'd moved in with his mom and told her he was there to take care of her whether or not she wanted him to, and that he promised not to bring up the past, but was willing to talk about it if she ever wanted to. He said that they then fought almost every day about normal things like the TV, and what she was (or more accurately was not) eating, and if she'd taken her meds, and why she wouldn't call her doctors back. As far as Kristen knew, his mom had yet to bring up the past, and Jack seemed to think she never would, but Kristen kept hoping for his sake.

"It's too bad you won't get to see each other at Christmas." Rosalee's statement brought Kristen back to the present.

"Mmhm." Kristen's vague mumble elicited a curious look from Rosalee, but the older woman didn't push her on it. Truth be told, Kristen was kind of glad that she and Jack wouldn't be spending Christmas or New Year's together. Those could be such pressure-filled holidays when two people were dating, especially when other people knew the two were dating.

The trio swayed as the tractor came to a stop. George climbed down and reached up to give Rosalee a hand. Kristen laid a hand on his shoulder for balance and jumped to the ground.

"All right!" she said, rubbing her gloved hands together. "Let's find us a tree!"

•   •   •

District Cafe was bustling when Celia, Kristen, and Rosalee walked through the door, full of what Kristen assumed were people out Christmas shopping. Not for the first time, Kristen was grateful that her Christmas list was very small, even this year when she was taking part in the McDonnell/Finch gift exchange.

The book club had still claimed one of the

meeting rooms, so the trio quickly placed their orders and headed back to the group. The sound of laughter and conversation greeted them as they walked through the door to the room, and they deposited their wrapped gifts on the coffee table that someone had centered in the room. Originally, the group had planned to have a book exchange for their December meeting, but Caroline had suggested having a literary-themed baby shower for Sierra and her now three-month-old instead. Sierra had clapped her hands in delight when Caroline had suggested it, and her excitement settled it.

As drinks arrived, everyone began taking seats in a loose circle, the conversation quieted, and everyone looked toward Sierra.

"Thank you all for doing this," she said, her face split by a wide smile. "You all are truly one of the best groups of women I've ever met, and I'm so glad I took a chance and came to that first book club meeting." There were murmurs of agreement, and Judy, who sat next to Sierra reached over and squeezed her hand. "But look, I can't open gifts in silence while y'all stare at me. So if you promise to just keep talking with each other, I'll start."

Everyone laughed, and slowly but surely the low hum of conversation returned. Kristen chatted with Caroline and Lois who were sitting nearest her, while keeping one eye on Sierra. She smiled as Mary and Ashley took turns snuggling baby Gianna.

"How long have you been in Riverton now?"

Caroline asked, taking a sip of her tea. "About eight months?"

Kristen nodded, her mouth full of pastry. She swallowed. "Yes. I'm impressed that you remember."

Caroline just smiled. "Eight months in. What is the best part, and what is the hardest part?"

Kristen tilted her head and thought. They were good questions. Questions that she might have asked someone in a similar situation, but not the kind of introspection she'd applied to herself lately. Her insides squirmed a little under Caroline's direct gaze. She wasn't used to being the one in the hot seat. She took a drink of her Earl Grey.

"I think... the best part has been the connections, the relationships."

"Old or new?"

"Both." Another excellent question, Kristen thought. "The time with Dad has been invaluable, but the new connections—friendships—" it seemed important to clarify that point, "have been surprising. In a really good way."

"And the hardest part?"

The answer came immediately to mind, but Kristen hesitated before answering. It was going to sound silly, she knew.

"This is going to sound ridiculous, but I'd have to say... the connections, the relationships."

Caroline grinned. "That's not ridiculous at all. Relationships are hard, especially if you're not used to them."

Kristen's eyebrows shot up. "Caroline," she said, "has anyone ever told you that you are an extremely insightful woman?"

This time, Caroline laughed. "All the time. That, and opinionated, and blunt. But I like insightful the best. Now tell me, are you glad you came?"

"Yes." There was no hesitation this time. For all the uncertainty and uncomfortableness the past eight months had held, it had definitely been worth it. She was looking forward to the next several months too, she realized. And longer? The squirmy feeling returned. She wasn't sure about that yet, but she pushed the question down for another time.

"We missed you last month," Kristen said to Caroline. "Rosalee said you and your husband were traveling?"

"Yes, we took a trip to Italy. We went a long time ago and decided to treat ourselves for our fortieth wedding anniversary."

Kristen, who had never been to Italy, began peppering her with questions. Their conversation drew in Lois who had lived in Italy for five years with her husband right after they were married. Before they knew it, Sierra had finished unwrapping her gifts, and the party gradually broke up. Celia caught Kristen's eye, and Kristen nodded to her before reaching out and taking Lois's hand.

"Ladies, I have thoroughly enjoyed this conversation, but I need to get going. My ride is leaving, plus I have an afternoon of baking and cooking waiting for me."

"It's that time of year," Lois said with a smile, squeezing Kristen's hand. "You know, my family doesn't arrive until late next week. If you have some spare time on Monday, come by my house and I can show you my photo albums from our time overseas."

"I would love that," Kristen said. She pulled out her phone and made a few taps. "Monday is perfect. Let me make sure I have your number so I can call you when I'm on my way. I can even pick us up some lunch if that works for you."

They finalized their plans and Kristen gave Caroline a hug goodbye before circling the room to wish the rest of the group a Merry Christmas.

Chapter 30

For the first time since moving back into his childhood room, Jack woke up without being disoriented. It had surprised him, this room. When he'd decided to give his mom more than just a day, to take care of her whether she wanted him to, it had become clear that he'd need to move back in with her. He hadn't wanted to. It had taken a phone call to his mom's doctor and half a day hiking to finally come to terms with it. He learned from the doctor that his mom didn't have much time, and that the end would likely be lonely and painful. He took to the woods to find peace in his soul about what his gut was telling him to do.

So he had told his mom he was moving in, and she had offered only minimal resistance—another sign that it was the right thing. When he'd walked down the familiar hallway and opened the familiar door, he'd frozen in surprise. His blue and green plaid comforter still covered the pine bed. His

Corvette and motorcycle posters still hung on the walls, and the cheap bookshelf in the corner still sagged under the weight of books stacked two deep on its shelves. For a second, Jack felt almost dizzy. It was as though everything he'd thought about his mom in the past two decades was a Jenga tower, and by opening the door he'd pulled out the wrong piece, and sent the tower crashing. Why hadn't she packed up that stuff years ago? Why wasn't it empty or full of junk?

The days had been rocky at first, Jack and his mom like two snarling dogs circling each other, on guard and wary. Eventually, as he'd told Kristen, they'd gotten used to each other. Jack stopped trying to boss his mom around, and she lost some of her combativeness. Jack fixed her simple meals, and she started swallowing the pills that he would set next to her plate with a glass of water.

Before moving in with his mom, Jack had a long conversation with his aunt and uncle. He'd wanted to know exactly the situation he was getting into. They'd told him she'd almost died 10 years ago from an accidental drug overdose, and it had actually scared her into allowing Henry and Susan to pay for an inpatient rehab program. When she'd come out she had been clean and sober, but no less prickly, and still not interested in renewing any kind of relationship with her family. On the bright side, his Aunt Susan had said dryly, she hadn't been interested in ANY kind of relationship, including any of her old so-called friends or romantic partners. She'd gotten a full-time job at the local grocery store, where she'd been a model—if perpetually grumpy—employee until she'd gotten too sick to come in regularly. Otherwise, she'd spent the past 10 years holed up in her house and avoiding people as much as possible.

Jack thought it was a bit of a miracle that his mom still lived in their old family home. He was sure she'd have sold it or lost it somehow. If he was honest, there were moments when he wished she had, when small, everyday acts poked and prodded his own half-healed wounds. Jack woke up in his old room, cooked in the little kitchen, watched television on the same set while sitting on the same sagging couch; and his sad and broken teenage self kept begging for his attention. Jack ignored the urge to self-reflect.

It was a Thursday evening, so the TV was turned to Jeopardy when Jack walked into the living room with a tray containing two bowls of homemade vegetable beef soup, a plate of crackers, two glasses of water, and one hot tea. He set the tray down on the coffee table and went to pull out a couple of TV trays from their stand in the corner.

"Any repeats tonight?" he asked his mom.

She shook her head. "All new contestants tonight."

Jack set up dinner and settled in on the couch with his mom. She glanced at him.

"Thanks."

Was it the first time she'd said thank you? He thought maybe it was.

"You're welcome."

They both tucked into their dinner and attempted to beat each other to the answers on all the game show questions. Jack pulled his phone out of his pocket and sent out a quick text to Kristen:

"My mom just thanked me for dinner. Does this mean we're getting along now?"

She must have already been on the phone, because her reply came right away:

"It's a good sign. That or she's softening you up for a new attack."

Jack smiled, sent back a cross-eyed emoji, and tucked the phone back in his pocket. He picked up his soup spoon again. He thought it was time to bring up a topic he'd been avoiding most of the week. When the show went to commercial, he found the remote and muted it. His mom immediately turned to him.

"What's going on?" she asked.

Jack knew he only had as long as the commercials lasted, so he kept it brief. "I'm going to start going over to Susan and Henry's house for dinner on Saturday nights. They invited you to come."

His mom immediately shook her head. "No thank you." The words were polite, but the voice was firm. She reached for the remote and unmuted to the sounds of a commercial for an antidepressant. Fitting, Jack thought. He muted the tv again, unfazed by the resulting glare.

"They also invited you over for breakfast on Christmas morning. I'll probably join them."

This time there was a flicker in his mom's eye, but before he could tell if it was interest or just irritation that he'd muted the tv again, the look was gone and she had yanked the remote control away from him.

"No. Thank you." She unmuted and tucked the remote in the pocket of her sweatpants, her eyebrows rising in challenge. Jack just rolled his eyes.

"Suit yourself. Offer's on the table." He turned his attention back to his soup and the show.

•   •   •

The Finches' home still glowed, the multitude of white lights along the trim giving it the look of an electric gingerbread house. Fat pillar candles sat in each window, their welcome glow spilling out into the yard. A warmth spread through Kristen's chest as she pulled up the gravel drive and parked. She turned off the engine and climbed out of the car, then walked back to the trunk where a cardboard box safeguarded a hot bowl of Buffalo chicken dip and a slow cooker full of her infamous green chili queso, plus crackers, chips, and celery sticks for dipping.

Someone must have been keeping an eye out the window, because Keira opened the front door as Kristen climbed the porch steps.

"Need any help?" she asked.

"Nope! Thanks though," Kristen said with a smile. She walked through the open doorway into the foyer, Keira following close behind and closing the heavy oak door behind her. They both followed the smells and sounds to the kitchen, where Elizabeth and Jonathan were arranging a large spread of snacks out on the island countertop.

"You made it!" Jonathan said, setting a basket full of napkins on one end of the island.

"I did! Thank you so much for including me. Do you have a spot near an outlet for this queso?"

Together they found a spot for her party offerings, then Elizabeth handed her a plate. "Dig in," she said with a smile. "No need to wait on the others. I think they're in the middle of a race on Super MarioKart. New Year's Eve is pretty casual. Oh, the coffee station has some more hot drink options if you want, and cold drinks are in the cooler."

Kristen chatted with Keira, Elizabeth, and Jonathan as the four of them began loading her plate with chips and dip, fruit kabobs, sweet and spicy roasted nuts, and little puff pastry bites. She held one up.

"Sweet or savory?" she asked.

"Blue tray is sweet, white tray is savory," Elizabeth answered.

As Kristen pulled a can of sparkling water out of the cooler, the distant sounds of laughter and conversation from the family room got louder, and other members of the family trickled in. The teenage McDonnell boys barrelled past their parents and older cousins, arguing about the race and loading up their plates as though it was their last meal. Kristen passed out one-armed hugs and relished the boisterous family sounds. She'd been mostly alone in her little house the past week, and while it had been nice to get some deep work done, by the time New Year's Eve rolled around she had been more than ready for some people time.

At Christmas brunch, Elizabeth had invited her over again for New Year's Eve, explaining that the McDonnell-Finch families always had a game tournament. They chose a different game every year, and this year had been George's turn to pick. He'd chosen Dominoes. The kids had all groaned, but George had assured them it would be more fun than they thought it would be. Only Keira seemed to believe him, but once the games got rolling, even Jessica—the grandkid least interested in any kind of game—admitted that it had been a good choice for the family tournament.

The action took place in the large family room, with the New Year's Rockin' Eve muted on the TV, and classical piano music playing the background.

They had taken the Christmas tree down to create more space for gaming, but the room still glowed with lit garland and candlelight. Twenty minutes until midnight, Kristen found herself curled up in one corner of the couch, a soft, cable knit blanket tucked around her knees, a steaming mug of spiced cider in one hand, and a plate with gingerbread balanced on her lap. She smiled, watching the championship match-up coalesce in front of her: George and Jonathan on one team, Keira and Corbin on the other. Austin and Chris had just returned from the kitchen with a giant bowl of freshly popped popcorn and cans of pop, and Rosalee lay on the love seat, her eyes half closed. Everyone else dotted the room, some with drinks and snacks, others with sleepy expressions on their faces, everyone placing their flag in the sand for one of the two teams. Kristen felt the cushions shift slightly and glanced over to see Elizabeth settling onto the other end of the couch.

"She always tries very hard to make it until midnight," Elizabeth said, nodding toward Rosalee, "but I don't think she's seen the ball drop since 1989."

Kristen laughed.

Elizabeth took a sip of her own hot beverage, then angled her body toward Kristen.

"So, what's going on with you and Jack these days? How long is he planning on being in Crofton?"

"We've been talking a lot, but not really about

anything like that. Our conversations are more focused on the present. But reading between the lines I get the feeling he's staying put until..." she hesitated, "... well, until his mom passes."

Elizabeth nodded. "So, how do you feel about that arrangement?" she asked. "Just talking...no future planning."

Kristen took a sip of her drink. *Did the room just get hot all of a sudden*? Her arm pits felt sweaty. How did she feel about her relationship with Jack? A cheer erupted over at the game table, but distracted Elizabeth only momentarily. She turned her perceptive and inquisitive gaze back toward Kristen.

"I think... I feel okay about it," Kristen said slowly. "Because, to be perfectly honest, I don't think much about it at all." she shrugged. "I enjoy spending time with him, and enjoy talking to him when we're not together. I miss his in-personness more than I expected." She stared off into the distance for a moment, then shook her head and looked back at Elizabeth. "I don't think I had actually realized that until just now. But yeah, I miss him being here."

Elizabeth nodded, and Kristen changed the subject.

"Are you a New Year's goals person?" she asked.

Elizabeth raised an eyebrow. "What do you think?" she asked, her mouth curving in a small smile.

"I think you're more of a quarterly goals person."

Elizabeth's laugh was both delighted and surprised. "I think you might be the first person ever to guess that about me. Everyone assumes I'm a make-the-resolution-and-knock-it-out-by-February-1 kind of person."

"I bet you used to be."

"I used to *try* to be," Elizabeth raised a finger, "but then I got tired of failing."

Kristen smiled. "Do you ever get tired of the expectations people have for you?" she asked. Kristen had met a lot of driven, hyper-focused people in her life—including Liz—and knew that it was easy to let the pressure get too heavy.

"I used to. But time has given me a lot more self-awareness. Well..." she made a self-deprecating face. "Time, therapy, and my mom getting remarried."

They both laughed, and this time Kristen was prepared for the tables to turn.

"What about you? I know you probably don't deal with the same expectations that I do, but I imagine people have put you in your own Kristen-shaped-box over the years. Especially as a single woman."

"You're very perceptive." Kristen took a sip of her cider and a bite of gingerbread. Her knee-jerk response was to leave it at that and ask another question, but her instinct told her to honor Elizabeth's candor with some honesty of her own.

"The number of people who would feel free to tell me about their expectations is small. I have always had... a wide circle of acquaintances, and a much smaller one of actual friends." Kristen lifted one shoulder in a half-hearted shrug. "For better or for worse, I'm probably more in danger of crumbling under the weight of my own expectations, to be honest."

Another cheer erupted from the dominoes game, and this time Kristen and Elizabeth got up to see what all the fuss was about. A short time later, after the ball had dropped, Keira and Corbin crowned the tournament champions, and Kristen said her goodbyes, she found herself thinking about the conversation with Elizabeth. She drove through the quiet, frosty streets, thinking about how they'd started the conversation talking about New Year's Goals, but never actually talked about what they were actually looking forward to or hoping for the coming year.

She thought about the book proposal that was out for submission, and the conversation she'd had with her dad and Rosalee about a possible trip to Argentina. She thought about the Halloween festival at the community center, and the enjoyment she'd gotten out of helping there. She thought about Sunday dinners with her new family, weekday lunches and spontaneous suppers with the Blairs, and walks through the neighborhood with funny, wise women. She thought about baseball games, and three friends who might as well be sisters. She thought about Jack.

As Kristen changed for bed and washed her face, she realized that the upcoming year was more of a question mark than she realized.

Chapter 31

Jack waved to Mrs. Lukens at the front desk of the Crofton Public Library as he slid two books through the return slot and made his way toward the stacks. He took a few moments to browse the new fiction titles, selecting the recent novel by Jane Harper before slipping down the "K" aisle. He was slowly making his way through the Stephen King oeuvre, after realizing that he had never read any Stephen King, and he had a lot of time on his hands. There were only so many projects to be done around his mom's house or his aunt and uncle's house.

He set his small stack down on the check-out desk, smiled at the librarian, and pulled his wallet out of his back pocket.

"Ah, you've made it to my favorite," Mrs. Lukens said as she slid the stack of books toward her. She tapped King's *11/26/73* which sat on the top.

"I've heard this is one of his more popular titles since it's not horror," Jack said as he handed Mrs. Lukens his library card. She scanned it.

"That's probably true," she conceded. "I'm a Stephen King fan though, and it's still my favorite."

"You're definitely convincing me to start it right away."

Mrs. Lukens finished scanning the books, printed his check out slip, and slipped it into one of the books.

"Oh!" she said, snapping her fingers. "Are you going to see Susan today? We have a book here she's been waiting for."

"I'm heading there next, actually."

"Wait right here."

Jack leaned against the counter and glanced around the library. It was an odd building, the way small town libraries often are, with various decades of architecture cobbled together. The children's section was the original building, which itself had once been a farmhouse. They had added the rest of the library on in two separate phases as the town grew, and it was a bit of a Frankenstein building. Jack still loved it though. Despite spending most of his time outside as a kid, he'd actually logged a lot of hours in the town library, the now-retired children's librarian Mrs. McCoy feeding him a steady stream of literature, even after he'd outgrown the children's section.

"Here you go, hon," Mrs. Lukens reemerged, quickly scanning the brand new hardback and handing it across the counter. Jack flashed his most winning smile.

"Thanks, Mrs. Lukens."

The sun was doing its best to break through the pearly gray clouds as Jack pulled up his aunt and uncle's gravel drive 20 minutes later. Susan's bright red Jeep Cherokee sat under the carport, with Henry's old GMC pickup truck parked right behind it. Jack pulled up behind them both. When he got out of his own truck, he could hear the faint tick-ticking of the GMC's engine cooling down. He grabbed the library book and a drink tray with three large coffees steaming in it and a box of donuts from Jerry's, which Jack privately maintained were the best donuts in the country. He shut his tuck door with his elbow and made his way to the kitchen door.

As he suspected, he could see Susan through the window of the door sitting at the kitchen table with a crossword puzzle, her long gray braid draped over one shoulder. Henry stood in front of the open refrigerator, head bent, searching the contents. Jack tapped the door gently with his foot, and both graying heads turned toward the door, faces immediately lighting up with smiles. Henry opened the door and took the box of donuts that Jack handed him.

"How'd you know I needed a snack," Henry said with a grin.

"And a fresh cup of coffee," Susan added, standing up to accept one of the paper cups and kiss Jack on the cheek.

"Just a hunch." Jack flashed his dimple. He

picked up the roll of paper towels from the counter and joined his aunt and uncle at the sturdy square table. He ran his hand lightly across the top of the scratched and dented top, worn smooth through years of use. It was an almost unconscious gesture, like fingering a string of rosary beads. He remembered the winter that Henry had made the table, two seven-year-old boys with oversized safety goggles shadowing his every move, taking mental notes and cleaning up after each work session for a few dollars that they would then immediately go spend at the nearby convenience store on candy and Mountain Dew.

"What are we working on today?" Jack asked, taking a sip of his coffee and reaching for one of the glazed donuts.

"I've got a set of bookcases that need sanding, and need to put another coat of stain on that table you helped me with last week."

Henry was a carpenter, and although he had spent most of his career as a cabinet maker, these days he mostly made furniture, beautiful and well-made pieces that sold for a premium. Jack wasn't the craftsman his uncle was, but since he'd been back in Crofton, he'd started joining his uncle in his shop once or twice a week, assisting in whatever way he could, mostly for something to do besides watch daytime tv with his mom.

"I went to see your mom yesterday while you were at the store," Susan said, taking a bite of her donut.

"How'd it go?" Jack's voice was heavy with skepticism.

"Better than I expected," Susan replied. She blinked her eyes rapidly. "It was... not like old times, but it was nice. We even laughed together."

Jack raised his eyebrows. "Wow. Well, I'm glad."

"And it's got me thinking; you need to take the weekend off. Go to Riverton for a couple of days. Relax. See that lady friend of yours."

Jack's mouth quirked. *Lady friend?*

"You're a good son, and you've been going above and beyond for your mom these past two months. But it's lonely work. You've told us she's stable at the moment, and now that I know she'll tolerate my presence again I can check on her while you're gone, make sure she eats and takes her meds."

"It's not a bad idea. Maybe I should dig out my winter hiking gear," Jack mused.

"No." Susan's voice was firm, her eyes locked in an expression Jack remembered well from the days he and Levi were full of teenage boy shenanigans. "You spend hours tromping around these woods, and what you need is some companionship, not more isolation. I won't do it unless you promise to go to Riverton."

He knew he was going to go along with it. Jack glanced at Henry, who was working on his second donut and calmly watching the discussion. He winked at Jack, because they both knew there was no point in arguing with Susan when she was this adamant. But Jack made a show of thinking about it, just because he never liked giving in too easily. If he were honest with himself the hiking suggestion was just a reflex. When he thought more about it, a weekend with some of his favorite people sounded a lot better than a weekend alone.

Susan fiddled with her coffee cup in a way that Jack knew meant she had something more to say.

"When your mom and I were talking, I happened to mention that you were seeing someone, and she didn't seem to know what I was talking about. Have you not mentioned Kristen to her?"

Jack shrugged, but got an uncomfortable tightness between his shoulder blades. "She just hasn't come up," he said. "I'm not used to talking about the women I date with anyone."

Susan raised an eyebrow, and Jack could practically read her mind. He *didn't* usually talk about the women he dated, and yet Susan and Henry had grown very familiar with Kristen in the past few weeks considering they'd never met her. Jack shifted in his seat.

"My guess," Susan continued, "is that this means you probably haven't talked much about your mom to Kristen either."

"Well, she knows I'm here, doesn't she?"

"That's not what I mean, and you know it." Susan's gaze was direct, but gentle. Jack knew what she meant. He thought back to the uncomfortable conversations with Kristen right after he'd gotten the news about his mom.

"Just think about... think about how you feel about Kristen and what that means when it comes to sharing about yourself, and your life. Playing all your cards close to your chest only gets you so far."

Jack glanced at Henry, hoping for a lifeline, but Henry just sipped his coffee and nodded. Jack sighed. "I'll think about what you said."

Susan changed the subject, asking a few questions about Julie's medicines and her appetite, then waved the men off to the workshop behind the house.

Chapter 32

Kristen woke up a good hour earlier than she needed to on Saturday morning, but her excitement kept her from going back to sleep. She peaked out her bedroom window, and while the sky was still a deep navy blue, it was clear, promising perfect weather for her upcoming day with Jack.

He'd gotten to Celia and Levi's the day before, and Kristen had joined them for dinner. She'd been surprised at how Jack's presence changed the energy. Having him back felt like using both hands after getting used to working with one tied behind your back. When he'd called Kristen to tell her he'd be in town for a few days, she'd cleared her schedule for Saturday, and as she expected, they'd ended up making plans for the day. A hike along the river, brunch at their favorite diner, and an early dinner and movie night with George and Rosalee.

Kristen went into the kitchen and made herself a cup of tea, then knocked out a few of her usual weekend chores before dressing in thick leggings, a long-sleeved shirt, fleece pullover, and her trail runners. She grabbed a couple of bananas and granola bars, and when she heard Jack's truck she slipped out the front door, locking it behind her. She climbed in the truck and gave him a big smile, which he returned.

"Hey!" she said, handing him half of the food. "I figure we might need sustenance before brunch."

"Hey yourself," Jack said. "Good thinking. And I brought water."

They talked about not much of anything on the drive to the trail, munching on their makeshift breakfast. Earlier in the week, Kristen had wondered if seeing each other in person would be awkward, or if they would have a lot to catch up on. It turned out to be neither—their frequent and regular phone conversations had bridged the gap even more than she'd realized. Of course, she also hadn't realized how much she'd actually missed his real life presence until he was there. The night before, she kept catching herself staring at him. Had he gotten a haircut? Had he lost weight? Had he always been this insightful and caring? Had his sense of humor always been so sneaky and dry? She'd forgotten how much he paid attention to the people around him. And if she were perfectly honest with herself, she'd forgotten how good looking he was, how much her heart fluttered every time he smiled his crooked smile with that one cheeky dimple.

The bright sun glinted off of the river, a blue ribbon winding its way through the rolling hills. Kristen tugged on her knit hat—the morning breeze had an icy bite to it—and was glad she'd remembered her sunglasses. She closed her eyes and took a deep breath, filling her lungs with air that smelled like ice and wood smoke. The truck "beep-beeped" behind her as Jack locked the doors, and she turned her head and opened her eyes to see him walk around the bed, pocketing his key before zipping up his quilted vest.

"Ready?" he asked.

Kristen nodded. "Let's go. I need to move before I start getting cold."

They walked to the trail head, then picked a direction that would keep the sun at their backs and out of their eyes. This was only the second time Kristen had hiked this section of the river trail. She usually walked or ran the paved section closer to town, often with her dad and Rosalee. The paved path ended just outside of town, but the dirt trail wound along the river for miles. Rosalee had told her that the trail technically went up the river all the way to Kansas City, but it was only officially maintained for about 20 miles where it connected to a park in the neighboring town of Sedalia. Jack and Kristen had briefly debated doing the whole 20 miles, but decided there were too many logistics involved, and that they'd rather have a good brunch than spend the entire day hiking.

The trail started out narrow, and for a little while, Kristen followed Jack. He set an easy pace, fast enough to keep her blood pumping, but not so fast that she was breathing too hard. Her thoughts drifted, her attention catching on a myriad of little things around her: the squirrels chasing each other around a nearby tree, the hawk soaring overhead, the gentle whooshing sound of the river that peeked occasionally through the trees.

Before long, the trail emerged from the trees, hugging the river more closely in an open area surrounded by fields and farms. The trail widened, and Kristen and Jack adjusted their pace until they were walking side by side.

"I owe you an apology," Jack said.

Kristen furrowed her brow and thought back to some of their most recent conversations, wondering what he could be referring to. Nothing came to mind.

"You trusted me with really vulnerable parts of your past," he said, "and I haven't exactly reciprocated. But when you tried to help me—when I first found out about my mom—I was really rude to you, and I'm sorry."

Now, *that* she remembered.

"Thank you," she said.

They walked a few more minutes in silence, and she thought that his apology felt like a relief of sorts, kind of like he'd removed a small wedge from between them. Yet somehow, removing the wedge only resulted in a...space. A hollowness. Well, he said it himself, she thought. I've been vulnerable with him, and now I see that he hasn't really been the same with me. She hadn't really thought about it directly, but now that it was there she couldn't ignore it.

"My dad and I were really close," Jack said, and Kristen almost stopped walking, she was so startled. Had she spoken out loud or had he just read her mind? She jogged a few steps to catch up.

"He was my best friend, my hero. He taught me about cars, and took me camping, and was the assistant coach for every single baseball team I ever played on. My mom and I got along fine, but it was more like we were only connected because of dad." he shook his head. "I don't know. Maybe that's just my interpretation I see through the filter of his death. Anyway, Dad died and Mom and I were broken. At first, our grief brought us closer, but it didn't last. Mom could barely get out of bed in the morning, let alone deal with a teenage boy who was suddenly filled with rage. We made it through the first year—Henry and Susan were great, and did everything they could—and then Mom started dating. Losers, mostly. Now that I'm older I can see that she just never stopped grieving. She was numbing the pain. But at the time, all I could see were a string of guys who treated her like crap, a growing pile of vodka bottles in the trash can, and a refrigerator that was mostly empty except for Aunt

Susan's rotation of casserole dishes. Which you better believe," he said, glancing over at her with a wry smile, "that I guarded from those losers like it was my job."

He paused, and Kristen forced herself not to ask "and then what?" Instead, she focused on her breathing, her steps, the sound of the river and the piercing brightness of the sun overhead.

"Eventually, one of her losers took a swing at me, and I punched right back. He was bigger than me, but pretty drunk at the time and not in great shape, so he definitely came out worse in the fight than I did. It was a turning point though. I stayed at Levi's that night and went the next day to talk to my mom when the guy wasn't there. I tried to get her to kick him out... leave... get help." Jack paused and cleared his throat. "It didn't work though. I wasn't—she couldn't see any other way. So I packed a couple of bags and left."

Dead leaves swirled across the ground in front of them in a brief gust of wind. Kristen pulled a strand of hair off her face and glanced over at Jack. His hands were stuffed into his jacket pockets, and his shoulders were hunched slightly, his eyes fixed firmly on the path. Kristen thought about a grieving teenage boy and the pain of feeling rejected. She felt a hot bubble of anger well up inside her at the thought of a mom so oblivious to her son's pain, then it quickly deflated as she thought about a woman who couldn't handle her own pain. What a mess, she thought. She racked her brain, attempting to find words. Instead, she simply slipped her arm through Jack's bent elbow as they walked.

It wasn't until later, when they were back at the truck, that she knew what she needed to say.

"I know that telling me about your dad was really difficult, and I want you to know I don't take it for granted. It means a lot that you trust me, and there are things I... understand better now." She leaned toward him and placed a hand on his knee. "I'm really sorry you went through that. It's bad enough to lose a parent, without piling more trauma on top of it."

He covered her hand with his own and squeezed gently. "Thank you," he said. "I won't say the wounds have healed completely, because the last few months have proven that. But I can say... well, it's a process. You know."

Kristen met his eyes. "Yeah, I do." More words welled up inside her, but his eyes looked tired and wary, like he needed a break from intense feelings and heartfelt conversation. Kristen shifted and leaned back against the seat, reaching from the seatbelt.

"Now." The word was punctuated with the click of the belt. "I don't know about you, but I have definitely worked up an appetite and there is a giant plate of waffles calling my name. Let's get this show on the road."

Jack grinned, and her heart flipped.

Chapter 33

"Can you play hooky for a couple of hours?"

The text from Celia had come just as Kristen hit "send" on an email containing the final round of revisions for an article that she had spent way too much time on. She had only written a few other articles for this publication, and the editor was proving to be extremely challenging to work with. With a sigh, Kristen closed her laptop and rolled her shoulders. It would be nice to just politely distance herself, but it was a very well-paying magazine. Kristen picked up her phone and tapped a few buttons, feeling an urge to text Lianne.

"Have you heard anything about the book proposal yet?" She sent the text, then stood up to find shoes, determined not to get worked up waiting for an answer—or hoping what that answer would be. So far she'd avoided asking too much about the proposal and how well it was—or was not—being received. But today, she couldn't help herself.

Celia pulled up and tooted her horn from the driveway a few minutes later.

"Hey!" Kristen said, as she slid into the passenger seat. "How's it going? I'm glad you texted. I needed a break."

Celia grinned and shifted into reverse. "I had a sixth sense," she said. "Actually, that's not true. To be honest, I needed to go to Target, and it just feels like the kind of day when you need someone to wander through a store with you."

Kristen frowned. "Anything wrong?"

Celia shook her head. "Nah. Levi's been working late the last several days, and it's been a lot of kid time and not much adult friend time, you know?"

Kristen nodded.

"I can imagine."

They chatted about inconsequential matters on the drive to the store, and when they were inside their conversation bounced between commentary on products and general life stuff. While Celia hunted for a book in the book aisle, a book blurb caught Kristen's eye. Across the top of a dark, brooding book cover were the words, " 'an immersive page-turner'—Stephen King". Kristen leaned down and picked up the novel. Celia, sensing her movement, glanced over her shoulder.

"I didn't think you read many thrillers." she asked, nodding toward the book in Kristen's hand. "I've heard that one's a nail-biter."

Kristen shook her head. "No, I noticed it had a blurb by Stephen King. Jack's been making his way through all the Stephen King novels."

"Oooh, you should definitely get it for him!"

Kristen tucked it in the cart. "I think I will."

They meandered down the aisle.

"So.. tell me to mind my business, but how are things going with you and Jack? Are you still..." Celia waved her hands vaguely. "... talking? Dating? Planning your futures and declaring undying love for each other?"

Kristen gave Celia a sideyed glance, and Celia just grinned, her eyes twinkling.

"We're still talking, yes," Kristen said. "Dating? I suppose it's silly not to call it that, but that is for *sure* as far as I'm willing to go with any labels." She shrugged. "Things are great. We talk often, and things have definitely shifted—for the better—since he told me about his parents. It's opened up our conversations if that makes sense."

"It does."

They walked down the throw pillow aisle and stopped. Celia picked up a bright yellow and green striped pillow and fluffed it. Kristen ran her fingers along a collection of nubby, textured pillows, but didn't really see them.

"I'm pretty sure his mom's taken a turn," Kristen said, glancing toward Celia, her hand still resting on the pillows.

Celia frowned. "I hate that."

Kristen nodded. "Jack hasn't said it specifically, so I'm really reading between the lines, but yeah, it's definitely the impression I get."

The shopping cart shifted gently as Celia dropped the pillow into the basket. They moved on, rounding the corner and by unspoken agreement passing over the storage section and walking toward the grocery section. There was more Kristen wanted to say about Jack, but she was having trouble finding the right words, and she hated talking when she didn't really know exactly what to say. But she knew that the words and feelings welling up inside her needed an outlet. Celia seemed to sense her struggle.

"I'm feeling too many feelings," Kristen finally said. "I'm really happy. I feel like Jack and I are really connecting and having fun, even from a distance. I'm sad, because his mom's dying, and that the circumstance that is finally bringing some healing is also going to hurt him. And I feel nervous because it feels like a change is coming that I can't predict or even identify." She glanced over at Celia with a small smile. "Maybe that part's just springtime, I don't know."

"Regardless, that sounds like a lot." Celia turned the cart. "Lots of feelings deserve lots of chocolate," she said, then reached out and pulled several large chocolate bars off the shelf. "I'm picking out a few of my favorites for you." She dropped them into the cart then reached out to squeeze Kristen's arm and looked her in the eyes, her expression full of compassion. "Levi tells me I try to lighten the mood too soon, so I want to make sure you know that I'm really sorry you're dealing with all of these emotions that seem so contradictory. I know it was probably hard for you to share it with me, and I hope it helped. You know I'm here, anytime."

Much to her surprise, Kristen felt tears prick her eyes. She cleared her throat. "Thank you."

Celia smiled, turned toward the cart, and changed the subject as she began pushing, telling Kristen a silly story about Aislinn. Kristen marveled at Celia's laser-sharp intuition, thinking that it wasn't the first she had seen Celia navigate a conversation knowing exactly when a person needed a listening ear and when they needed a shift in perspective or a bit of levity. What a gift, she thought.

• • •

A week later, Kristen's phone rang, and she knew Jack was calling to tell her Jules had died. There was nothing about the moment to indicate why he was calling, but she knew. It was the middle of the day on a Tuesday, and Kristen had the window next to her desk open as usual, letting in a sweet smelling breeze from the honeysuckle on the neighbor's fence. Her laptop sat open in front of her, a notebook at her elbow. Fluffy white clouds drifted by. The ringing phone felt like a welcome tug back to reality until she saw Jack's name and her heart sank. He always waited until after he knew she was done working for the day to call her.

"Hey," she answered. "What's up?"

"Jules passed this morning." His voice was a quiet rumble in her ear.

"Oh, Jack. I'm so sorry. What can I do?"

"Thanks." He was quiet, and she waited.

"The funeral is going to be on Tuesday. Just a graveside. Can you come?"

"Of course. Do you need me to come sooner? Do you need any help with anything?" Kristen assumed his aunt and uncle would help him with whatever needed to be done, but she had to ask. She felt a strong urge to be present with him.

"No, but thanks. There's not much to do in the way of preparations. Susan actually convinced her a few weeks ago to... make arrangements. Although..." he paused. "I'm going to pack up the house and list it as soon as possible. Would you be willing to stay a couple of days and help with that?"

"Absolutely," Kristen replied with no hesitation. She quickly ran through a mental list of all that she was working on. Nothing that she couldn't either finish before Tuesday or put on hold for a few days.

"Thank you."

They said goodbye and hung up the phone. Kristen drummed her fingers on the desktop, mind racing, then closed out the windows open on her laptop and set it aside. She needed to talk to Celia. Would Jack or his aunt have already called her? Maybe she would walk to Celia's house. That would give them time to call her if they hadn't already.

On the way, Kristen called Liz. Her husband Kole had lost his grandparents not long after the two had gotten married, and since it had been those grandparents who had raised him, it had been a difficult season. She knew Liz was the one to give her any advice on caring for someone who was grieving.

"Hello?"

"Hey, Liz, it's Kristen. Do you have a few minutes?"

Kristen heard the click-click of a keyboard in the background, before Liz responded, "Okay, now I do. What's up? Everything okay?"

Kristen quickly filled her in on the basics of the situation, including that she would help Jack go through his mom's house after the funeral.

"I'm really sorry," Liz said, her voice full of sympathy. "This is a tough thing to walk through with someone. I'm pretty sure you'll know what to do. Just trust your instinct. But if you want my advice, on the day of the funeral, just be there. Give him space if he needs it, stick like glue if he needs a lifeline. And when it comes to cleaning out the house, let him take the lead unless he seems overwhelmed. If that's the case, ask really specific questions that just have one or two options. And if he seems like he's in a 'chunk it all' mood, maybe ask about one or two things he might regret not keeping. That's tricky though," she added. "Not everyone needs... stuff. You'll know."

Kristen thanked her for the advice, and they chatted until Kristen reached the Blairs' driveway. She promised to call back in a few days to let Liz know how things went, then hung up. She took a deep breath and walked up to the front door. Celia opened it almost before Kristen had finished knocking.

"Hey," Celia said. The usual sparkle in her eyes seemed muted and dim, and her brow was furrowed. "Come on in. Jack called you?"

Kristen nodded. "Yeah. I had a few logistical questions and didn't want to bother Jack with them. Do you mind?

"Of course not. Would you like some tea?"

"That would be great."

They walked to the kitchen. Kristen grabbed mugs from the cabinet while Celia filled the kettle with water. In the silence, Kristen could hear music coming from the living room. She tilted her head and listened more closely.

"OK Factor?" she asked.

Celia nodded. "Always calms my nerves." She set the kettle on the stove and turned up the flame. "So," she said, leaning one hip against the counter as the water heated. "I talked to Susan, and she wants you to stay with us at their house."

Kristen shook her head. "I was going to ask you

about a nearby hotel. I don't want to be in the way, or make things weird."

"I understand your impulse, but I really think it'll be for the best. She's the one who mentioned it to me, if that makes a difference. They have the room, and he won't say it, but I think it'll make Jack feel better to have you there."

She turned to pull tea tins out of the cabinet, giving Kristen a moment to process. Staying at Levi's parents' felt both too intrusive and too intimate. On the other hand, refusing the offer to stay at a hotel felt like it would draw unwanted attention.

"You're sure they won't mind? Do they know Jack asked me to stay a few extra days?"

"They absolutely mean it, and yes, Jack talked it over with them too."

"If you're really sure, then I guess I'll do that."

The kettle whistled and Celia picked it up and turned off the heat. She filled the mugs and sat one in front of Kristen before settling into her own seat. "All right then, well, my next question is whether you'd like to follow us down when we go."

Kristen thought that was a good idea, and the two made plans.

•   •   •

The sun struggled to break through the gray clouds as Kristen followed Celia and Levi's truck up a long gravel driveway. The sky had looked heavy with rain the whole drive down to Crofton, but fortunately the rain had held off. Kristen hated driving in the rain. After a conversation with her dad and Rosalee, the latter of whom also assured her that the elder Blairs' hospitality was genuine, Kristen felt less nervous about staying with Levi's parents, but it still felt a little odd. *Oh well. There's no going back now.*

They approached the faded yellow farmhouse, where the driveway widened and curved to one side. A blue truck sat under a carport, but Kristen followed her friends just to the side of the car port and parked where the gravel gradually faded into a worn and packed patch of ground.

As Kristen gathered herself and her things, Aislinn and Tripp tumbled out of the truck, running and shouting, then launching themselves at the gray-haired couple that emerged from the side door of the house. Once the initial grandkid excitement ebbed, Levi made introductions, and the adults began carrying bags inside and getting settled in. Kristen followed Susan up the stairs and down the hall to another, more narrow set of stairs behind an open door.

"Celia said you wouldn't mind the attic room," Susan said over her shoulder as they climbed.

"Absolutely," Kristen agreed. "It sounds perfect."

"It has the benefit of its own little bathroom," Susan said.

The steps opened up right into the bedroom, directly across from a window framed with filmy white curtains. A small table sat under the window, with twin beds on either side, tucked under the sloping ceiling. The bathroom was to the right, almost directly at the top of the stairs. Kristen smiled as she got a glimpse inside, thinking that Susan wasn't joking when she'd said it was a little bathroom.

Susan asked if Kristen needed anything, then told her to take her time settling in and catching her breath.

"I'm going to head down and make a snack for the kids. Join us any time, or rest up here if you'd rather have some quiet. Jack said he'd be here in time for supper, maybe a little earlier."

"Thank you," Kristen said. "I really appreciate your hospitality."

Susan smiled, and Kristen could see Levi in her kind eyes. "It's our pleasure, truly."

Kristen could hear the distant sounds of the children downstairs, then a slamming door, then the sounds of childish laughter outside. She walked over to the window and glanced down to see Tripp and Aislinn racing toward a huge tree at the corner of the yard where a tire swing swayed in the wind. Although there was a part of her that wanted to conserve her energy and maybe take a nap, her curiosity got the better of her. She wanted to explore the house, and chat with Levi's parents.

A couple of hours later, Kristen sat at the big kitchen table—which, Kristen had learned, Henry had made himself with "help" from two small boys—slicing onions while Susan shredded the beef and Celia buttered hoagie rolls that would be toasted. Levi and his dad were outside with the kids. The cheerful sounds of their play drifted in the open windows along with the cool, early spring breeze. Kristen asked questions about life in a small town, and for once she didn't hesitate in answering the others questions about her own childhood growing up in a big city. The conversation was light, although there was a subdued undercurrent. No one had forgotten why they were gathered in the Blairs' kitchen.

Kristen was setting the knife in the sink when she heard the hum of a large engine and the crunch of gravel. Her pulse quickened, and she fought the urge to run out the door to greet Jack. Instead, she continued to help with supper preparations, one ear listening to Celia and Susan talk, the other listening to the sounds outside the open windows: the slam of the truck door, the muffled sounds of the men's greetings contrasted with the high-pitched shouts of "Uncle Jack!"

When Susan called out the back door for the others to come wash their hands, Kristen and Celia began setting the table. The kids rushed in first, not unexpectedly, going straight to the small powder room off the front hall. The men followed more slowly, wiping their feet on the door mat as they entered. Jack was the last one through the door, and

Kristen immediately noticed the dark circles under his eyes. Those dark eyes immediately began scanning the room as he walked through the door. When they found her, a smile touched the corners of his mouth. She stood at the opposite side of the table, her arms full with a stack of plates. He walked over to her and slipped an arm around her shoulders, briefly touching his forehead to hers when she turned her face toward him.

"Hey," he said, his voice low.

"Hey," she replied softly.

"I'm glad you're here."

"Me too."

He dropped his arm and took the plates from her, quickly setting them out around the table. Kristen, the tightness in her chest feeling much looser, grabbed silverware and followed him around the table.

The children kept the meal from being too subdued, although Kristen could still sense an undercurrent of quietness.

Later that evening, after the kids were in bed, the adults sat on the big front porch and Jack went over the timing of events for the next day. Since it was a simple graveside service, there wasn't much to it. Jack and Levi would leave in the morning for the funeral home—Jack said Levi didn't need to come, but Levi just raised his eyebrows and said, "I'm coming." Everyone else would meet them at the cemetery at 11, then after the service they would come back to Henry and Susan's house. The Blairs' church had wanted to host a lunch, but Jack had resisted, not wanting to feel the pressure to be social and grieve publicly. Susan had gently reminded him that the church members—many of whom had seen him grow up and known him his entire childhood—just wanted to be kind. So Jack compromised, and some of the church women would drop off a lunch at the Blairs' house for the family after the funeral service.

Levi and Celia went inside not long after the conversation, with Susan and then Henry following close behind. Jack didn't make any move to get up from his seat on the porch swing, and Kristen didn't feel tired yet so she also stayed put. She rested her head on his shoulder and they sat without talking, surrounded by the sounds of chirping crickets and the gentle snoring of the Blairs' ancient Basset hound who lay sprawled across the top step of the porch.

"Thank you for coming," Jack said at last, "and for agreeing to stay a few days."

"Of course."

Kristen debated with herself, words welling up in her, but her brain was wondering if it was the right thing to say, or the right time to say it. She thought of Liz's advice and decided to trust her gut.

"I'm really sorry, Jack," she said. "I know it's... complicated, but I also know right now is hard, and I'm sorry.

"Thanks." Jack scrubbed a hand along his jaw. "I

think the hardest part is not knowing how I actually feel, because it's all tangled up in how I've felt for so long, plus what people expect me to feel. I just can't work out what's actually going on in my own head."

"I think that's normal. This is just the kind of situation that takes a while to process."

"Mmm."

The silence stretched again, and the gentle rocking of the swing plus the comforting warmth of Jack's shoulder began to lull Kristen to sleep. When Jack shifted, she started, sitting up quickly and blinking rapidly. Jack's dimple appeared and his tired eyes held a hint of laughter. She narrowed her own eyes at him.

"Was I asleep? Was I drooling?"

"Yes, and no. Just snoring."

Kristen raised an eyebrow and Jack chuckled. "Just a little baby snoring. Nothing like Tom Selleck over there." Jack gestured toward the hound.

"I'm sorry, did you say Tom Selleck?"

Jack shrugged, his mouth still turned up in a smile. "What can I say? Aunt Susan is a fan from way back."

The interaction warmed Kristen's heart, even as she knew it was a transition to the end of their evening. She also knew she needed to resist the urge to make him smile, and instead lean into letting him be whatever he needed to be at that moment.

"I better go," Jack stood up, stretching his arms overhead. "It'll be a long day tomorrow."

Kristen stood as well. She slid her arms around Jack's waist and he wrapped his arms around her shoulders. They hugged for a long time, until their breath synced and their tension fell away. Until even the crickets were silent.

Chapter 34

A pink and orange sliver of light hovered above the horizon as Jack poured his second cup of coffee. With his other hand he rubbed his eyes, the sandpaper feeling a leftover gift from his mostly sleepless night.

Everything had gone well yesterday. The funeral home had executed the logistics seamlessly, and the minister from the church had conducted the graveside service exactly as Jack had asked, speaking words of comfort and encouragement without false platitudes. Lunch had been fairly subdued, save for the never ending cheerfulness of Aislinn and Tripp, a cheerfulness for which Jack was thankful. As they had sat around the house in the afternoon, Susan had brought out some photo albums from when Levi and Jack were kids, and had started telling stories. She went first, but eventually Levi, Henry, Celia, and even Jack chimed in with memories of both Jack's parents.

That had been the grief he wasn't prepared for. He'd stood beside the freshly dug grave of a mother with whom he'd had a complicated relationship, next to the memorial of a father whom he missed almost every day. As they told stories around the big kitchen table, Jack's grief felt deeper and more tender than he'd expected, a grief not just for his mom, but for the loss of his family.

The time at the farmhouse had been good, like a gentle massage of sore muscles; but it also left him feeling exhausted. He'd gone home early, after doing his best to express his gratitude for these people who had loved him during his darkest times. A part of him worried the whole day had been a lot for Kristen, but she seemed to take it all in her usual stride, and he'd reached for her throughout the day, her presence like an emotional anchor.

Standing now in the still-dark kitchen, Jack glanced at the pre-dawn sky and then at the clock and sighed. He'd been so tired it was a wonder he hadn't slept 12 hours, but apparently being tired was not a guarantee of sleep when you had a lot of feelings to process. He'd asked Kristen to come early, but that still meant he had a couple of hours on his hands. He glanced at the stack of collapsed boxes in the hallway. *May as well get started.*

Later, when Kristen's car pulled up to the house, Jack was taping up the last box of kitchen and living room items, most of which were heading to the local resale charity. One small box stood in the corner he'd designated as "save." It held two coffee mugs that he remembered being his parents' favorites, two framed family photos, and his grandmother's teapot that had miraculously remained safe in a high cabinet.

Jack stood and walked to the front door, hand still gripping the tape dispenser. He met Kristen on the porch.

"Hey," he said. "Thanks again for staying to help today."

"Of course," she replied. She held out a cardboard pastry box. "Henry told me to stop by Jerry's Donuts on the way in."

"Perfect," Jack said with a smile. "Did you have one yet?"

Kristen shook her head.

"Well then, let's not waste any more time. Although, I hope you brought napkins, because the only thing left in the kitchen is a mouse trap behind the refrigerator." Jack led the way inside. They each grabbed a chocolate glazed donut, but Kristen didn't make a move to sit down, and Jack was anxious to keep working. He led Kristen down the hall toward the bedrooms.

"I finished the kitchen and living room before you got here," he said over his shoulder, "So I thought we could tackle the bedrooms next."

"Just point me in the direction you want me to go." Kristen exuded a sense of calm purpose. Jack felt his shoulders drop a little, his wound-up self relaxing a little in Kristen's presence. After a moment of indecision over which bedroom to start in, he led the way into his childhood room. Kristen glanced around the space, munching on her doughnut. She swallowed.

"So," she said, a twinkle in her eye, "this is where the magic happened?"

Jack rolled his eyes. "Let's get started, smart-ass."

Jack's room had been the first one he'd sorted through, even before his mom had died.

He'd pulled a few of his favorite books off the bookshelf and found his dad's letter jacket in the back of the closet, but otherwise there wasn't anything else he was interested in keeping in the room. He told Kristen to box it all up. She rubbed her hands together. "Sounds good."

They worked in companionable silence and in just an hour were taping up the last box. As he stood surveying the now-bare room, Jack felt a slight pang, a tightness in his chest that he pushed aside for the time being. There would be time later to deal with his grief, both old and new. For now, he just wanted to focus on getting things done. He looked toward Kristen who was watching him with an unreadable expression on her face.

"Do you need some water?" Jack asked. "A soda?"

She shook her head, curly ponytail swaying gently. "Not yet," she said. "What's next?"

Feeling like a coward, Jack grabbed a box and pointed Kristen in the direction of the bathroom. "Everything in there is going," he said. "Trash what's used, leave the shower curtain, window curtains, and trash can, and box up anything that's left."

"Got it." Kristen took the box, then leaned forward and kissed his cheek. "Take a break whenever you need one," she said.

Jack cleared his throat. "Thanks."

She smiled at him and walked off with her box.

Jack watched her walk away, then took a deep breath, crossed the hall, and opened the door to his mom's room.

Once he'd come back home, the only time he'd gone into his mom's room had been during her final days, when she'd gotten too weak to get out of bed. The hospice nurse had stripped the bed and laundered the linens, which now sat neatly folded at the end of the mattress, but the room still smelled musty. He looked around, searching for traces of his mom, secretly hoping to find glimpses of his dad, but instead finding a room that was nearly devoid of any personality. There was the bed, a nightstand, a tall chest of drawers and a three-drawer dresser with a mirror, but the walls were bare and the surfaces were empty. He wasn't sure if that made things better or worse. With a shake of his head, he told himself to focus on the task. He picked up one of the boxes he'd tossed in the day before and started with the closet.

Kristen tapped gently on the open door before walking in, an empty box in her hand.

"Bathroom's done," she said. "Want some help here now?"

"Yeah. I'm about done with the closet. Why don't you start on the dresser."

Kristen nodded. Jack started on the chest of drawers which turned out to hold mostly winter clothes and a pretty astounding collection of socks. *What's with all the socks, mom?* He thought.

He heard Kristen's movements behind him halt, and when he turned to see what had given her pause he saw her kneeling next to the open bottom drawer, very still. He opened his mouth to ask if she had a question about something, when she stood up and turned, tears glistened in her eyes.

"Why don't you go through this drawer," she said. "I'll make sure there's nothing left in the nightstand."

As she passed him, she reached out and squeezed his hand, but moved to the other side of the room. Jack felt his heart pounding. Two long strides took him to the open dresser drawer. He gazed down at a manilla envelope with frayed edges and a small chipped teacup with a few pieces of jewelry inside. He reached into the teacup and pulled them out: a delicate chain with a pink seashell pendant and his parents' wedding rings. Clutching the jewelry he reached for the envelope and opened it. Inside were a handful of snapshots clearly taken before his dad died: pictures of him and his parents camping; pictures of Jack in his dirt and grass streaked baseball uniform, a gap-toothed grin splitting his face; a picture of his parents on their wedding day. Beneath the photos were a few letters, cards, and a folded piece of green construction paper covered in childish crayon hearts, and on the inside "I lov yu mom."

Jack's eyes burned and his chest ached. He felt emotion welling up inside of him, and clenched his jaw so hard he thought he might crack a tooth, desperate to keep the tide from overwhelming him. He felt the rough edge of the shell dig into his clenched fist, and remembered the one non-camping vacation his family had taken together—a trip to South Carolina, to the beach. He hadn't thought about that trip in so long. He closed his eyes, remembering the sound of his mom's off-key singing to the radio, the crunch of the ice his dad chewed while he drove, despite his mom's warning that he'd crack a tooth. He remembered the feel of his baseball card collection in his hands, the feel of the breeze through the open window. The hours staring out at an unfamiliar landscape. He remembered his first smell of the salty ocean air, the taste of it on his lips as they splashed in the waves. Jack felt his body curling in on itself, his hand clutched to his chest like he was having a heart attack. Maybe he was.

Tears dripped from his eyes, and Jack leaned against the dresser. The pain was so heavy. He felt a gentle touch on his shoulder and flinched, instinctively turning his head away from Kristen, but she didn't move away.

"I'm so sorry, Jack," she said softly." It's okay if you want to feel...it's okay if you want to feel something."

A shudder wracked Jack's body and after a moment he turned toward Kristen, his forehead against her shoulder. She wrapped her arms around him, and he leaned against her and cried.

Chapter 35

"That's the last of it." The slam of a tailgate punctuated Jack's statement. The bed of his truck was full of boxes headed to the charity resale shop, and the cab held the one box of things he was keeping and his duffle bag.

"Are you sure you don't want me to stay and help clean?" she asked, leaning against the hood of her car.

Jack shook his head. His eyes were still red from crying earlier. Of course, once he had moved through his moment, they'd gotten immediately back to packing and he hadn't mentioned it again. Kristen had opened her mouth several times to ask if he wanted to talk, but a little voice in her head told her now was the time to let him take the lead. There would be time to help him process later if he wanted to. She hoped, anyway.

"Well, I'm going to head back then. If you're sure."

"Yeah, I'm sure. Thanks for your help. It went a lot faster with two people."

"Of course."

An awkwardness creeped in between them. Their ease and closeness from earlier was buried beneath Jack's pensiveness and what she suspected was a vulnerability hangover. Kristen understood—grief was a funny thing. She knew it was something that would pass, but as they stood leaning against their respective vehicles, she realized with a sudden panic that she didn't know what Jack's plans were. He'd finished his job in Riverton. What was next?

Now is not the time, she told herself. She pulled her keys out of her pocket.

"I guess I'll talk to you soon." It was the most innocuous thing she could think to say.

Jack nodded, but didn't make a move to come closer, which she had to admit stung just a little. *It's not about you*, she reminded herself.

"Call me when you get home," Jack said, warming her heart a little. "Let me know you made it."

"I will." She opened her door and slid behind the wheel, waving as she backed down the driveway.

•   •   •

"I can't believe she's driving now!" Kristen shook her head and took a sip of her tea and adjusted the screen of her laptop. She was having a long overdue Zoom happy hour with Liz and Nora, and had just learned that Bella had passed his driving test that day.

"Honestly, I can't either," Liz admitted. "I am equal parts weepy and wondering where my baby girl went, and ecstatic that I can relinquish some of my chauffeur duties."

It had been a couple of months since Kristin, Nora, and Liz had synced their calendars for a virtual date. Their communication lately had been mostly quick texts, and although that served as a tether, sometimes it was important to see each other's faces.

Nora had just gotten back from another trip to Italy, and was apparently still talking with the man she'd met almost a year ago now. He'd flown back with her for a brief holiday that had included an evening out with Liz and Kole.

"Ooohh, so what did you think of him?" Kristen asked, working to hide her pang of envy.

"You know I usually try to keep Nora grounded in reality, but I have to admit, he seems pretty amazing," Liz admitted. "Kole liked him too. He was really easy to be around and treated Nora well." she shrugged. "Four out of five stars, and the fifth star is just being held in reserve since I've only met him once."

Kristen raised her eyebrows. "High praise!" She looked at Nora and could tell even through the tiny electronic square that she was glowing.

"He liked you guys too," she said. "Truly. He talked about Kole so much the rest of the night that

I almost felt jealous."

They laughed.

"Speaking of men," Liz said, "how's Jack? What's going on with him? How's he doing since his mom's passing?"

Kristen sighed. She had been waiting for that question, and it still felt... complicated.

"He's okay, I guess," she said. "Oh, he said to tell you thank you for the card and the donation, by the way." Nora and Liz had given a donation in Jules' name to a local addiction recovery center. Kristen hadn't been with Jack when he'd received the card, but even over the phone when he'd mentioned it, she could hear the sincere gratitude and surprise in his voice when he'd told her about it.

"Of course," Nora waved her hand in a dismissive gesture. "So, is he still in Crofton? Back in Riverton?"

"Neither. He's actually in California at the moment."

Two pairs of eyebrows shot up in surprise, and Kristen stifled another sigh. "He owns a condo in San Diego, stays out there between jobs sometimes, and rents it out the rest of the time. It didn't have any bookings lined up, and he said he hadn't been out to check on the place in a while"—*and it's far away from here*– "so he thought it was a good time to make a trip."

"You should have gone with him," Nora said, "and taken a vacation."

"It didn't seem like the time," Kristen responded.

And he didn't ask. "I've got a lot of work right now, and I think he needs some space. I think the past few months have given him a lot to process. But we're still talking." It had still stung just a little though, if she was honest with herself. The fact that he'd fled halfway across the country, even if they talked frequently and as though nothing had changed. What did she expect though, really? They didn't have a commitment, or an understanding, or an... anything, really. They had a connection, and an affection, but was that enough reason to orient your life around someone? Kristen pushed the thought away. This was not something she wanted to think about.

Chapter 36

Kristen stood, elbow-deep in a sink full of soapy water, humming along to the Johnny Cash album playing over her dad's speaker system. Her dad stood nearby, loading the dishwasher while Rosalee wiped down the kitchen table and counters. Kristen had joined the couple for a long walk along the river that Sunday morning, then waffles after. They had originally planned on playing cards, but it had started raining, and Rosalee said that always put her in the mood for a movie. She and George were currently discussing what movie they should watch.

"Do you have a preference, Kristen?" Rosalee asked.

"Not a one," Kristen said with a smile.

They were just settling onto the couch with fresh beverages when Kristen's phone started vibrating. She pulled it out of her pocket, and her brow creased in a frown. Lianne? Her heart started pounding. Lianne would only call with really good or really bad news. Kristen stood up, her thumb swiping.

"Sorry," she said. "I'll just be a minute."

George and Rosalee waved her away, but she was already halfway out of the French doors and onto the patio. She shut the doors behind her.

"Hello?"

"We got an offer!!!"

Kristen gasped. "Lianne! You did it!"

"*We* did it, you goof. And yes, we did! I'm on cloud nine and James is headed right now to the wine store for some champagne. I wish you were here to toast with us."

"Me too. But I still want to hear about the offer!"

"Well, first off I should probably have led with the fact that Becca thinks by the end of the day we'll have *two* offers."

Lianne summarized their first offer, and what their agent Becca hoped to see in the second, while Kristen paced along the edge of the patio, too excited to keep still. They made a plan to video conference the next day with Becca to go over all the details. When she hung up, Kristen couldn't stop smiling. She went back inside.

"Looks like good news," Rosalee commented.

"Our book proposal got an offer from a publisher, maybe two!"

"Oh, that's wonderful!"

Kristen sat on the edge of the love seat, still giddy with excitement. "I don't really have the details yet. We're supposed to talk with our agent tomorrow, but Lianne—my project partner—said that the first offer seems to meet most of our goals."

George stood up. "This calls for some celebrating." He walked into the kitchen, then returned with a bottle of wine under his arm and three glasses in his hands. He set it all down on the coffee table, opened the sparkling wine with a pop, and poured. They each reached for a glass, and George held his aloft.

"Here's to a brilliant daughter, and an exciting new project."

Warmth filled Kristen. "Thanks, Dad."

"Cheers."

The fizzy drink perfectly encapsulated Kristen's mood at that moment. Her brain was full of possibilities and questions, and her mental whiteboard was already filling up with ideas and lists and next steps. Her fingers itched to pull out her phone and call people, to shout it from the rooftops. It felt a little silly, but she hadn't been this excited about a project since the first time *Rolling Stone* accepted one of her article pitches.

She didn't remember much about the movie they ended up watching that afternoon, and once it was over she stood up from her seat almost immediately, apologizing to her dad and Rosalee for leaving early, but assuring them she'd be at the Finches' for Sunday Dinner, just as soon as she'd made some more phone calls. The other two didn't seem to mind, smiling fondly at her as she rushed out the door after hurried hugs. Back at her house, she immediately filled two pages of a spiral notebook with notes, hoping a brain dump would allow her to settle.

As soon as she set down her pen, she called Jack who didn't answer. She hung up without leaving a message and dialed Nora's number.

"Hello?"

"Nora! We did it! We got an offer on the book proposal!"

Nora squealed and told Kristen to hang up and call her on video chat. Kristen did, and—as she'd guessed—saw that Nora and Liz were together at the ballpark. Kristen repeated her news for Liz and laughed as the surrounding group got in on the congratulatory action. Eventually, Kristen said goodbye and ended the call. Since she was still full of that fizzy energy and had time to kill before needing to go to Elizabeth and Jonathan's, Kristen walked down to Celia's to share the news.

A few hours later, Kristen sat in the Finchs' kitchen watching Elizabeth chop up cabbage for a slaw, finally coming off of her afternoon high. The rain had stopped, so most of the family was outside, near the smoking grill where Jonathan monitored hamburgers and a selection of sausages. Kristen sliced the tops off of freshly washed strawberries.

"Have you done the research for the book already?" Elizabeth asked. She lifted her cutting board and slid the cabbage into a large mixing bowl that already held shredded carrots and shaved Brussels sprouts.

Kristen shook her head. "No. I'd like to think I have maybe a quarter of the research I'd need— mostly all scattered through my decades of article notes and files—but we would need a lot more."

"Hmm." Elizabeth squeezed lime juice into a smaller bowl and began adding olive oil, salt and other spices. "Sounds like the kind of thing that's better done in person," she said, picking up a small whisk. "Are you going to move back to Chicago, then? Your year's about up now."

The question made Kristen squirm, but she'd be lying if she said she hadn't thought about it, if she denied the fact that it was the only thing on her mind during the short drive to Elizabeth and Jonathan's house. She finished her strawberry task, glanced out the kitchen windows to the family gathered outside, smoke from the grill wafting across her view. With a sigh, she turned back to Elizabeth.

"I'll be moving back," she said. "Don't say anything to anyone yet. I want to talk it through with Dad first." She gave a sad sort of laugh. "It feels weird to say it so confidently, when I only just got the news about the contract today, but it's right, I know it."

"You're conflicted though, I can tell."

Kristen rested her chin in her hand. "Yeah, I think maybe I am. I mean, it's not going to be a surprise, necessarily. I'm still afraid it will be a disappointment."

Elizabeth reached over and gave Kristen's hand a squeeze. "He's your dad. He'll understand."

Chapter 37

Celia insisted on planning a going away party. Kristen tried to talk her out of it, but Celia insisted and brought Judy and Sierra on to her side. Once the three of them and Rosalee were unified, she knew it was a useless argument. And really, even though her instinct was to slip out quietly and draw no attention to herself, she knew she wanted and needed to say proper goodbyes.

"Do you think you'll make it back for the party?" Kristen sat on her screened porch, stretched out along the chaise lounge. She watched some birds building a nest in the tree out the window as she talked to Jack on the phone.

"Of course," he said. "I was actually planning to head that way in the next few days. Thought you might want some help packing."

"That's great! It'll be good to see you."

It had been three weeks now since Jack had gone to San Diego, on top of the months he had been in

Crofton. While they had continued their long distance rhythms, Kristen had to admit that the longer their relationship remained virtual, the more she wondered if they were simply meant to be friends and nothing more. Only, she wasn't sure how she felt about that, and if friendship even looked any different from what they were doing now.

"Have you found a place to stay yet?" Jack asked.

"Actually, yes. I'm moving in with Nora for now. She has a two-bedroom apartment now, it's in a good location, and this way I don't have to join the frantic brawl that is the Chicago real estate market."

"Why do you say for now?"

"Well, we've both been living alone for a while. And even though right now being housemates again sounds lovely, I'm not sure if it will be a long term solution or not. Especially depending on how things go with Nora's new boyfriend."

"Is it getting serious, then?"

"Eh... hard to say."

She changed the subject, asking Jack about his latest job that had just ended, a very temporary gig doing some decorative metalwork for a housing development. Kristen had been shocked when Jack had originally told her about the job, and it had taken quite a bit of mental shifting to picture Jack doing something that felt more artistic than practical. He'd teased her about stereotyping him, and she'd just marveled at the fact that she felt like she knew him so well on a soul level, and yet he still surprised her.

They chatted a few more minutes before saying goodbye, and after hanging up, Kristen just continued to lie in the chaise, staring out the window. She was having a tough time sorting through her emotions ever since she'd decided to go back to Chicago, in a way that was very reminiscent of her move to Riverton just a year ago. The move felt both simple and complicated in a way that left her feeling jumbled inside, which was not her preferred state of being.

When she was younger and faced with a big decision, she always went with the decision that felt solid. If she felt confident and sure down in her bones, that's how she knew it was the right decision. As she got older, she realized that any decision beyond what restaurant to visit or which movie to watch was rarely that clear cut. With a sigh, she sat up. If she lay there much longer, she was going to send herself into a morose, self-doubt spiral. She needed to move, and—although it was somewhat surprising to admit this—she kind of wanted some company. She tapped her fingers against her leg, thinking. Her dad and Rosalee were out of town for a few days, and she knew it was one of Tripp's days for baseball. With a swipe of her thumb she unlocked her phone and typed out a message, then went to change clothes. By the time she was lacing up her shoes, Sierra had responded an emphatic YES! to her invitation for a walk.

"I'm so glad you texted," Sierra said when Kristen approached her house 15 minutes later.

"I've been trying to take this munchkin out on a walk every day, but was really struggling to find my motivation today." Sierra and Gianna were waiting in the driveway, Gianna tucked into a stroller, furiously sucking on a pacifier, her big brown eyes wide and curious. Kristen crouched down in front of the stroller and tickled Gianna under her chin.

"Hey, precious," she said in a soft voice. "Are you being good to mommy today? Ready to go for a walk?" Kristen stood up and gave Sierra a hug. "Do you want me to just take her so you can get a nap, or veg on the couch or something?" she asked. "I'm happy to keep her occupied for a little while."

Sierra hesitated, then shook her head. "No. But thank you for offering. I need the fresh air as much as she does, and Jeremiah is getting off work early tonight so I can take a night off. I can make it until then."

"Good," Kristen said. "And good for you. I've known my share of new moms who would never take time for themselves like that."

They started walking, and Sierra gave a somewhat rueful laugh. "I'll be honest, it was hard for me to do, but Jeremiah was insistent, and told me he'd leave the house with her and drive around for a few hours if necessary."

They walked in comfortable silence for a few minutes, gradually picking up the pace.

"How long did you decide to take maternity leave?" Kristen asked after a bit.

"Six months," Sierra replied. "It's the maximum my firm offers paid, and it still puts me back at work well before our busy season."

"Makes sense. It's great that your company offers six months paid. My friend Liz had to take unpaid leave for about half of her time away from work."

"Yeah, we're lucky," Sierra replied, then shook her head. "Although, to be honest, I still think about how messed up it is that so many countries have a year of paid maternity leave and we're still stuck begging for time off."

"Yeah, it's one of the dark sides of the American work ethic."

For a while, they talked about economics and government systems, until Kristen finally held up a hand with a laugh. "You're making my brain hurt," she teased. "You forget I'm a word girl. We are veering way out of my lane, here."

Sierra grinned. "Sorry. I love nerding out on this stuff, and I've been spending a lot of my time while Gi's nursing reading political science and economics journals. I've actually started playing around with the idea of starting a newsletter to curate and distill all of this information I'm reading. I just can't decide if I want it to be more professionally focused and market it to other accountants, or make it more of a personal interest/education kind of publication."

"This is why I had a feeling you wouldn't be a full-time stay-at-home-mom," Kristen said. "I think it's a great idea, though. Although that's a tough call on which direction to go."

They rounded the corner at the far end of Kristen's street, and slowed their pace slightly, as though realizing the together portion of the walk was about to end. "I think I may just pick one and go for it, and if it doesn't end up feeling quite right, there's no reason I can't pivot later," Sierra said.

"That's smart."

"Well, I got the idea from you," Sierra said, glancing at Kristen with a smile. Kristen raised her eyebrows.

"Me?"

Sierra nodded. "Mm hmm. You wanted a change, so you made a change, but you were willing to pivot when the time came. I think that's a smart way to live. An honest way."

Kristen stopped abruptly in the middle of the sidewalk. She'd never thought about it like that. Sierra stopped a few feet down the sidewalk and turned to look at Kristen, a small smile on her face. She reached up and adjusted her baseball cap. "I just blew your mind, huh," she said with a laugh.

Kristen shook her head like she was waking up out of a daze and started moving again. "Maybe just a little," she admitted. "But in a good way. In a way that makes me feel less flighty."

"Girl, you're not being flighty at all. Who says life has to stay still. Sometimes we pivot or take chances or do something different for a while and then decide we're done with that thing. No shame in that."

They reached Kristen's house, and she reached out to give Sierra a hug.

"Sorry, I'm kind of sweaty," she said. "Thank you. Thank you for keeping me company and helping me process some things."

"Thank *you*," Sierra said. "And listen, between you and me, these postpartum hormones keep me sweaty about 90 percent of the time, even without the warmer weather."

Kristen laughed, then bent down to peek at Gianna, who was sleeping contentedly.

"Give the little one a cuddle for me," she said standing back up. "I'll see you all at the party?"

"Absolutely. Wouldn't miss it."

Sierra turned and walked off with a wave, and Kristen walked up the driveway feeling much lighter than she had earlier, and even motivated to get started on her packing. Now if only she could feel that same lightness regarding Jack.

•　　　•　　　•

"I hope you understand how much I love you," Nora said over the phone. "I've cleaned out an entire closet of my house AND one of my bathroom cabinets."

The ripping sound of box sealing tape punctuated Kristen's laugh. She adjusted her earbud and picked up the permanent marker sitting on the floor next to her. "I always knew it, but your sacrifice is noted and appreciated." She labeled the box "kitchen storage" then stood up, lifted the box and placed it in the growing stack against the wall, most of which was going straight into storage. When Nora had offered half of her apartment to Kristen, there had been some discussion over how they were going to merge their stuff. Eventually, Kristen had maintained that it would be easier for her to put as much as possible in storage until they determined how long they would be housemates again. Kristen also admitted—just to herself—that she wasn't ready yet to slide back into the same old routines and rhythms. As much as she was looking forward to being well and truly home, her year away had given her an opportunity to dust out the cobwebs in her soul, so why not carry that through to the external parts of life too?

"How's packing going?" Nora asked.

"Good. I've got almost everything packed up that I'll be putting into storage, which means I don't have a kitchen anymore. Fortunately, Rosalee and Celia are feeding me on the days I'm not just getting takeout. Everything else should fit into my car."

"You can bring as much as you want, you know."

"I know, and thank you. But we've talked about this. I'm going to live light for a while. I think. I am bringing the painting though."

"I've already got a spot on the wall picked out for it. And, not to change the subject too much or anything, but when does Jack get in?"

"Tomorrow," Kristen replied, her stomach fluttering at the thought.

"What's he think about the big move?"

Kristen sighed. "Who can tell? He's very supportive. Which is really nice, but is also kind of pissing me off."

"You wanted him to ask you to stay?"

"Maybe?" Did she? It surprised her that she admitted that out loud. But really, what did she expect? Was he really willing to commit to staying in Riverton? She knew he'd been getting restless even before he'd gone home to Crofton to take care of his mom. Did she want him to ask her to travel around with him from job to job? They'd never talked about the future, only the present or more lately, the past. She said as much to Nora.

"His loss," Nora said. "But my gut tells me it's going to come up. I don't think a long distance friendship or romance or whatever is going to last forever."

No, Kristen didn't think so either. And maybe that's why for the first time since she'd met him, she wasn't looking forward to seeing Jack tomorrow.

Chapter 38

The Blairs' backyard was full of laughter, childish squeals, and the sound of banjos and mandolins from Celia's favorite Bluegrass playlist. The scent of the grass that Jack had mowed that morning mingled pleasantly with that of wood smoke and charred marshmallows. Jack sat stretched out in one of the Adirondack chairs, his eyes following Kristen as she gradually made her way from one knot of people to another. He noticed the physical connections she made with each person she talked to, a hand on someone's elbow, a hug, or even just a brief touch to someone's back. It gave a weight to each goodbye, a silent communication that each person mattered to her. How different, he thought, from his own typical exit, where he avoided any extra show of emotion. Despite the bittersweet nature of the evening, Kristen gave off a relaxed, happy vibe, her smile never wavering, her eyes full of light. She was so beautiful. Jack felt an ache in his chest.

He sensed movement and looked up to see Levi settling into the chair next to him.

"How's Celia doing?" Jack asked.

Levi shrugged. "She's pretty sad, to be honest, but doing her best to hide it. I talked to Rosalee tonight, and she's going to plan a little weekend getaway with a couple of their book club friends in a month."

"It's kind of annoying how thoughtful you are sometimes. It's a lot of pressure for the rest of us."

Levi turned and raised his eyebrows. "Seriously? You don't seem to be feeling much pressure, man."

"What's that supposed to mean?"

Levi nodded toward Kristen. "Have you all had a conversation I don't know about? A woman whom you have been dating—don't give me that look, I don't know what else you would call it—for almost a year is moving to Chicago. You've run away to San Diego. No talk about the future, no breakup, no anything. I'm not dogging on you, it's your business. I'm just saying, you don't seem to feel much pressure in the relationship department."

Jack shifted uncomfortably in his chair. Several self-defenses came to mind, but they all seemed too... defensive. Eventually, he just shook his head.

"I don't know, maybe you're right. I was kind of hoping we could just carry on. I know, I know," he glanced at Levi who had an incredulous look on his face. "Those are the words of someone in denial." Jack sighed. "I'm still processing. I've never been here before, you know."

The pause was dense, heavy with something Jack wouldn't—couldn't—say.

"Do you love her?" Levi asked softly, no pressure behind his words.

Jack closed his eyes and leaned his head back. "I don't know. I just... being alone is a lot easier."

"But is it?"

They both fell silent after that, and the urge to do something other than sit there was nearly overwhelming. But despite Levi's remark, Jack was smart enough to know that he couldn't bounce on Kristen's going-away party. Not that he wanted to leave the party. He wanted to spend as much time as possible with Kristen before she moved. His breath caught. Kristen was leaving. Not just for a few weeks or months, but really leaving. There was no promise of reunification like there was when he went to Crofton to be with his mom, no end to the situation unless one of them chose to change the circumstances. And he certainly hadn't made any moves to change those circumstances. As painful as it was to hear, Levi had been right when said Jack had run away to California.

Kristen wasn't going to change her mind about moving to Chicago. Jack was as certain of that as he was of anything in his life. Chicago was her home, for one thing, and for another she had an amazing professional opportunity to pursue there. Her time in Riverton had always been temporary. But then again, his time in Riverton had always been temporary as well.

His gaze swept across the yard, the festive mood and twinkly lights growing more and more at odds with his mood. He found Kristen standing with her dad and Jonathan Finch. Even as his body relaxed slightly at the sight of her, the pressure in his chest tightened.

.   .   .

Kristen lay on the bed at her dad and Rosalee's, a book unopened on her chest as she stared at the ceiling. The moving company had come that morning to pack up her boxes and drive them straight to the storage unit, her car was packed, the keys to her perfectly, perfect rental house were back in the hands of the Mattoxes, and her eyes were dry and hot. The goodbye party a few nights before had been amazing. Wonderful, thoughtful Celia had allowed her the perfect opportunity to say goodbye to all the people she wanted to in a way that was fun, rather than sad. And it wasn't as though she would never be back to visit. Chicago might be home, but she had family in Riverton—more now than when she'd arrived. It was only a goodbye for now.

She heard a distant knock on the front door, and looked over at the bedside clock in the room, thinking it was a bit late for a visitor. Maybe one of the grandkids? A few minutes later there was a soft knock on the bedroom door. Kristen got up and opened it, surprised to find Celia standing on the other side, smiling. She held up a bottle of wine in one hand and a plate of brownies in another.

"I hear George and Rosalee have a nice little patio," she said. "Care to join me?"

"For brownies? Absolutely."

She followed Celia into the main area of the condo, pausing to grab four wine glasses and an extra plate. Celia uncorked the bottle and poured two glasses of wine for George and Rosalee who were sitting on the couch watching television. They made mild protests when Celia sat the glasses on the coffee table, but Celia just ignored them and added a few brownies to the extra plate and left it with the wine. Kristen kissed the top of her dad's head as she walked by, then opened the French doors to the patio. Celia followed her out, and the two of them settled into chairs, the plate of brownies and wine sitting on the table between them. Celia poured, and Kristen reached for a square of dark, gooey, chocolate.

"This is an unexpected treat," she said. "You, not just the actual treats. But those look good too."

Celia laughed, tucking one leg underneath her. "I just didn't feel like the party was quite the goodbye I wanted."

"Yeah, this is better." Kristen reached across the table, her glass held out in salute. "Cheers, friend. Here's to a good goodbye."

"Cheers."

They clinked glasses then each took a sip. Kristen

took a bite of her brownie, then another.

"It was a fun party, though. Thanks for that. I don't know if I actually told you thank you."

"It was fun, wasn't it?"

Kristen took a sip of her wine, sorting through the dozen things she wanted to say, none of them feeling quite right. Too sentimental, not sentimental enough, too glib, too serious. She felt like Goldilocks.

"I'm thinking I'll come down in August sometime for a visit. Dad's birthday is the 23rd."

"Oh, wonderful! Let me know for sure what days, and we'll have you over."

They slipped into silence again, and Kristen took another bite of her brownie. This was ridiculous.

"Why are we so awkward," she said with a laugh.

Celia grinned and shook her head. "No idea. But you're right. Maybe because I can't decide if I want to say something sappy or just tell you about my recent Target purchases like normal."

"Same. So how about a compromise." Kristen turned so she was fully facing her friend. "Celia. Thank you for being such a good friend. I'm so glad you reached out and didn't let me hole away in my house all by myself. Your friendship has taught me how to be more open and kind, and I am really just so lucky to know you."

Celia had a smile on her face, her eyes bright with tears. "I feel lucky to know you. Thank you for being willing to go to the grocery store with me, and eat lunch at my table with loud, sticky kids running around. Thank you for asking questions." She reached across the table and gave Kristen's hand a squeeze. "Don't disappear now, ok?"

"Absolutely not. I am an honorary member of the Blair family now, whether you like it or not." Both of them blinked away tears, and Kristen cleared her throat. "Okay, now tell me about your latest Target haul before I lose it."

<h1 style="text-align:center">Chapter 39</h1>

Kristen woke to the sound of a coffee grinder and the hum of traffic and distant voices. Her heart pounded as she fought disorientation. A breeze drifted in from the open window, thick with city smells: exhaust, concrete, and flour and sugar from the breakfast place on the corner. She blinked, her gaze catching on the striped wallpaper and stack of luggage in the corner. Chicago. She was in Chicago at Nora's apartment. No, *her* and Nora's apartment. The angle of the sun streaming in the window told her it was a bit later in the morning than she typically got up. Then again, she'd been exhausted when she'd arrived the night before, and had collapsed into bed like she'd just run a marathon.

She yawned and stretched, then sat up, figuring she might as well get moving. Several minutes later she entered the small L-shaped kitchen where Nora stood leaning against the counter drinking a cup of coffee and reading something on her phone. She glanced up and smiled.

"Ciao, friend. Sorry about the coffee grinder. I meant to grind the beans last night, but I forgot. I waited as long as I could."

"No problem." Kristen flipped the switch on the electric kettle and got a glass of water while she waited for the kettle to heat. "You off to work soon?"

Nora nodded. "Yes. Oh, and I'll be home early tonight. I'll pick up something we can cook for dinner. Does that sound all right?"

"Sounds great. Although I wanted to run to the store anyway and get a few things, why not send me with a shopping list."

They worked out their evening plan, then Nora finished her coffee and rinsed the mug in the sink. She took a few steps toward the other room, then paused. Kristen looked up from where she was pouring a bowl of cereal and raised her eyebrows.

"Something on your mind? You're going to be late."

Nora shook her head, but began speaking in contradiction to her body language. "How are you feeling about being back?" she asked. "In the cold— well, it's not cold, but you know what I mean—light of day, are you still glad you came back?"

Kristen nodded. "Absolutely," she said firmly. "I honestly have no regrets. I am so grateful for the year I spent in Riverton, but getting dressed this morning to the sounds of the city outside my window—yeah, this is home. It's good to be home."

Nora smiled. "Okay, good. I'm glad. I just wasn't

sure... with Jack..." she trailed off, her unfinished sentence a fitting illustration of the status of her relationship with Jack, such as it was.

Kristen shrugged. "I don't know what's going on there, to be honest," she said, "but this is where I belong. Things with Jack will... well, I guess we'll figure it out when it's time. Am I a little sad? Yeah, I think maybe I am. I care about him." It was the first time she'd said it out loud. "Despite my best efforts, I think maybe," she hesitated, the feeling and words solidifying in her mind even as she fully realized them. "I think maybe I was falling in love with him," she admitted. "But I'm not an idealistic teenager ready to give everything up in the name of love. We'll just have to see." She took a bite of her cereal, thinking that it was a very mundane and prosaic moment to admit that she might love Jack, in a cluttered kitchen eating cereal in her running clothes.

Nora's eyes lit up, and she clasped her hands under her chin in a gesture quite at odds with her tailored black suit and hounds tooth high heels. "You love him!" she practically sang. "I knew it!"

Kristen rolled her eyes. "I said I was maybe falling in love with him. There's a difference. And I don't know if it matters, anyway."

Nora shook her head. "Deny it all you want, but you've given me the most wonderful boost of hope for a Monday morning. Now I can dream of romance all day long." She grinned and waved her manicured fingers, walking toward the front door before Kristen could respond.

"Ciao, darling! See you tonight!" the door clicked shut behind her.

Kristen shook her head, a smile playing around her mouth as she took another bite. She'd always thought Nora's unshakeable romanticism was one of her more endearing qualities... unless it was trained on her. Then it was decidedly more uncomfortable. Well, at least she'd already planned on a run that morning. Thanks to that one minute interaction with Nora, her tired brain was spinning, and she knew she'd never be able to sort out the rest of her day. Time for some adrenaline and dopamine therapy. Lucky for her, it was a beautiful day.

⋅ ⋅ ⋅

The phone rang right on time.

"Jack, you're getting predictable," Kristen said, not even glancing at her phone when she answered it. She held the phone to her ear with one hand and stirred onions with her other. It was Thursday evening, just before 6 p.m., and Kristen marveled at how quickly life had returned to a new rhythm. She'd been back in Chicago for almost three weeks. After officially signing the contract on their book deal, she and Lianne had quickly created a routine for working on their project, and Kristen fit her other work in around it. She and Nora were rarely in each other's way, but it made Kristen inordinately happy that they were able to eat dinner together a few nights a week. And Jack called every evening, usually before 6 p.m. Sometimes they didn't talk for more than 10 minutes, and sometimes they chatted for more than an hour. While their conversations were the highlight of her day, they were also increasingly bittersweet. Kristen wasn't willing to give them up, but they no longer felt fully satisfying.

"You guys going to the game tomorrow?" Jack asked, ignoring her teasing comment.

"Absolutely. Nora's going to New York on Sunday, though, so it'll be just two of us next week." She hesitated. "Are you still in South Dakota? Want to make a quick trip to Chicago next week for a baseball game?" She knew the answer would probably be no, but couldn't keep from asking.

"I'm here today, but I'm leaving tomorrow. And I wanted to tell you I'll be out of pocket for a week or two. No predictable phone calls for a bit." she could hear the smile in his voice.

"Oh? Where are you headed?"

He gave a vague response and changed the subject to a book he'd recently finished. Kristen frowned at her slowly browning onions, feeling a powerful itch to question him further. She suspected Jack knew she would feel this way, because he talked more earnestly and loquaciously about his book than he normally did, and ended the conversation before she could ask any follow-up questions. He promised to call her when he could and hung up. Kristen just stared at the phone in her hands. What was he up to?

The sun was just a promise on the Eastern horizon when Jack threw his duffel bag in the back of his truck, the sky shades of navy and black, the stars mostly faded. A cool breeze blew across the prairie and tousled his hair. He stood for a moment with one hand resting on the tailgate and gazed across the shifting grasses, toward the mountains that called to him, a sweet song that promised clarity, simplicity, peace. With a shake of his head, he turned and looked toward the sunrise. He needed a different kind of clarity right now, and the peace that would only come once he'd navigated his current crossroads. Jack climbed in his truck and started the engine, then steered the vehicle toward the highway, where he began driving east. Toward Chicago.

He hadn't lied to Kristen. He was going to be out of pocket for a week or two. Just not for the reason she thought. Had he been slightly deceitful? Maybe. But he hadn't seen another way. Levi had been right. Jack had spent most of his adult life avoiding making any kind of permanent decision. As much as he hated to admit it, that kind of approach just wouldn't work with Kristen. He thought they could manage it—they were both on the same page after all. And maybe that's still where she was at. Maybe he was the only one who woke up in the morning and thought that waking up alone just wasn't as satisfying as it used to be. It was possible that he didn't fill her every waking thought, the way she filled his. He thought he saw her everywhere, and each time the woman was just a stranger, he ached just a little more.

Jules' illness and death had affected Jack more than he'd expected, leaving him feeling emotional and at loose ends. He'd done what he always did when he had no plan: he'd gone quiet and isolated himself, shutting out any and all noise so he could hear his own voice again. However, instead of feeling more settled, he ended up feeling lonely.

Kristen's announcement about her move made everything worse in Jack's mind, but he'd continued to ignore the real issue with his heart. He did all the usual things that kept him feeling at peace, but deep down he knew he was like a little kid with his eyes closed and his fingers stuck in his ears singing "nyah, nyah, can't hear you." He'd never tell him this, but Jack was grateful that Levi was willing to call him out on his bullshit. Jack needed to stop running away, and he needed to think, really think about what he wanted. Not just in the next few weeks or months, but what he wanted for his life.

Chapter 40

There were two benefits to the drizzly weather in Kristen's mind: one, it wasn't as hot as it had been the past week; and two, the weather matched her melancholy mood.

The past week and a half had made it glaringly clear that long distance with Jack was not a long term solution. As promised, he'd been out of touch, she assumed just him and a trail in his happy place. She had also been in her happy place—Cubs games, restaurant research with Lianne, shows, the energy of the city, runs along the waterfront, breakfast from the corner bakery, and nights in. There were countless moments she'd reach for her phone to call or text Jack, when she'd check her messages, forgetting that there probably wouldn't be one from him.

In some ways, Kristen felt content, but she missed Jack, and not just over the phone. She missed seeing his lopsided grin across a table while they shared good food. She wanted to spend an afternoon in the park or take a long walk through the neighborhood. She wanted him to tell her to read more books, and she wanted to introduce him to her favorite local musicians. Kristen didn't see any solution to her heart ache, because she couldn't ask him to move to Chicago and give up his freedom; and she wasn't going anywhere. If she wanted to protect her heart, it was time to tell Jack goodbye, to make a clean break and not prolong the inevitable.

That morning she'd had a long conversation with Celia about it, looking for reassurance that breaking things off officially with Jack wouldn't hurt their relationship. Celia, of course, was quick to affirm that Jack and Kristen's relationship or lack thereof would in no way make a difference with her and Levi. She reminded Kristen that Jack's extended stay in Riverton the year before had been quite an anomaly.

"Honestly," she'd admitted, "Levi and I worked really hard to hide how shocked we were that he stayed so long. But we talked about it a lot."

Kristen said nothing at that, but Celia's admission broke her heart just a little more. On the one hand, she should have known better than to think she and Jack could stay unentangled when they had behaved like two people who were seriously dating. On the other hand, why couldn't it have worked out? Kristen hoped a Cubs win might perk her up, but wasn't holding out much hope.

When she got to her row, Kristen's mouth dropped open.

"You're early!" she blurted out to Big Jim, who sat calmly in his seat, a half-eaten soft pretzel in his hand. One corner of his mouth lifted in a slight smile, and a smaller figure leaned forward from the seat next to Jim, his mop of curly hair longer than Kristen remembered. Big Jim's nephew waved and grinned, showing off the gaps in his teeth that were also new since Kristen had last seen him.

"Hi, Ms. Bowen."

"Zeke! I've been wanting to see you!" Kristen felt her spirits lift a little. "Tell me what's going on."

After Zeke told Kristen all about summer plans and his first time playing coach pitch baseball, Nora arrived, followed closely by Liz. The rest of their season ticket family began arriving, and for a few minutes it was a flurry of talking and catching up and people going in and out of the seats to get food and drinks. When they all stood for the National Anthem, Kristen caught a strange look pass between Nora and Liz. As she watched them out of the corner of her eye, trying to decide if she'd imagined it, Liz leaned close and whispered something in Nora's ear. Nora nodded at Liz, and glanced at Kristen, so quickly that if Kristen hadn't been paying close attention, she would have missed it. Kristen narrowed her eyes.

During a lull in the game, Kristen asked Liz what she and Nora had been whispering about, and Liz just waved her hand and said "Nothing. I was just asking her opinion about a new boutique that opened up near me, and it was so loud I had to lean close and whisper." Kristen raised an eyebrow and opened her mouth to ask Liz why she felt such a burning need to ask about it during the national anthem if it was so loud, but Liz changed the subject so aggressively that Kristen didn't push. But she noticed that both Liz and Nora had an excess of nervous energy throughout the entire game. They also seemed to leave their seats more to go to the bathroom or get concessions, although Kristen could admit that she might be reading into that a little.

Extra energy or not, something was going on, and Kristen couldn't stop thinking about it. She wracked her brain and even pulled out her calendar at one point, wondering if there was a birthday or anniversary coming up that she'd forgotten about, but nothing showed up that would warrant a surprise or secret of any kind. It was maddening. She couldn't concentrate on the game, and for one of the few times she could remember, she was glad when it was over.

Rather than stay and chat as they meandered out of the ballpark, Nora and Liz began saying somewhat hasty goodbyes to their seatmates, attempting to get a jump on the crowd as they left, dragging Kristen along with them. Now she was really confused, but she had no opportunity to ask them what was going on and why they were acting so strange. She nearly just stopped in the middle of the walkway, but the crowd was thick, pulling them along like a school of fish, and it seemed unnecessarily dramatic.

The trio exited the field into a mist that wasn't quite committed enough to be called rain, or even a drizzle, and the crowd dispersed quickly, many pulling up rain hoods or unfurling umbrellas as they did. Released from the crowd, Kristen stopped abruptly and spun to face her friends.

"What in the world is going on with you two!" she said. Her voice was spicy with exasperation.

Nora, one hand clutching a polka dotted umbrella, just smiled, grasped Kristen's shoulder with her free hand, and spun her 90 degrees. Kristen frowned, wondering why Nora wanted her to look at Segar's souvenir stand.

It was Jack.

Chapter 41

The sight of Jack standing in the awning's shelter chatting with Segar and holding a Cubs hat in one hand was so incongruous that she almost couldn't compute that it was real. Her heart pounded and her palms began sweating. What was he doing there?

Jack turned, as though sensing her stare, and the smile faded from his face, replaced with hesitation and an expression she couldn't quite read. Segar glanced back and forth between them, then pulled back to sit on his tall stool. Still, Kristen couldn't move, even though a part of her wanted to run toward Jack and throw her arms around him. As she watched, he began walking toward her, and his movement propelled her own feet forward. They met in the middle of the courtyard, now empty of everyone except a man packing up a hot dog cart, and her two friends who had taken Jack's place talking to Segar.

"Hey." Jack said. Kristen closed her eyes, her

stomach fluttering at the sound of his deep voice. She'd missed him so much. With a deep breath, she opened her eyes.

"Hey. What are you doing here? I thought you were... on walkabout or whatever."

"No, not walkabout." He hesitated, poised on the edge of continuing, but clearly struggling for words. When he opened his mouth to talk again, Kristen held up one hand.

"Wait," she said, then cleared her throat. Her mouth was as dry as a dessert. "I'm glad you're here. There's something I've been thinking about, and need to tell you." *Although I didn't actually want to break up with you in person. But in person is less cowardly.* "I mean, obviously I'm just glad you see you" *that's an understatement,* "but also I wanted to talk to you."

A crease appeared between Jack's eyebrows, and for a moment Kristen was distracted, overwhelmed by the urge to smooth it away. She clenched her fist at her side. Jack opened his mouth, but Kristen rushed on before he could say anything.

"Let me go first," she said, "or I'll talk myself out of it. Jack, I don't want to... I mean, I think it's time to... stop... talking. We should break up." Inside, she cringed at the awkwardness of the words and the effort of stuffing down the voice shouting at her to stop being an idiot. It took an effort to keep what she desperately hoped was a neutral expression on her face.

Jack's frown deepened. He took a step backward.

"Why?" he asked, his voice rough.

Kristen swallowed with some difficulty, desperately wishing she had some water. "Umm..well, the long distance thing isn't going to work, and it just seems...like one of us needs to call it. Before..." *my heart breaks...* "it gets awkward and uncomfortable."

The mist turned into a soft rain, and she pulled her hood up. Jack stared at her for several excruciating heartbeats, seemingly oblivious to the rain darkening his gray t-shirt. Then, much to her surprise, a grin lit up his face, dimple and all. In two quick strides he crossed the space between them and was standing so close she could smell the smoky, citrusy scent of his soap. *His old soap,* a distant part of her brain noticed. *Stop it. Not relevant.*

"You should have let me go first," he said. "I wanted to tell you about the job I got."

Now it was Kristen's turn to frown. What did that matter? Was he not listening?

He reached out with his free hand and took one of hers, rubbing his thumb across her knuckles, and sending shivers down her spine.

"I just got hired at Fuller Manufacturing as a crew manager. It's near Humboldt Park. I start in two weeks."

Kristen blinked rapidly. She understood the words he'd said, but what did it actually mean?

"You're moving to Chicago?" her voice cracked.

His smile dimmed, and the crease between his eyebrows returned. "I haven't said yes, yet," he said.

"I'm supposed to call them back tomorrow to let them know if I accept their offer. I wanted to talk to you first. It's not a temporary contract," he added, "just to be clear."

"Still not clear," Kristen said, shaking her head. "I don't... I don't understand."

"I've missed you. More than I've missed anyone in my life. You're right—long distance will not work, and I might have tried to convince myself that what we were doing was just casual, but I don't feel casual." By now, the rain had soaked the shoulders of his shirt, and had darkened his brown hair. He didn't seem to notice.

"But I thought you hated cities?" Kristen said. She felt like her brain was stuck in molasses. She couldn't process what he was saying. Jack just shook his head, his smile returning somewhat.

"I've been in Chicago for the past week, just to make sure. I've explored, I've gotten lost, and I made sure I could get out in an hour or less."

"I thought you didn't like to stay in one place too long?" her voice trembled, and her eyes burned, her body grasping what her mind wouldn't quite accept. She hated that her emotions were leaking out, that he'd caught her so off guard.

Jack let go of her hand, shoved his ball cap on his head and gently took her face in his hands. Her hood slipped off, and the misty rain cooled her flushed cheeks.

"I've been running, distracting myself," he said

gently. "I had no reason to stay anywhere. But nothing in the world sounds better to me right now than staying in one place. Possibly forever, but I'd at least like to give it a shot. I love you."

Kristen's chin trembled, and she searched Jack's eyes for any hint of deception or manipulation, but all she saw in the dark brown depths was openness and clarity. And yes, love. He was really willing to change up his whole life, for her. Tears slipped from her eyes, mingling with the rain on her face. With a shaky laugh, Kristen reached up and placed her own hands on either side of Jack's neck, her fingers curling in the ends of his damp hair. She pulled his head toward her own, resting her forehead against his.

"This is a gift, thank you," she whispered. "And I love you. But also... maybe we should get out of the rain?"

Chapter 42

The day Jack Blair officially moved to Chicago, the sun was shining in a cloudless sky, the wind was gusting off of Lake Michigan, and it was officially the hottest day of the summer so far.

Kristen sat on the front stoop of Jack's apartment building, a half-frozen bottle of water resting against the back of her neck. Nora sat next to her, and Liz stood in front of them, fanning herself with a stray piece of cardboard that had been in the back of Jack's truck.

"Did he buy a window unit yet?" Liz asked.

Kristen nodded, unscrewing the cap on her water bottle and taking a long drink. She heard the front door to the building open, and turned to see Jack, Kole, and the kids walk out. Noah asked Liz where the drinks were, and she pointed to the cooler sitting at Nora's feet. The kids jostled each other for first dibs on the cold drinks, but only half heartedly. It was too hot, and they'd been working too hard to put forth any real effort at fighting. Jack and Kole waited until the kids had moved out of the way and grabbed their own bottles of water.

"Please tell me that's all," Nora said, using her hand to shade her eyes as she looked up at Jack. Liz rolled her eyes.

"It was hardly that much stuff," she said before Jack could answer. "It took us all of what, an hour and a half?" she glanced at her watch.

"Yes, but it's so hot, I think that makes every hour count for two," Nora replied. "Not that I really mind," she added quickly, flashing a grin at Jack. "It's worth it to have you here."

Kristen caught Jack's eye, and they smiled at each other. Definitely worth the sweat and sore muscles.

"You know, it's not quite lunch yet," Kole said. "This feels like a good beach day to me. What do you all think?"

Nora sat up straight and the kids started a goofy dance. "That sounds amazing to me, but do you guys really want to go back home and get your stuff?"

"Well..." Liz said with a sheepish smile. "I looked at the forecast this morning and threw our beach bag and chairs in the car, just in case."

"I think it's a great idea," Kristen agreed. "Jack?"

He shrugged. "I think I can find my trunks. Water and sand sound pretty good to me."

"If you can't find them, there's a Target not too far out of your way, they should have some," Kristen said.

Liz clapped her hands together, and they quickly made a plan on where to meet, then temporarily went their separate ways, Jack offering Liz's family the use of his bathroom to change.

An hour later, the group had reassembled on a not-too-crowded section of the Lake Michigan beach with beach chairs, towels, takeout, and the cooler re-stocked with cold drinks. Kristen looked around at their little semi-circle and smiled. Her eyes landed on Jack sitting right next to her, who had just taken a giant bite of his gyro. He raised his eyebrows at her look, his mouth too full to say anything. She grinned, then reached over to wipe a bit of tzatziki sauce off the corner of his mouth with her thumb. He swallowed and returned her smile.

"You look happy."

"I am happy," she said, without hesitation. "It's a beautiful day, I'm with people I love, in a place that I love, and I feel.... light. Content. I almost feel like I should ask someone to pinch me to make sure I'm not dreaming."

Jack leaned forward and kissed her, long enough that when he pulled away, she was blushing, and not from the sunshine.

"Not dreaming," Jack said quietly.

"Not dreaming." she echoed, her eyes locked on his. "Is this happily ever after, Jack?"

"Probably not. But maybe it's the other kind of ever after, the one where the man and the woman love each other, and look out for each other, and make it work, and sometimes are miserable, and sometimes insanely happy. Maybe it's that kind of ever after."

"That sounds even better."

THE END

Acknowledgements

Thank you to the team at Black Rose Writing for helping bring Kristen's story to life, and for my fellow Black Rose Writing authors for being so supportive and encouraging.

As always, a giant thank you to my critique partner Dawn for keeping me accountable, sharing insights on messy drafts, and answering scintillating questions like "does this even make sense?"

Thank you to all my readers out there, and to every one of you who has shared my work with your friends. It's the highest honor.

And of course, thank you to Jeremy for supporting me in so many ways, and for reading my stories even though there's no magic or fight scenes.

About the Author

Amanda Waters is a former journalist-turned-librarian-turned author. Her latest novel, *With You*, was a winner in the romance category of the 2019 Writer's League of Texas Manuscript Contest. She's a midwestern girl currently living in Houston, Texas, with her husband and two children. When she's not writing or hiding from the humidity, you can find her on her back porch, reading, drinking way too much coffee, or playing endless games of *Skip-bo* and *Exploding Kittens*.

NOTE FROM THE AUTHOR

Word-of-mouth is crucial for any author to succeed. If you enjoyed *With You*, please leave a review online—anywhere you are able. Even if it's just a sentence or two. It would make all the difference and would be very much appreciated.

Thanks!
Amanda Waters